TAYLOR & ROSE

Secret Agents

NIGHTFALL IN NEW YORK

KATHERINE WOODFINE

Illustrated by Karl James Mountford

Farshore

Farshore

First published in Great Britain in 2021 by Farshore
An imprint of HarperCollins*Publishers*
1 London Bridge Street
London SE1 9GF

farshore.co.uk

HarperCollins*Publishers*
1st Floor, Watermarque Building, Ringsend Road
Dublin 4, Ireland

ISBN 978 1 4052 9327 3

Printed and bound in the UK using 100% renewable electricity at CPI Group (UK) Ltd

1

Typeset by Avon DataSet Ltd, Alcester, Warwickshire

For the next generation:
Rose
Frank & Lil

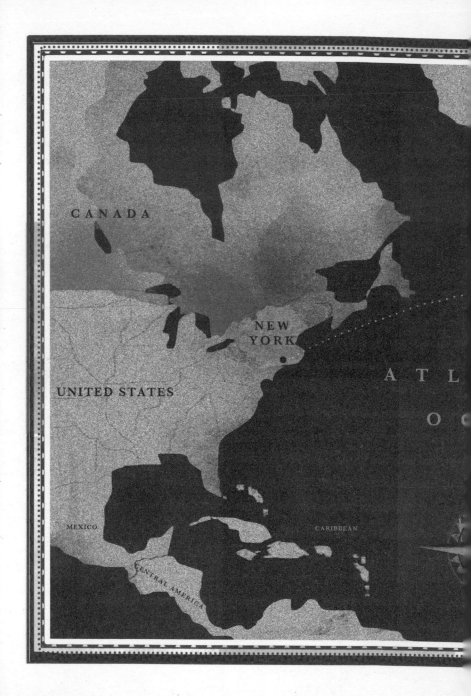

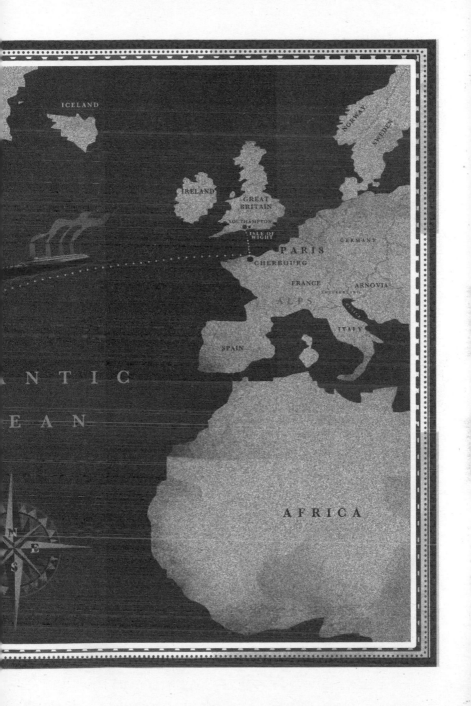

PART I

No. 2605   **A NORTON NEWSPAPER**   *One Half-Penny*

2nd March 1912

THE DAILY PICTURE

ATLANTIC LINE LAUNCHES WORLD'S LARGEST STEAMSHIP;

VAN BERGEN HAILS NEW ERA OF INTERNATIONAL PARTNERSHIP

Hundreds of spectators gathered in Liverpool today to see the launching of the Atlantic Line's flagship steamer RMS. Thalassa. Named for the Ancient Greek 'spirit of the ocean', the Thalassa is now the largest liner in the world, weighing 47,000 tons and exceeding even the White Star Line's Olympic steamers. She will undertake her maiden voyage next month, travelling from Southampton to New York via Cherbourg.

Established by American shipping magnate Theodore Van Bergen, the Atlantic Line has shipyards in Liverpool, Saint-Nazaire and Brooklyn, New York. 'The Thalassa is the very spirit of international collaboration,' Van Bergen told reporters at the launch. 'We are immensely proud that together with our partners in Britain and France we are making transatlantic travel faster, safer, more comfortable and more efficient than ever before.' However, some critics have begun to question the viability of Van Bergen's ambitious international partnership. (continued p5)

READ THE NEXT IN OUR EXCLUSIVE SERIES

as written by W. Parker of Taylor & Rose Detectives.

THE MYSTERY OF THE STOLEN JEWELS

When a priceless jewel is stolen from an elegant London department store, Miss Lilian Rose must investigate. But could this theft be the work of a sinister foreign secret agent? Read more on p10

HAVE YOU ENCOUNTERED A SPY ?

- Leading suffragettes arrested in London's West End – p2
- Coal miners strike continues amid calls to Prime Minister Lockwood for a minimum wage – p3
- International News: Marie-Adelaide succeeds to the throne of Luxembourg – see the latest pictures of the 17-year-old Grand Duchess – p6
- Sports News: British pair take Gold at World Figure Skating Championships – p18

CHAPTER ONE

10 Downing Street
London, England

It was midnight in London. Lights were being extinguished; the theatres and restaurants were closing their doors. Street lamps glowed and on Piccadilly Circus, illuminated advertisements glittered. The windows of Sinclair's, London's most elegant department store, shimmered gold in the dark.

In Covent Garden, people slept huddled on the doorstep of an old church, under the yellowing sheets of yesterday's newspaper. In Soho, a lone policeman strode down a narrow, cobbled passage. At the Inns of Court, all was silent – but on Fleet Street, the printing presses clattered through the night, churning out the papers that tomorrow the newsboys would be hawking on every corner.

In Westminster, Big Ben chimed midnight, slowly and solemnly. The policeman on duty outside 10 Downing Street heard it, and was glad. It was the end of his shift and he'd soon be home, toasting his toes before a warm fire.

Behind him, the Prime Minister's residence was dark, but for the first-floor window of the study, which still glowed with yellow lamp light. Arthur Lockwood was working late.

The Prime Minister had not noticed Big Ben chiming. He was engrossed in his work, making his way through the contents of a red dispatch box. Methodically he set aside one document to read later, before scrawling his initials upon another. The room was quiet but for the crackling of the fire, and the regular tick of the grandfather clock, marking time just as it had for every British Prime Minister since Gladstone. From an adjoining room came the tapping of the typewriter, and an occasional stifled yawn from the Prime Minister's private secretary who was hoping that Lockwood would soon retire for the night.

Just then, something made the Prime Minister pause. As he reached into the box to take out the next document, he saw something unexpected – a small envelope. It was still sealed, which was odd in itself. The other letters in the box had already been opened and reviewed by his staff. But this envelope was unopened, as if it had been slipped secretly amongst the rest by an unseen hand.

The Prime Minister slit the envelope open. Inside he found a folded sheet of paper. A new expression of sharp curiosity passed across his face.

'Horace,' he called after a moment. 'Set up a meeting

for me tomorrow. The Secretary for War and the Admiral of the Fleet.'

'Very good, sir,' came the secretary's voice, sounding a little weary.

'New York, eh?' murmured the Prime Minister to himself. Then he crumpled the letter, and tossed both it and the envelope into the fire, before turning back to his red box.

In the fireplace, the envelope flared up, and for a few seconds, the flames illuminated a symbol on its reverse.

It was so small it could easily have been dismissed as no more than an ink blot – a twisting shape that resembled a black snake, or perhaps a dragon.

It flamed orange-red for a moment, and then it disappeared.

CHAPTER TWO

Taylor & Rose Detectives
Sinclair's Department Store
Piccadilly, London

The clock was striking eight, as Sophie opened the door with the gold letters reading *Taylor & Rose Detectives*. It was early, but she'd already been awake for hours. At last, she'd given up tossing and turning, got out of bed, and come to the office. If she couldn't sleep, she might as well work.

The office of Taylor & Rose Detectives looked just as usual. There was the desk where Mei Lim, who worked as their receptionist, welcomed clients. There was the waiting area, with its comfortable chairs and illustrated fashion-papers. Beyond was the office that belonged to Billy Parker, the office manager, and then the little room — not much more than a cupboard really — where their technical expert Tilly Black spent hours experimenting with everything from fingerprinting techniques to an extraordinary-looking contraption called a *phonograph*, which she'd assured Sophie was going to be tremendously useful to them in future cases.

Last of all was the office that Sophie and Lil shared. Their desks, marked *Miss Sophie Taylor* and *Miss Lilian Rose* faced each other companionably. Her own was neat and well-ordered, exactly as she liked it; Lil's was, as usual, in chaos.

Sophie pushed back the window curtains to let in the morning light. She'd always loved this view and now she lingered for a moment, looking down at Piccadilly Circus, watching the city come to life. Shop shutters rattling up; blinds being opened in the windows; delivery boys on bicycles, weaving between the omnibuses carrying clerks and telephonists to work.

Everything seemed so ordinary. Yet it wasn't. The letter that had kept her awake half the night was sitting squarely in the middle of her desk, as if it was waiting for her.

It had arrived yesterday, wedged in the middle of a thick stack of envelopes. Taylor & Rose received a lot of correspondence these days – enquiries from potential clients, but other kinds of letters too. Flowery epistles, praising Lil's beauty. Disapproving notes, asserting that it was most improper for two girls to run a detective agency. Enthusiastic messages from other young ladies, who thought it would be rather a lark to become detectives themselves. This stack had also included a long letter from their newly retired mentor, Miss Ada Pickering, postmarked *Colorado, USA*; a picture postcard of blossoming cherry-trees addressed to Sophie from her friend Captain Nakamura in Japan; and a telegram for Lil from West End director Gilbert Lloyd, who wanted her to star in a new play. But all this had been forgotten when they had seen the envelope marked with the shape of a twisting black dragon. It was the letter they'd been waiting for: a second message from the *Fraternitas Draconum*.

Now, taking a long breath, Sophie sat down in her chair and read it all over again.

Miss S. Taylor,
Taylor & Rose Detectives,
Sinclair's Department Store,
Piccadilly, London W1

Miss Taylor –

Bring the Draco Almanac to New York City.
Travel alone. On arrival, await our instructions.
In exchange for the Almanac, we will return your friend to you.
Do not involve the authorities or he will suffer the consequences.
Tell no one about this message, or you will not see him alive again.

– The Black Dragon

For six months they'd believed Joe was dead – murdered by the sinister secret society known as the *Fraternitas Draconum*. Only Lil had refused to give up hope. But then another secret agent, Captain Forsyth, had been revealed as a double agent, secretly working for the *Fraternitas*. When he'd confessed to shooting Joe, even Lil had begun to accept that Joe was really gone.

Now everything they thought they knew had been turned upside down. Like something from an impossible dream, it seemed that Joe might be alive after all.

Alive, but a prisoner in the hands of their enemies.

The *Fraternitas Draconum*, also known as the Brotherhood of Dragons, was a shadowy criminal organisation whose influence stretched across Europe and beyond. Already rich and powerful, they would stop at nothing to increase their wealth, plotting to spark off a terrible war in Europe from which they could profit. The *Fraternitas* had cast a dark shadow over Sophie's life. They were responsible for the deaths of her parents, and it was because of them she'd been left powerless and friendless, all alone in the world.

But Sophie was neither powerless nor friendless any longer. Now, she was co-proprietor of Taylor & Rose Detectives, an agent of the British government's Secret Service Bureau, and a sworn member of the Loyal Order of Lions, dedicated to opposing the *Fraternitas*.

Now, in the cool light of a new day, she tried to look at

the letter as calmly and objectively as she would a piece of evidence in an ordinary case. Like the previous letter they'd received a week earlier, it was postmarked New York and signed by the Black Dragon. That was the code name used by Lady Tremayne – the sister of their old enemy, the Baron. After the Baron's death two years ago, Lady Tremayne had escaped to America, where she'd taken on a new identity as the mysterious 'Mrs Davenport'. She'd also taken her brother's place within the most senior ranks of the *Fraternitas*, becoming the Black Dragon. Now it seemed that she was the one behind Joe's disappearance.

Sophie's heart felt heavy as stone as she contemplated the message. It was blackmail, pure and simple. If they wanted to save Joe, they'd have to hand over the Draco Almanac – the ancient book which contained instructions for making a terrible weapon. They'd done everything in their power to stop the *Fraternitas* from getting the Almanac. Sophie had even tried to destroy it by plunging it into the waters of the Venice lagoon. But their Bureau colleague Captain Carruthers had rescued it, and now it was here – back in London, in this very office.

She leaned over to open the small safe in the corner of the room and reached inside. Taking out the book, she placed it on her desk beside the letter.

It looked so small and harmless. Just an old, battered book with a gilded cover, like something you might find in an antique shop, or the library of a grand old house. But

Sophie knew it was very dangerous indeed.

They'd worked for months and travelled across Europe to find the Almanac. They'd faced countless dangers. People had died. How could they even *consider* taking it to New York and putting it into the hands of the *Fraternitas*?

'There isn't a shred of proof that they really have your friend,' Carruthers had argued, when the Black Dragon's first letter had arrived a week earlier. 'We heard Forsyth say he shot him!'

'But he didn't say he *killed* him.' Sophie had been racking her brains to try and recall exactly what Forsyth *had* said in those moments underground, while all the time her heart had been pounding. *Joe could still be alive.*

'Even if they *do* have him – which hardly seems likely after all this time – what possible guarantee do you have that she'll actually release him in exchange for the book?' Carruthers had demanded. 'This is the *Fraternitas*, for heaven's sake! They're criminals. They can't be trusted!'

'But if there's even the slightest chance . . .' Billy had said in a hoarse voice. Looking at him, Sophie had seen the same emotions reflected on his face that she felt herself – astonishment and hope and excitement and fear all mixed up together. Nothing had been right since Joe had gone. He was their dearest friend, and the thought that he might still be alive was almost too much.

Carruthers hadn't understood that, but he didn't know Joe. He'd reached straight for the telephone. 'We need to inform the Chief at once.'

But Mei had dived in front of him. 'No!' she'd exclaimed. 'The letter says we mustn't tell *anyone*! If they find out we've disobeyed their instructions, the dragons could hurt Joe – or worse!'

'You can't possibly keep the Chief in the dark about something like this!' Carruthers had spluttered. He'd turned to Sophie and Lil, assuming they would back him up, but they'd both stayed silent. Lil had barely seemed to hear him. She'd been staring at the letter, pale as a ghost.

Sophie's heart had ached for her. This was awful for all of them, but worst of all for Lil. She and Joe had always been close, but before Joe had disappeared, it had seemed as though their friendship might be turning into something more.

Lil had worked harder than anyone to find Joe. She'd steadfastly refused to give up on him. Now, just as she'd begun to accept he wasn't coming back – this.

What did it mean? Was he alive – or not? For a moment, Sophie had felt a rush of desperation wash over her. But then she'd heard her papa's voice in her ear – brisk and practical and clear as a bell. *No sense in losing your head.*

'Mei's right,' she'd managed to say. 'The *Fraternitas* have spies everywhere. The last thing we ought to do is pick up the telephone and tell the Chief. Anyone could be listening.'

Carruthers had looked like he was about to explode.

'But this is a direct communication from a senior member of the *Fraternitas* – an *international criminal organisation*! It's imperative that we inform the Chief at once!' he'd blustered.

'But *not* on the telephone,' Sophie had insisted. 'We should meet the Chief at the safe house, where we can talk in secret.'

'Very well,' Carruthers had agreed. 'I'll go to him and arrange a meeting.' He'd reached out as though he was going to pick up the Almanac and take it with him, but Lil, like someone waking suddenly from a dream, had shot out her hand and snatched it back.

'I need to take that for safekeeping!' Carruthers had protested. 'It ought to be locked in the safe at the Bureau, under full official protection!'

But Lil would not let go of the book. 'We've got a perfectly good safe here. The Almanac is staying with *us*,' she'd said.

And now here it was. Sophie gazed down at it warily, as though it was a poisonous snake about to strike. There was something about it that made her uncomfortable – the way the gold eye on the cover seemed almost to *look* at you.

She slid it to the side, making room for a sheet of paper and a pen. Treat this like any other case, she reminded herself. Write everything down – beginning with exactly who they were dealing with. At the top of her paper she jotted: *Fraternitas Draconum*, and underneath it she made a list of the known members:

FRATERNITAS DRACONUM

The Black Dragon

Lady Viola Tremayne aka Mrs Davenport

Sister to John Hardcastle aka 'the Baron' (deceased)

Godmother to Leo Fitzgerald, formerly a close family friend of
the Fitzgerald family

Resides in New York, head of the New York branch

First female member of the society?

Organised the International Council meeting in Venice

The Gold Dragon

Identity unknown

Leader of the International Council

Connections in Arnovia (Countess von Wilderstein) and Russia
(Viktor)

The Red Dragon

Captain Harry Forsyth, formerly of the Secret Service
Bureau / British Army

New member of the society

Previously worked as a double agent passing secrets to the
society

Last seen in Venice

Current whereabouts unknown

Approx. 8 other senior members attended the International
Council meeting. All male — various nationalities and ages

Sophie ran her pen under the words *Gold Dragon*. There was no doubt he was the most important. They'd encountered his name more than once. Their friend Leo Fitzgerald had even seen him commanding the meeting in Venice. Yet Sophie still knew so little about him. He was not in the least like the Baron. She'd never faced the Gold Dragon on an East End dockside, or down a dark Chelsea alleyway. Even the letter in front of her hadn't come from Gold himself.

What little she did know had come from Leo, who had carefully described him to Sophie: 'I'd say he was around fifty. Greying hair. Smartly dressed, like all the rest. And he seemed like he was used to being in charge. He was practical – *businesslike*. Rather as though he wasn't addressing a secret society at all, but a board meeting, or something like that.'

'What about his voice?' Sophie had asked. 'Did he have an accent?'

'He was English, I think. He didn't have any particular accent. He just sounded . . . ordinary.'

But what was ordinary to Leo might not be ordinary to someone else, Sophie reasoned. Leo's father was a lord and she'd grown up in a grand country house. 'Ordinary' to her would mean something quite different than to Mei, who came from the East End of London. Likely what Leo meant was that he sounded upper-class.

Of course, the problem was that Leo's description could

have characterised hundreds of wealthy, powerful men. But there *were* some things that set Gold apart – like his connections in countries all over Europe, amongst quite different sorts of people. That was interesting, Sophie thought.

Just then, the door creaked open, and instinctively, Sophie reached for the Almanac to put it out of sight. But she soon saw it was only Lil with a copy of the morning paper in her hand. She looked tired and pale, as though she too had slept badly. She did not much resemble the glamorous young lady whose photograph was once again on the front page of *The Daily Picture*.

'Morning,' she said briefly.

'Did you sleep much?'

Lil shook her head. 'No. You?'

'Not really. Is that another one of Billy's stories?' Sophie asked, frowning at the paper in Lil's hand.

Billy had been thrilled when *The Daily Picture*'s Roberta Russell had agreed to print some of the detective adventures he'd been writing. But when they'd begun to appear in the newspaper, he'd been horrified to see that she'd changed them. Instead of stories, they'd been presented as reports of real Taylor & Rose cases, with glamorous young detective Miss Lilian Rose as the heroine.

Lil nodded. 'This time it's been altered so that the jewels were stolen by a *German spy*,' she snorted. 'Honestly, if you believed what you read in *The Daily Picture* you'd think there were thousands of the fellows popping up all over the place.'

Sophie knew what she meant. They *had* encountered a handful of German spies – most memorably, the secret agent they knew only as 'the grey man' who worked for the Berlin spymaster Ziegler. Yet they knew from experience that they were few and far between. In spite of that, the London newspapers were now so full of reports of German spies that readers might easily believe the city was overrun with them.

Lil saw the letter lying on Sophie's desk, and dropped into a chair beside her – all thoughts of spies forgotten.

'It was going round in my head all night long,' she said softly. 'I just don't know if we ought to believe a word she says.'

For a few minutes, they sat in silence. Sophie could hear the sound of the traffic in the street outside, and faintly, the tinkling of the piano downstairs.

'What do you suppose *Joe* would say to all this, if he were here?' said Lil suddenly, breaking the silence.

Sophie knew the answer to that at once. If *Lil* had been a prisoner of the *Fraternitas*, Joe wouldn't have hesitated for an instant. No matter how unlikely or impossible it might seem, no matter what risks he had to take, if there was even the slightest chance, he'd have gone after her. Just as Lil had gone after Sophie when she'd believed her missing in St Petersburg. Lil and Joe were alike in that way – they were loyal. It was one of the things Sophie admired most about them both.

In that moment, she knew what she must do.

'I'm going to New York,' she said decidedly.

'*What?*' Lil exclaimed. 'You can't really mean that you'll *give* them the Almanac?'

'We know how badly they want it,' Sophie said, a plan beginning to take shape in her mind even as she spoke. 'So let's use it to draw them out. If Joe really is alive, then it follows he must be in New York too. I'll go there, as if I'm following the instructions – and I'll track him down, and rescue him.'

Lil stared at her. She stared so hard that Sophie found herself beginning to blush. She knew it was a bold plan. She might be an experienced detective, but she was still just one young woman, talking of taking on a powerful criminal organisation in a completely unknown city on the other side of the world.

But then Lil began to smile. It was her old smile – a dazzling grin of the kind that charmed even the grumpiest elderly lady, and frequently flustered young gentlemen. Sophie realised that she hadn't seen Lil smile like that in rather a long time.

'Oh, well, then,' said Lil. 'In that case, I say we ignore *this*.' She pointed to the letter and the words *travel alone*. 'There's not the slightest chance I'm going to let you go to New York to rescue Joe without me.'

Sophie smiled back. Lil was right, of course: they'd spent more than enough time working apart. And with Lil by her side, anything seemed possible.

'But I suppose I'll have to travel undercover,' Lil continued. 'We don't want the *Fraternitas* to get wind of what we're planning.'

'Well, you've had plenty of practice,' Sophie pointed out. 'So – it's decided?'

Lil nodded. 'Yes. The two of us are going to New York.'

'Oh, no, you aren't,' came a voice from the doorway.

Sophie and Lil looked up to see Billy and Mei standing together on the threshold, looking in at them with very determined expressions. With them were the two dogs – Daisy, the Alsatian, and Lucky, the little black pug – whom they'd evidently taken for a morning run in the park.

'What on earth do you mean, we *aren't*?' repeated Lil.

Billy's cheeks turned pink as he hurried to explain. 'Not just the two of you, I mean. *We're* coming too.'

'If you're going to save Joe, you're going to need our help,' Mei added, her arms folded. At her side, Lucky gave a little *yip* as if in agreement. 'We're all members of the Loyal Order of Lions, aren't we? We *all* made a vow to try and stop the *Fraternitas*. So we'll *all* go to New York.'

Mei was right – Sophie saw that at once. This would be the most dangerous mission they had ever attempted, and they were rescuing one of their own. Of course they would need Mei and Billy's help.

But before she could say any of that, Tilly appeared behind them in the doorway. 'New York? Are we really? Excellent. I hoped we would.'

Lil laughed. 'Of course. My mistake. We're *all* going to New York to rescue Joe.'

Sophie nodded. This was a job for the whole Taylor & Rose team — together.

Lil grinned, her eyes sparkling. 'So,' she said. 'When do we leave?'

CHAPTER THREE

The Kensington Select Seminary for Young Ladies
Cromwell Road, London

It was four o'clock in the afternoon, lessons were over for the day and the young ladies of the Kensington Select Seminary were in the common room. Some were playing parlour games, while others sat sedately, talking or reading. Several letters and packages had arrived by the afternoon post, and now one pupil was handing around a box of Sinclair's chocolates sent by a generous aunt. In the window seat, another was engrossed in the new issue of *Boys of Empire* – which she kept carefully concealed inside a copy of *Lady Diana DeVere's Etiquette for Debutantes*, since such magazines were not considered suitable reading material by the strict headmistress, Miss Pinker.

Anna and Evangeline had flopped down on the rug to open their letters. Anna – or, to give her her full title, Her

Royal Highness, Princess Anna of Arnovia – had been a pupil at the Kensington Seminary for less than a year, but she was already quite used to being at school. Indeed, there were times when her old life at Wilderstein Castle seemed rather like a dream.

In many ways, school was like being dropped into the pages of one of the school stories she'd always loved reading. There were dull things, of course, like arithmetic and end-of-term exams, but plenty of jolly things too – playing tennis and art classes and having buns for tea. She still had to learn needlework, and the proper way to dispense afternoon tea. But there were also singing lessons and lacrosse matches and splendid times in the common room. Best of all, there was Evangeline.

'Grandmother has engaged a French governess to chaperone me home for the holidays,' huffed her best friend now, looking up from her letter. 'Miss Pinker told her my French could use more work. So now I s'pose I'll have to spend the whole voyage practising verbs. I don't see why I have to have a chaperone anyway. I'm nearly fourteen! Why, there are lots of girls who go out to work at that age!'

Anna nodded – though she knew very well that Evangeline was not 'lots of girls'.

Like Anna, Evangeline had never been to school, and like Anna she was not British. Apart from that, the two girls couldn't have seemed more different. While Anna had been at lonely Wilderstein Castle, Evangeline had

22

grown up in the most fashionable part of bustling New York City. Her uncle was one of the richest men in America and her grandmother was a pillar of New York society. Evangeline was tall and confident; she spoke with an American drawl; she dressed in marvellous Paris frocks, as fashionable as any debutante; and she seemed impossibly sophisticated and grown-up.

But although they might seem different, Anna had soon realised that she and Evangeline actually had a lot in common. Like Anna, Evangeline was curious about everyone and everything. And like Anna, Evangeline loved the idea of travelling and having adventures. Anna could have listened to Evangeline talk about New York all day long – the people, the theatres, the shops. In return, Evangeline seemed to adore hearing about Anna's home country, Arnovia – the crooked little streets of the capital, Elffburg, and the gloomy old castle in the mountains where she'd grown up with only her brother for company.

Before long, the two of them had become best friends. And then something really exciting happened: Evangeline had invited Anna to spend the Easter holidays with her in New York.

'We'll have the most marvellous time! We'll go riding in Central Park – and have tea at the Waldorf-Astoria. Uncle Teddy will take us to the beach, and we'll go sailing in his yacht!'

Anna had listened, captivated, as Evangeline talked.

She couldn't imagine anything more wonderful than seeing it all for herself – but she knew there was not the slightest chance she could go. Her grandfather, the King of Arnovia, would never let her travel all the way to New York. It was remarkable enough that she'd been allowed to go to boarding school in London.

But before she could say any of this, Evangeline had continued in excitement: 'And *that's not even the best part!* We'll be travelling there on the *Thalassa!*'

Anna's eyes widened. The young ladies of the Kensington Seminary did not read the newspapers very often, but even *they* had heard of the *Thalassa* – the glamorous, state-of-the-art ocean liner that was now the largest in the world.

'Uncle Teddy is the founder of Atlantic Line, you know. He's in Europe on business, and he says we can travel back to New York with him on the *Thalassa*'s first voyage. Isn't that something? In the very best suite – good enough even for *royalty!*' Evangeline had added, flashing Anna a grin.

Anna did not think that Grandfather would be impressed even by grand ocean liners. But she had not reckoned with Evangeline's grandmother, Mrs Alma Van Bergen. 'She's thrilled with the idea. Having a real-life European princess to stay – why, it's all of her dreams come true!' Evangeline said. A string of messages had flown to and fro across the Atlantic: long, persuasive letters from Mrs Van Bergen, and short telegrams in reply from Grandfather's private secretary.

Now, Anna looked down at the envelopes in her lap. There was a rather inky, scribbly one which she recognised as a letter from her brother, Alex. There was a postcard from Elffburg from their footman and great friend, Karl. But to her surprise there was also a fat letter with the Arnovian royal crest on the envelope. It must be from Grandfather, she thought – no doubt confirming that she would not be allowed to go to New York.

She tore the envelope open, but as she scrutinised the letter inside, she went suddenly quiet.

'Hey, Anna – are you listening?' demanded Evangeline, who was still complaining about governesses. Anna did not reply, so she added more gently: 'It's not bad news, is it?'

But when Anna looked up from the letter, her eyes were shining. 'I don't believe it!' she said. 'Grandfather has given me permission. Eva – I'm coming with you to New York!'

CHAPTER FOUR

A Secret Location
Soho, London

The hidden room was silent, but for the crackling of the fire and the pattering of rain against the window. For once, the Chief of the Secret Service Bureau was completely lost for words.

'Miss Taylor . . . Miss Rose . . .' he muttered, looking at first one and then the other through his spectacles. 'Let me see if I have understood you correctly. We have finally acquired the Draco Almanac – containing within it the instructions for making a powerful secret weapon. Obtaining it has required a great deal of hard work and considerable risk to your own safety – let me remind you, Miss Taylor, that barely two weeks ago in Venice, you were almost *drowned* in an underground tomb. Now you propose going to New York to give the Almanac to the *Fraternitas Draconum*? The very people we have been working *against* all this time? And you are actually asking for my support in this?' There was silence for a moment, and then he continued mildly: 'Please do forgive me if I seem a little confused.'

'We're not *really* going to hand over the Almanac,' said Lil excitedly. 'We'll only appear to be following the instructions.'

'Once we arrive in New York, we'll begin an investigation,' Sophie explained. 'Starting with the Black Dragon herself – Mrs Davenport.'

'We'll locate her, find out where she's keeping Joe, and rescue him,' Lil continued. 'And we'll investigate the New York branch of the *Fraternitas*. We may be able to learn more about the society and its members. Perhaps even the identity of the Gold Dragon himself!'

'Of course, anything we can learn about the *Fraternitas* would be of great value,' the Chief acknowledged with a nod. 'And now more than ever. All our intelligence suggests that as we've closed in, putting them under increasing pressure, the society has grown more determined – and more dangerous. Reports indicate they're planning something big.' He frowned. 'The problem is that in order to *act* on anything you might learn in New York, we would need *hard evidence* to back it up. That has always been our trouble with the *Fraternitas*. They're generally very careful to avoid leaving any kind of trail.'

'That's just it,' said Sophie. 'We know how much they want the Almanac. We can use that to our advantage. And if they're under pressure, they may take risks and slip up.'

The Chief nodded. 'I do see what you are getting at, Miss Taylor. But if that is your plan, why take the Almanac with you at all? Why not leave it safely at the Bureau?'

Sophie hesitated. She knew that the Chief had expected her to deliver the Almanac to the Bureau the moment they'd returned from Venice. But Sophie had stalled. She knew that as soon as she handed the Almanac to the Chief, his experts would go to work to decipher it — and the Chief would share whatever they learned with his superiors. What if the British government decided to make the deadly weapon for themselves? What if they used it against their enemies? Sophie couldn't let that happen. She was glad that their plan now provided her with a valid reason not to hand him the Almanac straight away.

She couldn't say any of that outright to the Chief, of course. 'We have to give the appearance of following their instructions,' she said instead.

'We can't risk them becoming suspicious – not when they have Joe,' said Lil.

'But taking the Almanac to New York would be a far *greater* risk,' argued the Chief. 'I understand your fears for your friend and I sympathise. But you must see that he is just *one person*. If the *Fraternitas* were to get hold of the Almanac, then *thousands* of innocent lives could be at risk.'

'With respect, sir, I think there may be innocent lives at risk either way,' said Sophie softly.

The Chief gave her a very sharp look. His expression was difficult to read, and Sophie's heart began hammering in her chest. She shouldn't have said that. The Chief was a powerful and important man. He was connected to the highest levels of the War Office and the Admiralty, and reported directly to the Prime Minister. If he wanted to, she knew he could stop them in their tracks. He could forbid their plan, have his men sweep into the office and seize the Almanac for himself. He could shut down Taylor & Rose altogether, or even arrest them, if he felt like it. He was frowning, and Sophie felt dread sweep over her. It had been idiotic to think there was even a chance he'd agree to this.

Then the Chief turned abruptly to his secretary, Captain Carruthers, who was sitting at his side. 'What do you make of this plan?'

Carruthers looked awkward, and Sophie watched him unhappily. She knew he believed that the Almanac belonged in the hands of the British government. She was certain she knew how he would answer, and so she was startled when he cleared his throat and said: 'I think Miss Taylor and Miss Rose are right.'

The Chief looked surprised too, and Carruthers hastened to explain. 'We know the *Fraternitas* desperately want the Almanac. We have no idea how this proposed *exchange* will work but there's no denying it offers a real chance to get close to them. Yes, it's a risk, but it's a calculated one. And Miss Taylor and Miss Rose have kept the Almanac safe so far, haven't they?' he added, flashing Sophie a quick, pointed look. The Chief still did not know that Sophie had tried to destroy the book in Venice. 'There's no reason to suppose that they could not continue to do so now,' he finished.

The Chief said nothing for a moment. He eyed Carruthers thoughtfully, then looked at Sophie and Lil. 'No, I am sorry. I cannot possibly endorse this,' he said at last, slowly and heavily. 'No matter how much of an opportunity it may present. The Bureau cannot support anything so reckless. It is out of the question.'

Lil looked horrified. 'But what about *Joe*?' she protested. 'You can't expect us to just *leave* him!'

The Chief held up a hand. 'Listen to me, Miss Rose,' he said, speaking carefully. 'I cannot *endorse* this. *The Bureau* cannot support it.' He looked at Lil again, then at Sophie, more intently this time. Sophie stared back at him in wonder. Did he mean what she thought he meant?

'But –' Lil began again.

The Chief was still looking at Sophie, and in that moment, she was certain. She grabbed Lil by the arm. '*Lil!*' she hissed – and Lil fell abruptly silent.

'We understand,' said Sophie. 'Do you have any other orders for us?'

The Chief shook his head. 'I won't be needing you again for a few weeks. Captain Carruthers will call at your office in a few days, just to ensure that all of our paperwork is in order,' he said, taking a casual puff of his pipe. 'Make sure you have everything ready for him. Tell him if there is anything you need – anything at all. And needless to say, I will expect you to deliver the Almanac to me at the Bureau, in due course.'

'*In due course*,' repeated Sophie, getting to her feet. She pulled Lil up beside her. 'Thank you, sir. Thank you very much indeed.'

'Goodnight, Miss Taylor, Miss Rose,' the Chief said. He spoke in the same casual tone, but his eyes flashed as they met Sophie's one final time. 'Good hunting.'

The door had barely closed behind them before Lil exploded. '*Sophie! What on earth* –' she began.

Sophie squeezed her arm again, but more gently this time. 'It's all right, Lil,' she said softly. 'We're going to New York.'

'But – the Chief said –'

'He said he couldn't *endorse* it. He said the Bureau couldn't *support* it. But he didn't forbid it. He didn't say we *couldn't go*.'

Lil's eyes widened as she understood. The Chief had made it clear that he could not give them official permission to take the Almanac to New York. But without saying it in so many words, he'd made it known that they *should* go, just the same.

CHAPTER FIVE

Taylor & Rose Detectives
Sinclair's, Piccadilly, London

'It's a good plan,' said Billy, nodding earnestly. It was after closing time, and the five of them were sitting in a circle in the office, with cups of hot cocoa and a plate of currant buns.

'But what about our tickets?' asked Mei. 'Our identity papers? The Bureau has always organised everything like that.'

'Carruthers will take care of it,' explained Lil. 'He came this morning and said he would organise everything for us.'

'*Unofficially*, of course,' added Sophie. She remembered what else Carruthers had said to them. 'Are you absolutely *sure* you want to do this? It won't be a Bureau mission. You'll be travelling as private citizens, without any of the protections afforded to agents of the British government. That means if anything goes wrong . . .' His voice had trailed away, but Sophie hadn't needed him to finish his sentence. She'd known what he was getting at. Without the Chief and the Bureau, they would be absolutely on their own.

'So we'll all be travelling undercover – except for Sophie,' Billy said.

Sophie nodded. 'I'll be bringing the Almanac, as though I'm following the Black Dragon's instructions.' She tapped the gilded cover of the book as she spoke.

Tilly had been listening in silence. Now, she frowned at the book, and spoke up. 'Listen, there's one thing I've been thinking about. I know why you don't want to hand the Almanac over to the Chief and his experts – but why shouldn't we look at it ourselves? It could help us understand why it's so important to the *Fraternitas* – and exactly what the secret weapon is. What did you say it was called – sky fire?'

'But we'd never be able to understand it!' said Mei. She reached out a fingertip and flipped open the book's cover, revealing wrinkled pages covered in cryptic symbols, peculiar diagrams, Latin words and Chinese characters – some of them now rather blurry from being submerged underwater. 'Just look at it – how would we even begin?'

'Well, it mightn't be easy,' said Tilly. 'But we could try. After all, I know something about chemistry, and I'm sure Leo would be able to interpret some of these pictures and symbols.'

'I say – that's true!' exclaimed Lil. 'Perhaps your father could help us with the Chinese characters, Mei? And Jack could help too. He's studied Latin and Greek.'

They looked excited – all except Sophie. She'd already seen more than enough of the Almanac, when she'd flicked through its pages in Venice. She knew nothing about old documents – after all she hadn't been to university like Tilly, or boarding school like Lil, or even studied at night-classes like Billy. The only formal education she'd had was the French and fancy embroidery stitches she'd been taught by her old governess, Miss Pennyfeather – unless you counted her ability to identify a Paris hat. But she didn't have to be able to read the book to feel that something dark and sinister seemed to seep from its pages. She didn't think anyone should try to decipher it — not even themselves.

'There could be all kinds of valuable scientific information in there,' Tilly was saying.

'And we might learn more about the origins of the *Fraternitas*. Those legends about dragons and lions!' added Billy, looking rather thrilled at the prospect of mysterious old tales.

Sophie got to her feet. 'I'm sorry – we just *can't*,' she said shortly. Before any of the others could argue, she wrapped up the Almanac, put it in the safe and shut the door.

Tilly looked annoyed and the others disappointed. But as soon as the door was locked on the *Almanac*, Sophie felt better. Silly as it sounded, the book seemed to give off a bad feeling. If it weren't for Joe, she'd wish heartily that it was still at the bottom of the Venice lagoon.

Several days later, Carruthers returned, bringing with him a thick folder. The outside was neatly labelled, *Taylor & Rose: Contracts and Invoices*, but inside was something rather different.

34

NEW YORK

Population c.5million
(growing rapidly)
Currency: Dollars (100 cents =
1 dollar)
... of five boroughs - The Bronx, B...
...ens and Staten Island.
...est and most de...

NATIONAL
REGISTRATION
IDENTITY
CARD

OCEAN TICKET
RMS THALASSA
TITLE   MISS MATILDA MORTON
...   ...'S MAID

OCEAN TICKET
RMS THALASSA
...ATION   MISS MEL...
...ass, De...

OCEAN TICKET
RMS THALASSA
TITLE   MISS SOPHIE TAYLOR
OCCUPATION   DETECTIVE
SECOND CLASS F4
...MPTON To   NEW YORK

OCEAN TICKET
RMS THALASSA
MR WILLIAM SMUGGS
...ATION   CLERK
THIRD CLASS G60
...PTON To   NEW YORK

THE
RMS THALASSA
VOYAGE
№ 3443

№ 3457

№ 34...

THE
RMS
VOYAGE

CONFIDENTIAL
CONFIDENTIAL

NAME Mrs Zhang
D.O.B.
Occupation None

NAME Matilda Mor...
D.O.B.
Occupation

'Well . . . here we are,' said Carruthers, a little awkwardly, taking a seat beside Sophie's desk. 'Papers . . . tickets . . . boarding passes. I've secured passage for you on the new RMS *Thalassa*. You'll have seen it in the papers. It's very large – the largest transatlantic steamer there is, in fact – which should make it easier for you all to blend in amongst the other passengers.'

'Everyone apart from Lil will be using their own first names. They're far less likely to slip up and make mistakes that way.' Carruthers pointed to a ticket. 'This one is Lil's. She'll be posing as a governess. She's done it before, so it should be straightforward. But just the same, she'll need to be careful. After all, her photo *has* appeared on the front pages of a London newspaper, strongly implying she's a British secret agent!' He looked disapproving. 'It makes her rather conspicuous!'

'You don't have to worry about Lil,' Sophie said. 'Undercover work is – well, it's rather her *speciality*.'

'Hmmm,' said Carruthers. 'That's as may be. But the other person I'm concerned about is Miss Lim.'

'*Mei?*' repeated Sophie in surprise.

'The United States of America has a law called the Chinese Exclusion Act,' Carruthers explained briskly. 'It prevents Chinese nationals from going to live there.'

Sophie frowned. 'But why?'

'The American government thought there were too many Chinese immigrants coming to America, I suppose,' said Carruthers.

'What a perfectly horrid law,' said Sophie. She knew that the Chinese community in London had to put up with people spreading idiotic stories about nefarious goings-on in sinister opium dens, which bore no resemblance whatsoever to the real East End Chinatown she knew. That was bad enough, but actually being banned from a country simply because of where you came from seemed extraordinary.

'Even though Mei *isn't* Chinese, but British, because of her appearance the New York port officials may be suspicious of her on arrival, and begin asking awkward questions,' Carruthers explained primly. 'Especially if she's travelling third-class, among people who are immigrating to America to live.' He tapped another ticket. 'That's why she'll be travelling First Class. She'll take on the identity of the wealthy daughter of a rich Shanghai merchant. She'll be the pupil, and Lil will be her governess. As for Miss Black, I know she's posed as a lady's maid before. She'll be doing the same here, playing the role of Miss Lim's maid. That seems the most *suitable*,' said Carruthers, pointing to another ticket.

Sophie frowned. She knew what Carruthers meant by *suitable*. A girl who looked like Tilly would not be expected to travel aboard a grand ship like the *Thalassa* – not unless she were in the guise of a maid. For all the difficulties that Sophie faced as a young lady detective, she was always learning of the many more that Tilly and Mei had to deal with.

Carruthers had already moved on. 'This is a briefing on New York City. And here is some information about the *Thalassa* which may be useful.'

'Thank you,' said Sophie. But as she reached for the documents, greatly to her surprise, Carruthers reached out and took her hand.

'Be very careful, Sophie,' he said in a low, warning tone. 'And when you come back from New York, whatever happens, you *have* to give the Almanac to the Chief. You'll be in fearful trouble if you don't.'

'I know,' said Sophie, feeling a sting of guilt as she spoke. Papa had taught her she should always tell the truth, but she could not possibly admit to Carruthers that she was still planning to destroy the Almanac. The words *fearful trouble* made her uneasy, but she knew she had no choice.

'Give me your word,' said Carruthers, without letting go of her hand.

Sophie hesitated, not knowing what to say. To her relief, just then the door opened, and a young woman came unexpectedly into the room. She was tall and upright, plainly dressed in a brown tweed suit, a high-necked blouse and a hat without any trimmings. Her hair was drawn back into a neat bun, and she wore spectacles on the end of her nose.

Carruthers started in alarm, snatching his hand away and shoving the papers out of sight, but Sophie grinned.

'Good afternoon, Miss Carter,' she said.

The young woman grinned back, and the serious-looking bluestocking vanished and became Lil again. 'I jolly well had you fooled, didn't I?' she said to Carruthers, quite delighted with herself.

'Only for a minute,' said Carruthers, crossly.

'I *told* you that you didn't have to worry,' said Sophie, with a laugh. It was wonderful to see Lil back to her old, effervescent self. Ever since they'd made the plan to go to New York, she'd seemed transformed. The prospect of getting Joe back had filled her with cheerfulness. Looking at her now, Sophie hoped more than ever that it was all true, and that Lil's optimism was not misplaced.

Lil performed a little twirl before the looking-glass, and then gave a sigh. She'd always loved clothes, and was drawn to bright colours and beautiful fabrics. Wearing Miss Carter's dark, plain suits and sensible shoes gave her no joy. How could anyone choose to go about without even as much as a dusting of rouge, or a bow on their hat?

But it was worth it. *Anything* would be worth it, she decided, as she walked home later that evening. Wearing dreadful clothes. Posing as a governess – again. The elaborate plans they were making to travel across an ocean to the other side of the world. Putting off Gilbert Lloyd, who wanted to stage a new play about a young lady detective – with herself as the star. It was something she had dreamed of for as long as she could remember. Yet now it hardly seemed to matter at all.

What mattered was finding Joe and bringing him back to London, so they could be together. She had a very clear vision of exactly how it would be.

The Taylor & Rose office on a wet afternoon – rain against the windows, the lamps lit. Sophie pouring the tea, and Billy getting buns out of a paper bag, while they chatted and laughed. And there would be Joe in the midst of it all, listening to what everyone was saying and smiling his slow, kind smile at her.

As always, the thought of Joe made her heart skip and pirouette in the air. She remembered when she'd last seen him, when they'd said goodbye on the station platform, and she'd thought, for a moment, that he was going to kiss her. Then, like the air rushing out of a balloon, her heart plummeted. There was so much they didn't know. Where was he? What had the *Fraternitas* been doing with him all these months? Had they hurt him? Worst of all – was he really alive, or was it all a dreadful trick?

There was no way of knowing for sure. But if Joe *was* still alive, then one thing was certain: they had to find him. She began humming a little song to herself as she walked – a very silly sort of song, from a show she'd been in back when she was a chorus girl at the Fortune Theatre. It was called 'The Fairest of Them All' – a perfectly idiotic song, really, but somehow it always raised her spirits.

She began to feel better at once. She might not know

how they would do it, but she had no doubt they would do everything they could to find Joe and bring him safely home once more.

But Lil might not have felt quite so confident if she had been able to see what was happening at Taylor & Rose at that very moment.

In the darkness of the empty office, the door creaked softly open. A stealthy figure came inside, sliding through the shadows, making their way towards the safe.

A careful gloved hand reached out, and then quickly spun the dial – first this way, then that. A moment later, the metal door gave a *clunk* as it unlocked and swung open.

The gloved hand reached inside, moving over the identity papers, the boarding passes, the tickets, the secret briefings, and a thick stack of dollar bills. At the back of the safe, all by itself, lay the Draco Almanac.

There was a moment's pause – and then the gloved hand reached out and took it.

CHAPTER SIX

London & Southampton

The next two weeks rushed by. There was a great deal to prepare, as well as all the usual work of a busy detective agency to do: clients to meet, letters to answer, bills to pay. They were all working hard to give the impression that everything at Taylor & Rose was 'business as usual'. Officially, only Sophie was travelling to New York. But behind closed doors, suitcases were packed, and quiet conversations took place with their most trusted friends.

In a cosy Bloomsbury sitting room, Lil and Tilly talked late into the night with Jack and Leo. In the kitchen of their home in Chinatown, Mei had a long conversation with her older brother, Song. Over what appeared to be an ordinary afternoon tea in the Marble Court restaurant, Sophie spoke to two young socialites, Veronica and Phyllis. Behind the door of her private office, Billy had several confidential talks with Mr Sinclair's secretary, Miss Atwood, who placed a short transatlantic telephone call on his behalf. With their help, the offices of Taylor & Rose would remain open – and no one would guess what was really going on.

...parture came. Early in the morning, ...office to collect the last things she ...ting out for Southampton – and to ...who would be staying behind with ...gave the dog a final pat, and Daisy ...siastically. 'We'll do our very best to ...,' Sophie whispered in her ear. Daisy ...e Joe's dog than anyone else's; now ...e, as if she understood every word

...already packed and waiting by the ...as left was to put a few things in her ...ather battered now, after travelling ...s, trains and even aeroplanes. She'd ...tray with ordinary supplies that any ...e on a journey: a book, a magazine, ...ns, and a bottle of *eau de cologne*. But ...rtment beneath were supplies of a ...pers and the letters from the Black ...merican dollars, her lock-picks, a ...all camera disguised to look like an ..., and her little pearl-handled pistol. ...the safe and unlocked it. There, at ...left it, was the Draco Almanac, still wrapped in brown paper. She tucked it away into the secret compartment of her case, shutting the lid with a firm *click*.

She took one last look around the quiet office. A peculiar feeling swept over her suddenly – a prickle of excitement and anticipation, of something about to happen. What lay ahead of her, she had not the least idea.

But as she turned out the lights, she realised that there was something else too. Wherever she'd travelled before, she'd always taken one of her mother's old diaries along with her. Sophie's mother had travelled a great deal when she was young, but her travels had never taken her as far as America. Now Sophie would be venturing right across the Atlantic – and she'd be doing it alone.

But she wasn't really alone of course. For one thing, hidden beneath the collar of her blouse, she wore her mother's green necklace, like a secret talisman. For another, as she stepped off the train and on to the railway station platform in Southampton, she could sense that her friends were not far away. They might be travelling separately, but they were together, just the same.

The docks were crowded with people: passengers saying goodbye to loved ones; porters pushing trolleys stacked high with steamer-trunks; smart officials inspecting tickets and boarding cards. High above all the bustle and noise and smoke, the immense ocean liner towered. For a moment, Sophie stood still and gazed up at it from beneath the brim of her hat.

The RMS *Thalassa* made every other ship she'd travelled on before look like a tiny rowing boat. Smoke was already unfurling from the enormous funnels, and passengers were streaming aboard. Holding tightly to the handle of her attaché case, Sophie went forward to join them.

PART II

CHAPTER SEVEN

Aboard the RMS *Thalassa*

A door swung open. A smart doorman bowed low.

'Welcome to the RMS *Thalassa!*' The steward beamed as he came forward to greet them. 'Please, allow me to escort you to your suite.'

Growing up beside the docks of the East End, Mei thought she knew something about ships. After all, her own uncle was a sailor. But this immense ocean liner was like no ship she'd ever seen.

There was almost too much to take in. Elaborately carved statues, chandeliers, a grand staircase sweeping regally downwards, a domed glass ceiling arching high above her head. Everything seemed to gleam and glitter and she felt suddenly giddy. It was so strange to be here, dressed in a rustling silk frock with frilly petticoats, silk stockings and an enormous bow in her hair. Her skirts swished as she walked, and her big hat wreathed in ribbons and flowers felt very heavy on her head.

The steward, who had introduced himself as Mr Talbot, gave her a smile. Mei clasped her gloved hands, trying to look like Miss Mei Zhang – or to use her proper Chinese name, Zhang Chan-Mei – the pampered daughter of a rich Shanghai merchant who had never been anywhere near a Limehouse grocer's shop in her life. She suddenly wished that she was back at Taylor & Rose, with her telephone and typewriter. She always knew exactly what she was doing there.

'Here are the elevators, and this is the main staircase, reserved *exclusively* for the use of First Class passengers,' Talbot was saying.

'What about the other passengers?' asked Lil. Her voice was low and very proper; she looked every inch the prim governess, though behind her spectacles, Mei could see that her eyes were sparkling. She was in high spirits, and Mei understood why. Lil had always had a gift for undercover work, and loved nothing more than dressing up and playing a role. What was more, this time she was doing it for Joe.

By contrast, though she looked the part in her trim maid's uniform, Tilly did not seem to be enjoying it much. Tilly had grown up 'below stairs' in a grand country house, where she'd worked as a maid herself, so she knew exactly how to play the part, but Mei knew she found it dull. She was clutching a carpet bag protectively under one arm: Mei guessed it contained books, or scientific papers, or other such things that a lady's maid would not be expected to have in her luggage.

'Second and Third Class have their own staircases *elsewhere* on board,' Talbot explained as he led them along a wide corridor. Through open doors, Mei glimpsed bedrooms that looked like they belonged in a smart London hotel. Inside, maids and valets were unpacking trunks and hanging up evening gowns. 'They also have their own promenades, dining room and lounges. The First Class quarters are kept *quite* separate.'

Lil nodded, her face unreadable, and Mei tried to keep her own expression just as blank. Inwardly, she was grimacing. The steward made it sound as if even catching sight of a lowly Second or Third Class passenger would be quite revolting.

'You are travelling in one of our Deluxe Parlour suites – the *largest* of our suites on board. Each has three bedrooms, a bathroom and a private promenade.' He opened a door with a flourish, revealing a large and luxurious sitting room with panelled walls, soft rugs and comfortable chairs. You wouldn't have known you were aboard a ship at all, Mei thought, were it not for the doors opening on to a private section of the deck, framing magnificent views of pale grey sea and sky. It was all she could do not to gasp aloud, and even Lil faltered.

'It is a *very* fine suite,' said Talbot, looking pleased at their reaction. 'I hope you'll be most comfortable here. Here are the bedrooms, where you will find your luggage waiting for you, and this is the bathroom – equipped with every modern convenience.'

Peeping into the lavish bathroom with its enormous, gleaming bath tub, fluffy towels and hot water taps, Mei's eyes widened. At home in Limehouse they didn't even *have* a bathroom – Mei was used to the tin bath in front of the fire.

'This is your bell. You can ring for anything you may require, day or night!' added Talbot. 'And *here* is today's luncheon menu from the restaurant – though, of course, I can have your meal brought to your suite, if you would prefer to dine in private.'

Mei looked down at the impressive luncheon menu, and then up at the others. Lil was grinning and even Tilly looked pleased. Perhaps, she reflected, going undercover on the *Thalassa* was not going to be so very difficult, after all.

As the ship steamed out across the Atlantic Ocean, Sophie was hanging up her frocks in the wardrobe in her cabin. It was a very comfortable place. There was a neat bed, spread with a fresh white eiderdown, and a little sofa where she could sit and read. There was a dressing table complete with wash basin, looking glass and clever compartments to keep her belongings tidy. She was glad that her cabin was so pleasant – for she'd made up her mind she'd be spending a great deal of time in it over the next few days.

She wanted to keep a low profile on the voyage. She'd go to the dining room for her meals, of course, and take some walks on deck for fresh air – but she wasn't going to linger in the public areas chatting to her fellow passengers. Better to stay in her cabin, Better to stay in her cabin, reviewing her notes, and studying the map of New York's criss-crossing streets.

Already though, she felt restless. Perhaps it was the rumbling of the engines, or the splashing of waves against the porthole? Or perhaps it was simply that she always felt excited and nervous at the start of a new assignment – and this time, more than ever.

She picked up her small travelling clock, and saw that it was time for luncheon. Perhaps a change of scene would help? She glanced down at the information sheet which had been left on her dressing table.

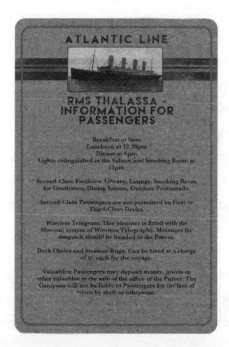

ATLANTIC LINE

RMS THALASSA –
INFORMATION FOR
PASSENGERS

Breakfast at 8am
Luncheon at 12.30pm
Dinner at 6pm
Lights extinguished in the Saloon and Smoking Room at
11pm

Second Class Facilities: Library, Lounge, Smoking Room
for Gentlemen, Dining Saloon, Outdoor Promenade.

Second-Class Passengers are not permitted on First or
Third-Class Decks.

Wireless Telegram: This steamer is fitted with the
Marconi system of Wireless Telegraphy. Messages for
despatch should be handed to the Purser.

Deck Chairs and Steamer Rugs: Can be hired at a charge
of 1/- each for the voyage.

Valuables: Passengers may deposit money, jewels or
other valuables in the safe of the office of the Purser. The
Company will not be liable to Passengers for the loss of
items by theft or otherwise.

Sophie looked thoughtfully at her attaché case, containing the Almanac. She'd kept tight hold of it as she'd come aboard, in spite of several porters offering to carry it for her. But what now? She couldn't risk leaving the Almanac unattended in the cabin – one glance at the door showed her it would be an easy job to pick the lock. Yet she was not going to put it in the Purser's safe either. She'd dealt with the *Fraternitas* long enough to learn that they were rich and powerful enough to bribe chambermaids, stewards, sailors, or perhaps even the Purser himself to do their bidding.

She would have to bring the Almanac with her. She took it out of the case and slipped it – still in its wrappings – inside a handbag, looping the long strap securely over her shoulder. She locked everything else inside the attaché case and slid it into the bottom of the wardrobe, out of sight.

There. Now to keep a low profile. But as she stepped out into the passageway, a familiar voice startled her.

'My goodness . . . Miss Taylor! Is that you?'

Sophie's heart fell. Even before she turned around, she knew that voice. It was Miss Roberta Russell – the inquisitive young journalist from *The Daily Picture* and the very last person Sophie wanted to see aboard the *Thalassa* – emerging from a cabin directly opposite her own.

'What *are* you doing here? I suppose you have a case to solve in New York?' Miss Russell's eyes gleamed. 'Or aboard the ship itself perhaps? Do tell – what's it all about?'

54

Sophie frowned. 'I'm not going to tell you anything about my work, after the way you twisted Lil's interview,' she said shortly. It wasn't only Billy's stories that Miss Russell had altered. Her interview with Lil in *The Daily Picture* had been full of wild exaggerations and sensational additions.

But Miss Russell just shrugged. 'Twisted it? Oh please! Miss Rose knew exactly what she was doing – she's got a sharp eye for publicity. Anyway, you ought to be grateful to me. I'll bet Taylor & Rose has had queues all the way down the street ever since!'

'That's not the point,' Sophie argued – though as a matter of fact Miss Russell was right, which only made it all the more annoying. 'Why did you put in all that made-up stuff about *spies*? And in Billy's stories, too! You more or less rewrote them.'

'We made a few tweaks, that's all,' said Miss Russell. 'I *told* him we'd have to make some changes. That's how it works. As for *spies*, well, that wasn't my doing. Mr Moorhouse, the editor-in-chief, is frightfully keen on spies – absolutely obsessed. He's even appointed a *spy editor*. He's got a bad case of spy fever, if you ask me!'

Miss Russell tutted as though she thought it was all terrifically silly, but for Sophie, her offhand phrase chimed like a bell. In Venice, senior members of the *Fraternitas* had talked about stirring up *spy fever* in Britain. Obviously it was working.

'Cabin numbers, please,' said a voice suddenly – and Sophie realised that they had come to the dining room, where a waiter was ushering them to a small table. It occurred to her too late that she was going to have to have lunch with Miss Russell.

'Look, I've helped *your* business,' the journalist said, as the waiter handed them each a menu. 'Now why don't you help *me* by dropping a hint about what you're investigating? We working women should stick together, after all. I rather think it would add some extra excitement to the piece I'm writing – a feature on the world's largest ocean liner and its passengers. Charlie Walters is aboard too, taking the pictures. There are a lot of famous people in First Class, you know. Movie stars, millionaires – even royalty, or so I've heard, though of course they're keeping *that* hush-hush.'

Sophie's heart fell further. Having Miss Russell aboard was bad enough, but if she and Charlie Walters were going to be nosing about First Class, there might be trouble. If either of them caught sight of Lil, the cat would be out of the bag at once.

'Of course, Moorhouse loves all that. The only thing he likes more than *spies* is *royalty*. What he wants is a piece full of celebrities and fashions – which is all he thinks lady journalists are capable of writing. If it were up to him, I'd write about nothing but princesses and weddings and *the season's loveliest debutantes*. Awful rot! When of course the *really* interesting story is the Atlantic Line itself.'

'What do you mean?' asked Sophie, drawn in despite everything.

'Well, transatlantic shipping is so important these days,' Miss Russell explained. 'There's a lot of money in it, of course – but imagine if there were to be a war! Whoever has control of the ships will have a tremendous amount of power. Just look at the way Britain and Germany have been vying for the biggest and best navy. Then along comes Van Bergen and the Atlantic Line. A *joint venture* involving three different nations: America, Britain and France. That's something quite new!'

The waiter brought them a bread basket. Miss Russell took a roll and began buttering it vigorously as she went on talking: 'I bet the Germans don't like it one bit. Their ships simply can't compete with the likes of the *Thalassa*! I'm going to ask Van Bergen about that – he's aboard and I've set up an interview with him tomorrow. Not what Moorhouse asked for, of course, but I'll soon change his mind when I get to New York.' Seeing Sophie look surprised, she explained: 'Moorhouse is out there already, with Sir Chester Norton. Sir Chester is buying the *New York Evening Telegram*, you know. He plans to expand Norton Newspapers into the United States. Of course, *Sir Chester* will quite understand why I'd interview Van Bergen. *He* knows that I'm capable of more – and that I want to write about something other than idiotic frocks and hats.'

'There's nothing wrong with frocks and hats, you know,' Sophie pointed out.

'Oh, *well*, I suppose not, if that's the sort of thing that interests you,' said Miss Russell, wrinkling up her nose. 'You read the fashion papers, then, do you?'

'Sometimes,' said Sophie. 'But that doesn't mean I don't read the *Financial Times* as well.'

'Interesting,' said Miss Russell. 'Do you know, I'm glad I ran into you, Miss Taylor. You're giving me some good ideas.'

Sophie wasn't quite sure how that could be as she'd barely opened her mouth since they'd sat down at the table. But she was grateful Miss Russell had been distracted. Kept busy talking about her own work, she had stopped asking awkward questions about Sophie's – for the time being, at least.

CHAPTER EIGHT

Aboard the RMS *Thalassa*

Anna was fizzing with excitement. She'd always longed to travel, but she'd never imagined anything half so fascinating as this enormous ship, with its huge smoking funnels and deep rumbling engines. She could still hardly believe Grandfather had allowed her to come at all. She couldn't wait to tell Alex every thrilling detail. He was beside himself with jealousy that she was going to New York – a city he knew well from the pages of his film magazines. He was usually the one who got to do things, and for once, Anna found it delightful to be the one who was setting off on a new adventure.

Grandfather had sent her a long letter before she left London, full of instructions: *at all times be a gracious guest . . . remember that you are a representative of Arnovia wherever you go.* She was trying not to think too much about the end of his letter, when he'd concluded: *Most of all, I want you to enjoy this splendid opportunity to see something of the world,*

without undue ceremony or (Mrs Van Bergen has assured me) the
attention of the press. Remember that in only a few years' time,
when you leave school, we must begin thinking seriously of your
future, and the official role you will play.

Anna knew what that meant. There was only really one
official role for a princess like her. It would be Alex who
would inherit the throne of Arnovia; she would be expected
to make a diplomatic marriage to a prince or duke, in order
to forge an important alliance for her country. Only last
year, Anna had been to Schwarzau Castle for the wedding
of her cousin Princess Zita of Bourbon-Parma, who'd been
married to Archduke Charles of Austria while she was still
in her teens. There had been a great deal of fuss and
photographs in all the newspapers. The thought that in
only a few years' time that could be *her* made Anna shudder.

She wouldn't think of that now. She would do as
Grandfather had told her – enjoy being here, aboard a
grand ocean liner, having a marvellously exciting adventure
in the company of her very best friend.

To Evangeline, of course, none of this was so thrilling
or remarkable. She was used to transatlantic travel– though
even she had never been aboard a ship quite as big or
impressive as the *Thalassa*.

'She's the biggest there is!' Teddy Van Bergen told them
proudly. 'Nothing else can hold a candle to her. There's
never been a ship like her before!'

Uncle Teddy, as Anna had already begun to think of

him, was not how she had imagined a tremendously rich businessman. She'd expected someone rather stiff and serious, but Mr Van Bergen was energetic and cheerful. He'd been dashing about all over the ship ever since they'd come aboard – meeting with the Captain and the Chief Engineer, chatting to all the most important passengers, posing for photographs – but he'd still managed to make time for his niece and her friend.

He'd arranged one of the best suites aboard for them, which they shared with Mademoiselle Esmé, the French governess who had been engaged to look after them on the voyage. 'Marvellous for you to practise your French!' said Uncle Teddy, beaming enthusiastically at them and at Mademoiselle Esmé, a pale young woman who seemed always to be clutching a lacy handkerchief. 'Foreign languages are very important in this day and age. The world is getting smaller all the time!'

When Evangeline had protested, Uncle Teddy had stood firm. 'We can't have the two of you rattling round the ship by yourselves. Mother wouldn't stand for that – and I'm quite sure His Royal Highness wouldn't either! Especially with journalists aboard. We've promised to keep Princess Anna out of the limelight.'

But as it happened, they *had* been allowed to rattle round by themselves a good deal more than they had expected. From almost the moment they'd left Southampton, Mademoiselle Esmé had gone from pale to decidedly green. Complaining of *mal de mer*, she'd shut herself in her room, leaving Anna and Evangeline free from French lessons, and able to roam around their new surroundings to their hearts' content.

'What luck!' exclaimed Evangeline. 'Oh, of course, I'm sorry she's ill and all, but now we can explore properly without a governess hanging about. We're going to have a lot of fun on this trip, Anna – just you wait and see!'

Anna was having the most tremendous fun already. She'd adored every minute aboard: standing on deck with Evangeline as they came into Cherbourg and seeing all the people waving; eating delicious meals in the First Class Restaurant where the chefs had come from the Grand Hotel Continental in Paris and the smart waiters made a great fuss of them because they were sitting at Mr Van Bergen's table. Sitting on deck in steamer chairs, watching the sparkling waves whipped by the wind, and seeing the elegant passengers promenading in the latest fashions. Finding her way about the ship through its maze of corridors, and peeping through open doors into the First Class staterooms.

Now, as they returned to their suite for afternoon tea, she saw that a nearby door was open. A steward was taking in a trolley of tea, and Anna's mouth began to water at the sight of it – scones topped with cream and fresh strawberries, a delectable-looking chocolate cake, and cucumber sandwiches cut into perfect triangles. She glanced curiously past the steward and caught a glimpse of the people inside. There were only two of them – a girl of about Anna's own age, dressed in a pale-pink frock, her long black hair tied back with an enormous bow. Opposite her, with her back to the door was a tall young woman dressed in a plain tailored suit, her hair in a neat bun. Although she couldn't see her face, the strangest feeling suddenly swept over Anna – the feeling that she *knew* her.

Just then, the steward came bustling back out of the suite, closing the door behind him with elaborate care. He saw Anna and Evangeline and beamed at them.

'Good afternoon, Your Royal Highness, Miss Van Bergen,' he said with a little bow. Anna had noticed that all the stewards and stewardesses seemed to know exactly who they were – and whether it was because she was a princess, or because she was the personal guest of Mr Van Bergen, or both, they seemed in a great hurry to do whatever she asked them. It was hard to believe that only last week she'd been at school, being scolded for inkblots in her arithmetic book.

'Good afternoon – er, could you tell me who is staying in that suite?' she asked.

'But, of course, Your Royal Highness,' said the steward. 'It is occupied by a young lady named Miss Zhang.'

Miss Zhang. She must be the black-haired girl in the pink dress. Anna was sure she had never heard that name before.

'Is she alone?' she asked.

'She's travelling with a maid and a governess.'

A *governess*. For a moment Anna stood still, frowning, but Evangeline had become restless. 'Come on – I'm hungry after all that exploring. Let's have some tea.'

Anna followed, thinking of chocolate cake and cucumber sandwiches – but even as she did so, she couldn't help glancing back over her shoulder to the closed door.

Sophie peered cautiously out into the passageway, checking for any sign of Miss Russell before she left her cabin. She'd spent most of the afternoon puzzling out the best way to get a message secretly to Lil in First Class. She wanted to let Billy know too; even though Miss Russell was less likely to be poking about Third Class, if she *did* see him, she would certainly recognise him.

By the time she'd worked out a suitable method of sending them each a message, and made her arrangements, it was dinner time. To her relief, Miss Russell was nowhere to be seen in the passageway or in the dining room, but still, Sophie did not linger over her meal. She didn't want to be caught by Miss Russell and subjected to more questions about what she was doing aboard.

She'd planned to go straight back to her cabin as soon as dinner was over, but as she left the dining room, she began to feel restless again. It was strange just waiting to arrive in New York, with no idea what would be waiting for them when they got there. She'd felt so certain of the plan when she'd been with Lil and the others, but now she was alone, she began to feel worried. Were they doing the right thing? Her thoughts kept slipping back to Joe, and the question she didn't want to ask herself – whether he could really be alive at all.

Sophie was usually quite happy in her own company, but now she suddenly longed for someone to talk to. In the Lounge, she could see groups of passengers gathering to drink after-dinner coffee or play card games, and the sight of them made her feel lonelier than ever. Turning away, she headed out on deck. A breath of fresh air would soon set her right.

The promenade was almost empty now. One or two people had been taking a stroll to watch the sunset, but most of the pink had ebbed away from the sky, and darkness was falling. It was cold, and Sophie wished she had brought a warmer jacket. She walked briskly along the promenade, feeling the chilly wind against her face, and pausing to lean against the balustrade, looking down at the dark water below.

She couldn't have said what it was that first gave her the feeling that something wasn't right. There was no sound to alert her, only the sudden, peculiar sense that she was being watched. At once, she whipped around – and as she did so, she caught sight of a man disappearing quickly through a door that led inside, the hem of a dark coat flapping behind him.

Sophie did not hesitate. She raced after him, but the

man was moving fast. She could hear the sound of his footsteps ahead of her, disappearing down a staircase. Making up her mind to follow, she ran lightly down the stairs after him, until she emerged in a long passageway stretching in both directions, lined with neat cabin doors. She caught a glimpse of a man in a dark coat and hat disappearing into one of the cabins, closing the door swiftly behind him.

Sophie made straight for the door, which she saw was numbered *D56*. But before she could reach it, she heard someone coming down the passageway, and at once she dropped to the floor, as if fastening a bootlace that had come untied. Glancing sideways, she saw that a stewardess was approaching, carrying an envelope. She stopped at the door of *D56* and tapped on it gently.

Sophie stayed where she was, fiddling with her bootlace. There was no reply, so the stewardess tapped again, a little louder this time. 'Excuse me – Herr Fritzel?' she called. 'There's a Marconigram for you. It's marked urgent.'

The door jerked open a crack – much too narrow for Sophie to see anything inside. A hand snatched the envelope from the stewardess and the door was shut again in her face.

'Er, shall I wait for an answer, sir?' the stewardess called through the door, looking rather startled by this rude behaviour. There was a curt grunt of assent in reply.

'Are you all right, miss?' asked the stewardess politely,

glancing down at Sophie.

Feeling that she couldn't possibly stay where she was for any longer without appearing most peculiar, Sophie stood up and smiled. 'Oh, yes, thank you – my bootlace snapped,' she explained. She wished she could linger to see the door open again with the answer, but she couldn't think of any possible reason to stay. Instead, she walked quickly back to her cabin to think. *Herr Fritzel.* It was a German name. Had he really been following her?

But even before she opened the door to her cabin, that strange feeling swept over her again. *Something wasn't right.* Swiftly, she unlocked the door and went inside. Everything seemed just as usual. There was nothing out of place – no footprint on the floor, no snippet of loose thread, not even so much as a faint whiff of tobacco to suggest an intruder. Yet someone *had* been here, she was sure of it.

She opened the wardrobe, noticing that the clothes were hanging in almost but not quite the same order that she had left them. Her attaché case was still in the bottom of the wardrobe, but it had been moved, just slightly. Someone had handled it; perhaps, if they were clever at picking locks, they had even looked inside. But everything was still there – papers, money, camera, even her little pistol. Whoever had been in her room, they were no ordinary thief.

She shut the case and replaced it in the wardrobe, then sat down to think things through. Was the intruder the same man who'd been following her on deck – the mysterious Herr Fritzel? Had he been sneaking around in her cabin while she'd been in the dining room? If so, there was surely only one reason for that. Herr Fritzel must be working for the *Fraternitas Draconum*.

But why would the *Fraternitas* send someone to search her cabin? Had they hoped to find the Almanac and steal it? Why would they take it from her, when as far as they knew, she was bringing it to them in New York? Then something dreadful crossed her mind. If they intended to steal the Almanac on the voyage, could it be that the exchange really was a trick, after all? What if they'd simply used Joe's name as a way of getting her here alone, so they could take the Almanac from her?

She went over to the door, locking it securely, and then wedging a chair behind the handle. That would keep her safe for tonight, at least. She'd keep the pistol close beside the bed and carry it with her from now on.

Tomorrow she would get to work investigating Herr Fritzel. It was a good job she'd already sent messages to the others, she reflected. With an agent of the *Fraternitas* aboard the *Thalassa*, she was certainly going to need their help.

CHAPTER NINE

Aboard the RMS *Thalassa*

'Peppermints,' said a voice, from somewhere above Billy's head. 'That's the thing.'

'No, no – it's a dose of port wine and a pork chop, that's what Auntie Mary always said,' said another. 'And *she* would know, with the way that Uncle Colm always used to carry on.'

'You're all wrong, Jimmy. It wasn't a pork chop. It was a *dish of strawberry ice-cream* that Uncle Colm used to take for his sickness.'

There was a dismissive snort. 'A dish of strawberry ice-cream, is it? And where exactly are we going to get *strawberry ice-cream*? Are you proposing to stroll up to First Class and ask for some?'

Billy let out a miserable groan. 'Can you both please stop going on about food?' he demanded weakly.

It was the second day aboard the *Thalassa*, and from

where he was lying on his narrow bunk, Billy was vaguely aware that the corridors of Third Class were full of cheerful activity. Children were running up and down the passageways; plates and glasses were rattling as the tables in the dining room were laid for lunch; and somewhere, a gramophone was playing. But Billy could scarcely lift himself from his bunk. Now that the ship was out on the rolling waves of the Atlantic Ocean, he'd been struck down with powerful seasickness. He'd never felt so dreadful in all his life.

'Cotton in the ears, maybe? That's one I heard from an old sailor,' said Jimmy O'Hara. He was one of Billy's cabin-mates, a talkative young fellow from Dublin.

'Or a pinch of smelling salts, perhaps?' suggested his brother Patrick. They were a high-spirited pair, both excited about going to live with their uncle and aunt in Brooklyn, and keen to help Billy if they could.

'Give the poor kid a break,' said the third of his cabin-mates with a grin. Danny Quinn was a young New Yorker, heading home after spending some time working in Europe. Billy didn't know much about him, but he felt disposed to like him because of his ready sense of humour – and because he was often to be found reading a book. Now, Danny nodded towards the door. 'Cheer up. Here's the steward with something for you.'

A plate of biscuits and a steaming mug appeared at Billy's side. 'Not feeling too well, I hear?' said a cheerful voice. 'It can take some folk that way. We need to get you up on deck in the fresh air, that's the best thing. But have this to perk you up first. A good strong cup of beef tea and some cabin biscuits. Drink up, there's a good lad.'

Billy didn't feel like he could bear to drink anything, never mind beef tea, but the steward looked like a no-nonsense sort of a fellow and, besides, he didn't have the strength to argue. Propped up on some pillows, he managed to take a small sip of the savoury liquid.

'That's the way,' said Jimmy, nodding approvingly. 'You'll soon feel better, Bill.'

He'd told them that his name was Bill Smuggs, according to the cover story he'd rehearsed with Lil back at the office, the storyteller in him rather enjoying the chance to spin a tale. He'd said that he worked for Mr Edward Sinclair, who was travelling in the States, and had instructed Billy to travel out there to bring him his pet dog – an idea which the other fellows found very amusing indeed.

'You need to get well so you can go down to the kennels and check on that dog,' said Pat now with a chuckle. 'What's her name again?'

'Lucky,' said Billy, taking another sip of beef tea, and bravely nibbling a biscuit. 'She's a little black pug.'

Jimmy shook his head. 'I didn't know you could *bring* dogs aboard the ship!'

'Oh, you can – if you can pay for it,' said the steward, nodding sagely. 'Lots of First Class passengers have their dogs in the ship's kennels. There's a prize Pekingese, a champion bulldog and one or two pedigree cats as well. Even a canary, if you can believe it. They each have to have their own First Class ticket, of course.'

'Even the canary?' asked Quinn, with an amused grin.

The steward nodded, and Jimmy gave a hoot of laughter. 'So you mean to say this dog is living the high life in First Class – while you have to put up with the likes of us? That's a laugh, that is.'

'She's probably sleeping on silk pillows and eating roast chicken and dishes of cream!' said Pat.

Billy shuddered at the mention of chicken and cream, though to his surprise, he was beginning to feel a little better.

'Oh, that reminds me – this is for you,' said the steward suddenly. 'A note from the ship's kennels.'

He handed Billy an envelope with *Bill Smuggs* written on it. The other fellows were already chuckling.

'A letter! From the kennels!'

'Reckon the dog wrote it, then? She *must* be quite a creature!'

'Let's take a look, Bill – is it signed with a paw-print?'

But when Billy opened the envelope, he saw only a copy of the information he had already been given about the ship's kennels:

ATLANTIC LINE

RMS THALASSA – INFORMATION FOR DOG OR CAT OWNERS

RMS Thalassa – Information for dog or cat owners

Important: all pets travelling on board require a ticket.

Dogs and cats must be housed in the ship's kennels, located on the Boat Deck.

Owners may visit the kennels between 9am – 12 noon and 2 – 4pm only. Please note that there is no access to the kennels at night.

Dogs will be exercised twice daily on the poop deck.

Pets are not permitted in cabins or suites, or in First Class reception rooms, including the Entrance Hall, Reading Room, Smoking Room, restaurants or cafés.

Please talk to your steward if you require further information.

Billy frowned at the note for a moment, his eyes flicking over it, taking in the words marked in pencil. *Important. Boat Deck. 12. At night. First Class Entrance Hall. Talk.*

He didn't need to see the tiny pencilled initials *S.T.* to know who the note was from. He understood at once that he would have to get over his seasickness as quickly as possible, because he needed to meet Sophie – tonight.

On the other side of the ship, the First Class restaurant was full of the polite sounds of glasses tinkling and the chinking of fine china. From where they were sitting at a round table, Lil and Mei could see waiters moving efficiently to and fro, while sunlight streamed in through tall windows that opened on to the First Class promenade.

Mei was studying the menu, full of intriguing dishes called things like *Consommé Olga, Chateau Potatoes* or *Waldorf Pudding.*

'Just look at all these different kinds of cheese!' she murmured in an awestruck voice. 'I had no idea there were so many. Oh – *apple meringues and custard pudding!* Tilly would love that.'

Tilly had decided to stay behind in the suite, since a lady's maid would not normally be found dining alongside her mistress in the grand restaurant. She'd seemed quite happy to be left alone with a plate of delicious-looking sandwiches. She wasn't very interested in looking around First Class, preferring to keep to her room, preoccupied with the papers she'd brought in her carpet bag. Still, Mei thought it a shame she was missing all this.

'What do you think we should order?' she asked Lil.

But for once, Lil was not interested in what she was going to eat. She was frowning down at the note that had just been delivered to their table, addressed to *Miss E. Carter*. When she'd first opened it, she had thought it was simply a printed sheet with information about the swimming pool. But just as she'd been about to discard it, she'd noticed that some of the words were underlined faintly in pencil – and concealed in the header were the initials *S.T.*

'I say! It's a message from Sophie!' she murmured in a low voice. 'She wants to meet us – at midnight tonight!'

Mei dropped the luncheon menu at once. 'She wants to *meet*? But why?'

'I don't know – it doesn't say. But you know Sophie. She wouldn't deviate from the plan unless there was a jolly good reason for it.'

Instinctively, Lil glanced around the restaurant. There was nothing out of the ordinary to see – only waiters and expensively-dressed passengers tucking into a fine luncheon. She looked down at the message again, at the pencilled initials. Something must be wrong, she thought, with a sudden shiver of unease.

'I *knew* it was you!' exclaimed a voice suddenly. 'It's so *wonderful* to see you again! Are you going to New York too?'

For a moment, Lil was thrown off balance. Looking up from Sophie's note, she was astonished to see that standing in front of her was Princess Anna.

The young Arnovian princess looked quite different to when Lil had first met her at Wilderstein Castle. Then, she'd seemed so small, dressed in stiff black velvet, her dark hair hanging smooth and limp on either side of her pale face. Now she was a pink-cheeked, jolly-looking schoolgirl, wearing a pretty blue frock with a sailor collar. Behind her was a smart gentleman and another girl of a similar age, though rather taller and wearing a sophisticated gown with lace trimmings that Lil noticed was very much *à la mode*.

'Mr Van Bergen, Eva – this is a very dear friend of mine,' Anna was saying. Lil swept in quickly before she could say any more.

'I'm Elizabeth Carter,' she said, rising politely to her feet. 'I was Princess Anna and Crown Prince Alex's governess for a time – at Wilderstein Castle, in Arnovia.' She could see Anna looking at her, puzzled by the false name, and she placed the slightest emphasis on the words *Wilderstein Castle* and *Arnovia*. She hoped it would remind Anna of what she'd been doing there – posing undercover on an assignment for the Secret Service Bureau. She knew Anna was quick and clever – and sure enough, Anna picked up on the hint.

'Miss Carter was our favourite governess,' she said, her eyes flashing curiously at Lil. 'The best we ever had.'

The gentleman stepped forward and shook Lil's hand warmly. 'Miss Carter! I'm delighted to make your acquaintance. My name is Theodore Van Bergen and this is my niece, Miss Evangeline Van Bergen,' he said, speaking with an American accent.

'Eva is a very good friend of mine, from the Kensington Seminary,' Anna put in. Lil gave a vague nod, as if she only distantly recognised the name of the school – though, in fact, she herself had been a pupil there, and one of the desks in the back row of the schoolroom still had the place where she'd carved her name during an especially boring lesson.

'We're so pleased that Her Royal Highness is joining us on a little trip to New York, to spend the holidays with Evangeline at our home,' said Mr Van Bergen, with a wide smile.

Lil nodded politely, thinking that she would hardly call going all the way across the Atlantic in the world's grandest ocean liner a *little trip*. But judging from Mr Van Bergen's affluent appearance, he was the sort of man who was forever flitting to and fro between America and Europe.

'And who is this young lady?' Mr Van Bergen asked, turning to Mei, who had been sitting still, listening to all of this – inwardly horrified, but trying hard not to show it.

'Oh, I do beg your pardon,' said Lil hurriedly. 'This is my pupil, Miss Zhang.'

Mei smiled but said nothing. When she'd been

preparing her undercover identity back at the office, she'd decided that Miss Zhang was going to be rather shy. She'd thought it would be easier to keep up the pretence if she didn't have to *say* too much. Now, she felt very grateful indeed that she'd made that plan.

'Have you ordered luncheon yet? Well, then – come and join us at our table. I absolutely insist!' said Mr Van Bergen.

A waiter was already hurrying over to set two extra chairs at a large table. Evidently Mr Van Bergen was the sort of man who made things happen, and Lil saw at once that there was no point in arguing. She quickly folded Sophie's message and tucked it away into her pocket. Was *this* what Sophie had wanted to tell her? Had she learned that Princess Anna was aboard?

Well, it was too late now. She and Mei would have to put on a jolly good performance – there was nothing else for it.

'How kind, Mr Van Bergen,' she said. 'We'd be delighted.'

CHAPTER TEN

Aboard the RMS *Thalassa*

It was after eleven o'clock that night when Billy crept out of his cabin. His cabin-mates were all asleep – and if any of them *did* happen to wake up and wonder where he was, he could always say he'd felt sick again and had to rush off to the bathroom. For the first time, he was rather grateful for his seasickness.

The Third Class corridor was quiet now. Most people were asleep in their cabins – although he could hear the distant sound of voices and music coming from the common room, where a few passengers were still enjoying themselves. He went softly past the door and continued in the direction of the Laundry Room on F Deck.

He'd known as soon as he got Sophie's message that getting to the First Class Entrance Hall wouldn't be easy. Not only was First Class out of bounds to Third Class passengers, the Entrance Hall was right on the other side of the ship. But he'd spent the afternoon in a deckchair, apparently engrossed in Montgomery Baxter's adventures in the latest edition of *Boys of Empire*, while really studying the plan of the ship he had hidden inside to work out a route. After a while, Danny Quinn had appeared and struck up a conversation about detective stories, but by that point, Billy had made his plan. Assuming it worked, the route that he'd chosen would be swift – and more importantly, secret.

Now, he opened the door to the laundry room – which, as he'd expected, was empty at this time of night. Adjoining it was a drying room, where sheets and pillowcases and stewards' uniforms were hanging up in rows. Billy hunted about until he found what he was looking for – a hatch in one corner.

The plan of the ship had revealed that there were several long air vents, running up all eight decks of the ship, from the furnaces in the basement, to the Boat Deck at the top. When he opened the hatch in the air vent, he saw that inside was a long service ladder stretching up into the darkness. From deep down below came the whirring of fans and the sound of men stoking the furnaces. They would be working all night to keep the ship steaming across the ocean.

He looked up, appraising the climb. There was plenty of room in the vent, and the metal rungs of the ladder looked sturdy. Just the same, it was a long way up, and he wished he was as good at climbing as Mei. The ship rocked beneath him, and he felt another wave of seasickness wash over him. No, no – this was no time for *that*.

'Come on, Billy. Get on with it,' he whispered to himself. He rubbed his hands together, took a deep breath, and then clambered into the vent.

Inside, it was very dark. The rungs of the ladder felt slippery in his grasp, and although he tried his best to concentrate on climbing, it was difficult not to begin imagining what might be lurking above him in the dark. Just think what a good scene this would make in a story, he told himself, as he kept climbing.

A tale about a band of intrepid young detectives stowing away on an ocean liner to investigate a sinister criminal was already beginning to form in his mind as the vent grew lighter, and colder. To his relief, he realised he had almost reached the top. At last, he clambered out into the freezing night air, on the roof of the Boat Deck.

The First Class promenade looked strange at night – eerily silent and empty. There were no sounds but for the flapping of the ship's flags in the wind, the throb of the engines, and the rush of waves against the prow as the *Thalassa* surged onwards, into the night. Below, the water was ink-black while above, the sky stretched high and clear, glittering with hundreds of stars. For a moment, Billy stopped in his tracks, gazing upwards, but he knew he shouldn't linger. It must be close to midnight now, and so he crept on, over a railing, past shadowy lines of ropes and rigging, and down to the promenade.

But there, he stopped still. There was someone a little way ahead of him in the dark. It was a man, leaning on the balustrade, staring down at the water almost as if he were looking for something. In his dark coat, the collar turned up against the cold, he looked so much like the sinister criminal Billy had just been thinking about that for a moment, he felt as if he had conjured him straight out of his imagination. But then the man felt in his pockets, removing a packet of cigarettes, and Billy shook his head. Clearly this was a perfectly ordinary First Class passenger who'd come out on deck to smoke.

He moved a little closer, keeping low behind a lifeboat, wondering if he dared try to creep past the man and through the door into First Class. If he saw him, the man was certain to wonder where he had come from and what he was doing out in the dark at this hour – and that might be awkward. But even as he was thinking it over, the man struck a match to light his cigarette. The flare of light lit up his face – and Billy stopped still.

He *knew* that man. For a moment, he felt dazed, his thoughts racing to make sense of what he was seeing. If *he* were here, aboard the *Thalassa*, it could be no coincidence. Billy hung back in the shadows, watching breathlessly as the man finished his cigarette and tossed the end over the rail, into the water below. Then he turned and walked swiftly along the deck, glancing around him, before opening a door marked: *No Entry*.

In the distance, Billy heard a clock striking midnight. He looked at the door that led into First Class, where he knew that Sophie would be waiting. Then he turned away, moving quickly and quietly in the same direction the man had gone.

Sophie slipped through the door to the First Class Entrance Hall, her bag looped carefully over her shoulder, the Almanac stowed safely inside. She found herself in a very large room with a domed roof and a sweeping staircase leading downwards – in darkness now, but still with enough moonlight to see how grand it was, with its glittering chandeliers and ornamental clock.

She'd chosen the location of the meeting carefully. The First Class Entrance Hall was far away from both the sleeping quarters and the First Class Lounge, where passengers might still be lingering even at this late hour. In a corner, there was a little group of chairs and sofas where they could sit and talk – and as she glanced around, she saw Lil's head pop up from behind the tall back of a sofa.

Sophie felt better as soon as she saw her. Lil was sitting with Mei and Tilly in an excited huddle. All three of them were wearing dressing gowns – Tilly's plain and neat, Mei's a grand quilted satin affair with bows, quite in keeping with Miss Zhang's wardrobe, though not in the least like something Mei would choose. As for Lil, she looked every inch a governess even in her night-things, still wearing her spectacles and with her hair skewered up into a bun. Surely that was taking her undercover identity a little *too* far?

But there was no time to remark on that now, for Lil had already begun: 'It's too late, I'm afraid. She's already seen us!'

'Oh, goodness – Miss Russell has seen you *already?*' Sophie said, as she dropped into an armchair.

'*Roberta Russell?*' repeated Lil. 'I say! You don't mean *she's* aboard too?'

'In the cabin opposite me, worse luck. And Charlie Walters is with her. They're doing a story for *The Daily Picture* about grand ocean liners and celebrity passengers. They're certain to be poking about First Class, so you'll have to be on your guard. But wait – who were you talking about? Who has seen you?'

'Princess Anna,' said Lil. 'She saw Mei and me in the restaurant today – and very nearly let the cat out of the bag! Luckily for us, Anna isn't slow on the uptake. She didn't give me away – but having her on board is going to make things jolly difficult.'

'She's here with Theodore Van Bergen – the founder of the Atlantic Line,' Mei explained. 'Anna is friends with his niece, Evangeline, and they're all travelling to New York together on the *Thalassa!*'

'It's rotten luck,' said Lil. 'Mr Van Bergen is awfully keen to be friendly. It seems that the governess who's supposed to be looking after the girls has been dreadfully seasick and so he's suggested they chum up with us, and that I supervise them instead. He offered to pay me – jolly generously too! I couldn't think of an excuse fast enough, so I ended up saying *yes*. But it's the absolute last thing we need!'

'Luckily Princess Anna hasn't met Mei before,' said Tilly. 'But she could recognise me from the airfield in Paris.'

'And she knows who I really am, and she'll guess I'm here undercover,' said Lil. 'She's bound to be wondering what I'm doing. She's so terribly inquisitive. And clever too – she was the one who worked out I wasn't really a governess when I was in Arnovia.'

'You'll have to talk to her,' said Sophie. 'Make sure she won't let slip who you really are. Then you'll have to keep up appearances with the Van Bergens until we get to New York.'

Lil nodded, as if she'd been thinking the same thing. Now Sophie understood why she'd been so careful to make sure she looked like a governess, even in the middle of the night.

'At least the voyage is only a few more days,' pointed out Tilly. 'The *Thalassa* is so fast. Twenty-three knots at top speed. That's more than twenty-six miles per hour!' she added admiringly.

The ornamental clock chimed the half hour, and Sophie

frowned. Surely Billy ought to be here by now? It might take him a little while to get here from Third Class, but even so . . . She hoped he'd received her note safely.

'Roberta Russell and Charlie Walters are a bigger problem,' Lil was saying. 'If Miss Russell finds out there's a princess aboard, she'll be straight on Anna's trail. And *she* won't keep any secrets. Oh bother her!'

'And there's something else, too,' Sophie added. Quickly, she told the others about the figure she'd glimpsed on deck, who she believed had also searched her cabin. They exchanged worried glances.

'Do you think this Herr Fritzel is working for the *Fraternitas?*' said Mei.

'I can't be sure,' said Sophie. 'But I'm going to have to be awfully careful from now on.'

Even as she spoke, they heard the door that led on to the deck creak slowly open. Quickly, they ducked out of sight in their secluded corner. Sophie peeped around the edge of her chair. Could it be Fritzel – had he followed her here?

To her relief, she saw it was only Billy. She waved to him and he came rushing over – looking rather pale but tremendously excited.

'You'll never believe who I've just seen aboard,' he burst out, as if he couldn't keep the words inside for even a second longer.

'Yes, we will,' said Lil with a groan. '*Roberta Russell.* I suppose she was poking about the ship at night, looking for more things to put into her beastly story!'

Billy's eyes widened at the name, but he shook his head. 'No,' he said eagerly. 'No, it's –'

'Surely not Princess Anna? *She's* not up in the middle of the night, wandering about, is she?' Lil interrupted again.

'No!' said Billy, beginning to look impatient now.

He stared around at them all and then spoke in a hoarse whisper, as if he didn't quite like to say the name aloud: 'It was *Captain Forsyth!*'

CHAPTER ELEVEN

Aboard the RMS *Thalassa*

'And what will you young ladies be doing this afternoon?' asked Mr Van Bergen, smiling at them over the gold rim of his coffee cup, as they sat in the restaurant after another splendid luncheon.

It was a good question, Anna thought. This was their third full day aboard the *Thalassa*, and already she felt they'd seen every corner of the ship. They'd explored everywhere from the library to the hairdressing salon. They'd enjoyed ice-cream sodas in the elegant café; tried out the *Thalassa's* magnificent salt-water swimming pool; and even watched an array of pedigree dogs being exercised on deck, where Anna had taken a particular fancy to a funny little black pug with a curly tail.

Most of all, though, they liked sitting in the Lounge or on the sun-deck, watching the other passengers. Evangeline was especially intrigued by the beautiful actress, Vera Lennox, whom Anna recognised from the pages of Alex's film magazines. Yesterday Eva had insisted that they hang about on deck for over an hour, watching Miss Lennox pose for a photographer. While he'd taken a series of pictures, several others had looked on – including the fashionable dressmaker Henrietta Beauville, who Eva said had designed the rose-pink embroidered coat that Miss Lennox was wearing.

Yet while watching the other passengers was intriguing, Anna found her attention wandering. What she was *really* interested in was what Lil was doing on board the ship.

By contrast, Eva was in no hurry to spend more time with Lil. 'As if *one* boring governess wasn't enough, now we have two!' she grumbled.

Anna nodded – though in truth, *boring* was the last word she'd choose. Lil was not a bit like any other governess she'd ever known. In fact, she wasn't a governess at all – though, of course, Anna couldn't tell Evangeline that. She'd solemnly promised that she wouldn't give away Lil's real identity, not even to her best friend. She was proud that Lil had confided in her that she was travelling to New York undercover, as part of her secret work. She hadn't said anything about what her mission actually *was*, but Anna knew it must be something important for the British government. She was itching to know more, and she felt intensely curious about the girl, Miss Zhang, who was travelling with her. Perhaps Lil was protecting her – just as she'd once protected Anna and Alex from the sinister society called the *Fraternitas Draconum*.

Miss Zhang seemed like someone who might need protecting. She must be older than they were – probably at least sixteen, Anna thought. Yet she still dressed like a little girl, unlike Evangeline, who was quite the glamorous young lady in an elegant striped travelling suit with a fashionably narrow skirt. And while Evangeline talked confidently, just as if she were a grown-up herself, Miss Zhang only listened, letting Lil do most of the talking and rarely saying very much at all.

'Do you live in New York, Miss Zhang?' Eva asked.

'Oh – no,' said Miss Zhang.

'Miss Zhang's father is currently in New York on business,' Lil explained. 'We're on our way to meet him there.'

Evangeline looked at Miss Zhang curiously, and Anna guessed what she was thinking. If Miss Zhang's father could afford to pay for his daughter, a governess *and* a lady's maid to travel First Class on the *Thalassa*, just to join him on a business trip, he must be very rich and important indeed.

'What kind of business is your father in, Miss Zhang?' she demanded.

It was not a question that Anna would ever have asked. She'd been taught that business and money were not subjects that young ladies – especially princesses – should ever discuss.

Miss Zhang looked uncomfortable, and Mr Van Bergen

jumped in. 'Now, now, Eva! You mustn't ask so many questions!' he chuckled, smiling kindly at Miss Zhang.

But Anna was rather sorry he had interrupted. She was puzzled by Miss Zhang, and wanted to know more. She was also puzzled by her lady's maid, Tilly, who never seemed to be tidying Miss Zhang's clothes, or brushing her hair, or doing any of the other things you'd expect a lady's maid to do. In fact, they barely ever saw her.

'I can't think why she *needs* a proper lady's maid,' said Evangeline with a sniff. 'She doesn't have a single grown-up evening frock. And look at the way she wears her hair – just as if she were still six years old!'

Eva took matters of clothes and hair very seriously. Now, she explained to her uncle, with her most grown-up air: 'We will have to leave *plenty* of time to dress for dinner with the Captain tonight. But before that, we've got tickets for the gymnasium.'

'They've got something called an *electric camel*,' Anna added. 'It sounds extraordinary. Perhaps you'd like to come with us?' she suggested, looking at Miss Zhang.

But at that moment, a steward appeared at their table. 'Are you ready, Miss Zhang?' he asked smilingly.

As usual, it was Lil who replied. 'Yes, of course – we'll come now,' she said, getting to her feet. Miss Zhang stood up too.

'Where are you going?' asked Anna, at once.

'We've arranged for Miss Zhang to visit the Marconi

wireless telegraph room this afternoon,' said Lil.

'The *wireless telegraph room?*' repeated Eva, with a laugh. 'Why would you want to do that?'

'Mr Zhang's father suggested it. He's very interested in new technology,' said Lil. 'He wanted Miss Zhang to see it.'

'Quite right too,' said Mr Van Bergen. 'The set-up on the *Thalassa* is state-of-the-art! Wireless telegraphy is quite remarkable. Whoever would have thought that we could send messages across oceans, using radio signals?' He shook his head, in delighted disbelief. 'These new communication technologies are extraordinary. Telephones in people's homes! Dictation machines in offices – and the most remarkable new cameras! It's fascinating! I'm sure you'll find it most interesting, Miss Zhang.'

'Shall we come too?' said Anna, getting up. Seeing Eva pull a face, she added quickly, 'We've got plenty of time before we go to the gymnasium – and we did say we were going to explore every corner of the ship.'

'Our wireless operator, Mr Hamilton, will be *delighted* for you to join the party,' said the steward. But Anna noticed Lil frowning a little as Evangeline sighed and got to her feet.

To Anna's surprise, Tilly joined the group too, walking beside Miss Zhang.

Evangeline gave Anna a quick sidelong glance. 'What's *she* here for?' she whispered. 'Surely Miss Zhang doesn't need *two* chaperones to go and look at some *machines.*'

The steward led them up a staircase, and through a door marked: *NO ENTRY*. 'Passengers are not normally allowed into this part of the ship, but we have obtained special permission from Captain Walker for your visit,' he announced.

Through the door, it was quite different from the elegant First Class quarters. There were no plush carpets here: instead everything was plain and neat and practical. As well as the thrum of the engines, Anna could hear the sound of purposeful activity in the distance – the clank of machinery, footsteps and voices.

'*That way* is the most important part of the ship,' the steward explained, pointing along the corridor. 'There you will find the wheelhouse, the navigation bridge and the Captain's own quarters. *This way* is the Marconi Room.'

He led them around a corner and into a small room entirely lined with telegraph equipment. A young man sat at a desk, before a bank of wires, levers, dials and switches. He got up and bowed politely as they all squeezed inside.

'This is Mr Hamilton, our wireless operator,' said the steward.

'Good afternoon,' said Mr Hamilton. He had spectacles and untidy hair and seemed a little awkward. Anna guessed he wasn't much used to groups of visiting young ladies, though he was doing his best to be polite.

'And *this* is the equipment,' said the steward, flinging out an arm in the direction of the machines.

'The most modern wireless set-up there is,' said Mr Hamilton. 'Designed by Guiglielmo Marconi himself.'

They all looked around politely. To Anna's surprise, it was Tilly who asked a question. 'How powerful is it?' she asked, examining a machine.

'Extremely,' said Mr Hamilton. 'Most ships only have a 0.5-watt rotary spark generator, but on the *Thalassa* we have a 5-watt.'

'In order to cover a greater distance, I suppose,' remarked Tilly. 'What kind of range do you have?'

The wireless operator adjusted his spectacles. 'About two hundred miles radius by day, and around three hundred and fifty miles at night. It's more by night because –'

'Because of the refraction of long-wave radiation?' said Tilly.

The wireless operator looked rather stunned. 'Er – yes, that's right,' he managed to say.

How very *peculiar*, Anna thought. She'd barely heard Miss Zhang's maid say two words together until now, but she certainly seemed to have plenty to say about wireless telegraphy. Watching her, she suddenly had the odd feeling that she'd seen Tilly somewhere before. Beside her, Evangeline was also staring at Tilly, frowning.

'Do you get a lot of messages to send from the passengers?' Lil asked quickly.

Mr Hamilton snorted, and then as if remembering himself, turned the sound into a polite cough. 'Yes, rather a lot,' he said carefully. 'Over two hundred on the voyage so far. Passengers do seem to enjoy sending Marconigrams to their friends and relations. It's a novelty, I suppose.'

'*Over two hundred?* But we've only been at sea for a few days!'

'I know,' said Hamilton wearily. He waved to several stacks of telegraph forms piled high in trays behind him. 'Such heavy use puts a great deal of pressure on the machinery.'

'And are you the only operator aboard?'

Mr Hamilton looked glum. 'I'm afraid so. I'm always working like the devil – er, that is to say, awfully hard – to get all the messages through, as well as news from other ships, or warnings of storms and icebergs.'

'Could we send a message to someone?' asked Evangeline suddenly. She turned to Anna. 'Let's send one to Muriel. She was staying on at school for the holidays. Just think how surprised she'll be to receive a telegram from the middle of the Atlantic!'

Anna thought it was rather silly to use all this impressive machinery simply to send a message to a schoolfriend they'd seen just a few days ago. She rather thought Mr Hamilton did too. But seeing the steward giving him meaningful glances from behind Evangeline's back, the wireless operator said: 'Er – certainly, Miss Van Bergen. I'd be delighted to send your message. Here is a telegraph form. Write down the message and I'll send it for you.'

Evangeline took up the form and the pencil. 'What shall I say, Anna?'

But Anna wasn't listening. She was watching Lil, who was frowning at the trays of telegraph forms. She glanced quickly at Miss Zhang, and then over at Tilly. For a moment, Anna felt that some invisible communication was passing between the two of them, but then, as if nothing had happened, Tilly turned back to the wireless operator. 'Is it Continental Morse you use to relay your messages? Or American Morse?'

Evangeline nudged Anna. 'Look – what do you think of this?' she demanded, pointing to her message.

Anna turned reluctantly away from Lil, who now appeared to be listening attentively to the wireless operator, while Miss Zhang leaned over the desk, examining some of the large dials. Lil was *up to something* – Anna was sure of it. And it seemed that Tilly was in on it too.

What it might be she had no chance to find out. The moment that Evangeline had finished writing her message, Lil hustled them all away.

'Thank you *so* much, Mr Hamilton. We've taken up quite enough of your valuable time.'

'It's been a pleasure,' said Mr Hamilton formally. 'I'll send your telegram at once, Miss Van Bergen – and if I receive a reply, I'll have it brought to your suite.'

As they walked back to First Class, Lil made polite conversation with the steward, and Tilly walked sedately beside Miss Zhang – once more a smart lady's maid, and not at all the sort of person you could imagine talking about Morse code.

It was all decidedly peculiar. And more than ever, Anna felt a sharp longing to get to the bottom of it.

CHAPTER TWELVE

Aboard the RMS *Thalassa*

At eight o'clock that evening, a young stewardess was walking briskly along a First Class corridor. She looked like any other stewardess on duty, wearing a neat black dress and white apron; the only thing that was perhaps a little unusual was the handbag she wore over her shoulder. At the door to one of the Deluxe Parlour suites, she stopped and knocked – three staccato taps.

First Class was rather quiet just then. Most of the suites were empty: the passengers were in the restaurant, arrayed in evening gowns and dinner suits, enjoying another delicious meal. But someone was evidently still inside this particular suite, for almost at once, the door opened a little way, allowing the stewardess to slip inside.

'Come in,' said Tilly, waving Sophie through and closing the door behind her. 'Is everything all right? No more *visitors* to your cabin?'

Sophie shook her head. 'No, thank goodness. But I did

what you suggested and wrapped up a book in a bit of brown paper, and hid it in my attaché case. If Forsyth does come snooping again, then perhaps the decoy will throw him off the scent.' She stopped short, staring around, and then said in a very different tone: 'Gracious! I thought Second Class was comfortable, but this is something else!'

Billy grinned at her from where he had already made himself at home on a sofa. Like Sophie, he was wearing a uniform. It had been his idea to borrow them after he'd seen them drying in the laundry room. 'After all, no one in First Class is going to look twice at a steward and a stewardess,' he'd pointed out, and Sophie had agreed. They knew all too well that staff – whether stewards and chambermaids or shop girls and porters – were more or less invisible to the wealthy upper classes.

'It's quite a place, isn't it?' said Billy. 'And just look at the food! Lil ordered it for us before she went off to her dinner with the Captain. The food in Third Class is jolly good, but it isn't anything like *this*.' Appreciatively, he surveyed the delectable cakes, buns and sandwiches which had been spread out on a well-polished wooden table. Now he had got over his seasickness, he was feeling very hungry indeed.

But Tilly was already busy with a stack of telegraph forms. 'We can eat later. First, we've got work to do.'

Sophie hurried over to look. 'You got them, then?'

'Mei pinched them while I distracted the wireless

operator. These are all the telegrams sent or received by Second Class passengers on the first day of the voyage.'

'Didn't the wireless operator notice what she was doing?' Billy asked.

Tilly shook her head. 'No one suspects Mei of *anything* when she's dressed up in all those frilly petticoats and ribbons,' she said with a little snort. 'She slipped them inside the puffy sleeve of the frock she was wearing and he never even blinked.'

She pushed aside a plate of chocolate éclairs and strawberry tarts to make room on the table. 'I've been through them already, and these are the telegrams we want,' she said, laying two forms side by side.

It had been Tilly's idea to track down the telegrams, after Billy had told them all about seeing Forsyth on the deck.

'I followed him, of course,' Billy had told the others excitedly. 'He went through a door, and down a spiral staircase – one the crew use, I think. I stayed a good way back, so he wouldn't spot me, but I managed to stay on his tail down the stairs, and along some corridors.

'Eventually he came to the cargo holds at the front of the ship, where they keep all the luggage and things. He went into one of them – Cargo Hold 4. I thought at first that he was going to snoop about in some of the crates there, but instead he just moved one or two of them around in a corner. Then after a bit, he moved the boxes back again, brushed off his hands, and left.'

Billy had paused for breath. 'That was when things got a little bit dicey,' he'd admitted. 'I had to get out of the way fast. Luckily there was a simply enormous motor car down there (fancy taking a whole *motor car* on a ship!) so I hid behind that. Then I followed him back up again. This time he went to Second Class, where I saw him go into a cabin – cabin D56. Then I came straight here,' he finished up triumphantly.

'*It's the same cabin*,' Sophie had realised at once. '*Forsyth* is the man who followed me – the one who ransacked my room!' She waved the Second Class passenger list, which she'd brought with her. 'He's travelling under a false name. *Cabin D56 – Herr Fritz Fritzel*. F for Forsyth, F for Fritzel.'

It made complete sense that Forsyth was the one on her tail. Until recently, when his treachery had been revealed, he'd been a Bureau agent himself. No one else could be so well placed to follow her, and anticipate what she might do. What was more, he would be especially determined to finish the job, after failing to take the book from her in Venice. But she still didn't understand why the *Fraternitas* would send him to steal the Almanac when she was bringing it to them in New York. And if that *was* why he was here, then what had he been up to in the cargo holds?

'*Fritz Fritzel?* Honestly! That's exactly the kind of idiotic name that Forsyth would come up with if he was pretending to be German,' Lil had snorted. 'He might as well have called himself *Herr Berlin Deutschland* and be done with it.'

'But why pretend to be German at all?' Tilly had asked.

'To help with his cover?' Mei had suggested.

Lil had nodded. 'He always made such a fuss about being such a proper jolly old *English chap*. Maybe he thinks pretending to be German is a clever disguise.'

'Hardly what you could call *clever* with a name like Herr Fritz Fritzel,' Sophie had pointed out.

Now, as she looked down at the telegraph forms in front of her, Sophie wondered if there was more to it than that. She tugged at the edge of an idea – something someone had said to her recently about Germans . . .

'Here's the telegram you saw Forsyth receive – marked for *Fritzel*,' Tilly was saying. 'This one must be his answer. They're clearly in code. Quite unlike the other telegrams, which all say things like *Wish you were here* or *Hope Grandmother is feeling better.*'

'Surely the wireless operator thought that was odd?' said Billy, wrinkling up his forehead.

'Maybe. But he said he was very busy. With so many telegrams to deal with, perhaps he doesn't have time to fuss about what's in them.'

Sophie was already examining the telegraph forms. 'Look at the address,' she said.

Form. No. 4|4|LTD Forwarding Charge —— April 12th 1912   deld. Date

THE MARCONI INTERNATIONAL MARINE COMMUNICATION CO. LTD

RT

OFFICE

No 17 Words

Prefix ___ Code ___

Office of Origin ___ RMS THALASSA

Service of Instruction: ___

Office Rec'd from ___ Time Rec'd ___ m. By Whom Rec'd

Messenger ___ Time Sent Out 14·32 m. By Whom Sent

FROM: FRITZEL, RMS THALASSA

TO: FLORENCE ANDREWS, WALDORF–ASTORIA, NEW YORK

2PL GIH HBIM 6DG71 IMGH H60 GHA

Form. No. 17 3 – 17 Forwarding Charge —— April 12th 1912   deld. Date 16/12

THE MARCONI INTERNATIONAL MARINE COMMUNICATION CO. LTD

No 12

Prefix S/7 Code ___ Words

OFFICE

RT

Office of Origin ___

Service of Instruction: ___

Office Rec'd from KCM Time Rec'd 21·17 m. By Whom Rec'd F2

Messenger ___ Time Sent Out ___ m. By Whom Sent

TO: FRITZEL, RMS THALASSA

FROM: FLORENCE ANDREWS, WALDORF–ASTORIA, NEW YORK

GHIG 7HK IM H3P PE H1707 N6IH
K6B 3HG 4HB 6JI7K6 IH AHK77HIP
97BE IMH 9 M7D GHD1N IP JPB 27G0
170H

'New York!' exclaimed Billy.

'The Waldorf-Astoria is a hotel – a very grand one,' said Sophie. 'But who do you suppose is Florence Andrews?'

Tilly was already handing them both paper and pencils. 'Let's get to work on decoding the messages,' she said. 'Maybe then we'll find out.'

Mei looked down at the array of shining cutlery and the exquisitely folded napkin that lay in front of her. Watching carefully to make sure she was doing exactly the same as everyone else, she picked up the napkin, unfolded it and laid it on her lap.

Outside the long windows it was very dark, but the restaurant seemed full of brightness. The ladies' jewels glittered, and shimmering strains of music came from the string quartet who played on a platform nearby. At the head of the long table was Captain Walker himself, white-haired and dignified in his uniform. On either side were some of the most important people aboard. These special dinners took place each night of the voyage, giving a handful of carefully chosen First Class passengers an opportunity to dine with the Captain – and tonight, it was their turn to attend.

Mei was certain that if it were not for Mr Van Bergen, she and Lil would not be there at all. They might be travelling in a Deluxe Parlour suite, but a young Chinese girl and her governess were not the kind of people who might normally be found at the Captain's table.

Mr Van Bergen smiled at her reassuringly. He was at the centre of everything – making introductions, praising the *hors d'oeuvres* and talking to everyone. Opposite him was Mr Roberts, the naval architect who'd designed the *Thalassa*, who was nervously conversing with a glamorous woman in glittering diamond earrings and a fur stole – the American film actress, Vera Lennox. Beside her was London *modiste* Henrietta Beauville, very smart and severe in wine-coloured velvet, talking to a beautifully dressed gentleman whom Mei recognised from the newspapers as the Duke of Roehampton. Finally, there was a couple who had been introduced as Colonel and Mrs Wentworth. They seemed rather put out to have been seated beside the younger guests: Mei heard Mrs Wentworth muttering to her husband: 'Girls of that age . . . quite unsuitable! They ought to be in bed . . . in the nursery with a bowl of bread and milk!'

Mei glanced over to where Evangeline, in a Paris evening frock, was confidently demonstrating to Princess Anna the proper way to eat an oyster and had to hide a smile. It was very, very difficult to imagine anyone sending Evangeline Van Bergen to bed in the nursery with a bowl of bread and milk.

Mr Van Bergen had evidently caught a few words too. 'Things certainly are different for young girls today,' he said genially, speaking with a warmth and familiarity that made

Mrs Wentworth flinch. 'And it's not only the American girls, either. I met a dashing young Englishwoman today – a young lady newspaper reporter.'

'A *reporter*? Here on the ship?' repeated Mrs Wentworth, looking appalled, but Captain Walker was nodding from the head of the table.

'Ah, yes – Miss Russell of *The Daily Picture*. She interviewed you, I suppose, Van Bergen?'

Mr Van Bergen nodded. 'Most intelligent questions, I thought.'

'A young lady newspaper reporter?' Colonel Wentworth snorted in disgust – or possibly disbelief. 'Never heard of anything so ridiculous in my life!'

'I don't see why young ladies shouldn't be newspaper reporters,' spoke up Vera Lennox. 'Haven't you heard of Nellie Bly?'

Colonel Wentworth blustered. 'It's exactly that kind of thing that gets them all riled up and then they begin expecting to be able to *vote*, and who knows what else!'

Beside her, Mei felt Lil twitching in her chair. Under normal circumstances she'd have been the first to leap in and argue, but as Miss Carter, she had to stay respectfully quiet. Luckily, before Colonel Wentworth could say more on what was obviously a favourite topic, the Duke of Roehampton deftly changed the subject. 'Do tell us a little more about this fascinating ship, Mr Roberts. Is the *Thalassa* really the largest man-made moving object there has ever been?'

'Yes, that's right,' said Mr Roberts – shy but rather proud. 'Forty-seven thousand tons of steel. Nine hundred feet long and almost two hundred feet high.'

'And she's fast too,' said Mr Van Bergen. 'Why, at this speed we'll be arriving in New York a day ahead of schedule!'

'Well, we shall see,' said the Captain more cautiously. 'We're making excellent progress, but we mustn't overtax the boilers. Although it's very true that the *Thalassa* is remarkably swift – particularly given her size.'

'And is she really *unsinkable*, as the newspapers have reported?' asked the Duke of Roehampton. 'Can that really be true?'

Mr Roberts flushed. 'We would never make a claim like that, Your Grace. No ship is *absolutely* unsinkable. But we have indeed designed a system of watertight compartments and electronic doors that makes the *Thalassa* exceptionally safe.'

'No ship could be safer!' said Mr Van Bergen, nodding enthusiastically.

'And that, in turn, has allowed us to allocate more space to passenger facilities,' Roberts went on. 'We've been able to cut down considerably on the number of lifeboats aboard, you see. On a ship like this, they're really just a precaution. With our new design, even if the *Thalassa* were to hit a rock – or – or an iceberg, say, she could still stay afloat.'

'An iceberg?' repeated Mrs Wentworth, dropping her fork in alarm.

'*Theoretically* speaking, of course,' said Mr Roberts, turning redder still.

'Icebergs are fairly common in this part of the Atlantic,' said Captain Walker reassuringly. 'We've had several warnings of them this afternoon, in fact. But that's quite what we'd expect at this time of the year, so there's no cause for concern. You can be assured our lookouts are keeping a careful watch and the *Thalassa* will be giving any icebergs a very wide berth!'

Mr Van Bergen nodded enthusiastically. 'I propose a toast,' he said, raising his champagne glass, where it shone gold as it caught the light. 'To Captain Walker, the RMS *Thalassa*, and the Atlantic Line!'

Far from the music and conversation of the restaurant, the Deluxe Parlour suite was very quiet. There were barely any sounds at all but for the rustling of paper, the scratching of pencils, and – frequently – the munching of cakes.

This was not the first time that Taylor & Rose Detectives had had a secret code to crack. In fact, Sophie and Billy had been dealing with codes and ciphers ever since they'd first solved the case of the Clockwork Sparrow. They'd learned a great deal since then of course – and with her quick, logical mind and knowledge of mathematics, Tilly was the perfect person to work alongside them to solve the puzzle.

Yet when Mei and Lil returned, close to midnight, they found the three of them still sitting, frowning over the telegrams, surrounded by plates of crumbs.

'Haven't you got it yet?' asked Lil, taking off her spectacles and pulling the pins out of her hair with relief.

Billy threw his pencil down in frustration. 'No, we haven't *got it* yet. I'd like to see you try!' he snapped.

'We have to keep going. We can't let this get the better of us!' said Tilly, bracingly.

Mei had already changed out of her frilly evening frock. With her long hair fastened in its usual plait, she looked like herself again. 'What have you tried so far?' she asked, coming to sit beside Tilly.

'We've looked for all the obvious things,' Billy said. 'Shift ciphers. Keyword ciphers. Nothing's worked. So we've had to resort to letter frequency analysis.'

'What's that?' asked Mei, who had not had as much experience of codes and ciphers as the rest.

'We're assuming that each of these letters or numbers stands for a letter of the alphabet,' explained Sophie, tapping the telegraph form with the end of her pencil. 'We know that some letters tend to appear more frequently in English – like *E*, for example. In these messages, we can see that some letters and numbers appear much more than others. There are lots of *Is* and *Hs* for example. So we might guess that one of those letters stands for *E.*'

'We can also look at patterns,' said Tilly. '*IMH* appears a couple of times, so we could guess it's a commonly-occurring combination of letters – perhaps a word like *AND* or *THE*.'

'The problem is, it takes such a jolly long time,' sighed Billy. 'It's all guesswork and half the things you try turn out to be wrong.'

'We think we've got some of the letters,' said Sophie, pushing her scribbled notes over to Lil. 'But I'm afraid we've got a lot still to do.'

'I think I'm going to need some more chocolate cake,' said Billy with a yawn.

'Don't even *mention* chocolate cake,' said Lil, groaning. 'We had *ten* courses at dinner. I don't think I've ever felt so full in my life. Look, why don't you three take a break and let us take over? We're coming at it fresh. Perhaps *we'll* be able to solve it.'

Rather to Billy's annoyance, it *was* Lil who solved it. After only half an hour had passed, she put down her pencil.

'I say, I think I've got this one!' she exclaimed. She pushed her paper into the middle of the table where they could all see it. 'FOURTEENTH APRIL THREE AM - RED,' she read aloud.

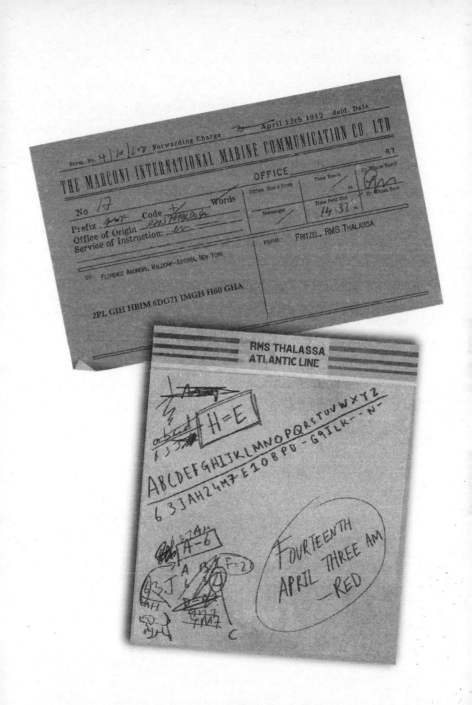

'Red!' exclaimed Mei. 'Isn't that Forsyth's code name – the *Red Dragon*?'

'And the fourteenth of April is *tomorrow!*' exclaimed Billy.

'Not tomorrow – *today*,' said Tilly, pointing up to the clock on the wall, which showed that the time was now a little after one o'clock. 'But what does it mean?'

'Let's look at the other telegram,' said Lil. 'I think I've got most of the letters and numbers worked out now.'

Sophie had already grabbed her pencil, and was busy filling in the missing letters. The others sat breathlessly as her hand moved across the paper. Then she sat back, frowned, and read the message aloud:

'*RETRIEVE THE BOOK. ELIMINATE VAN BERGEN. ACTIVATE DEVICE TO SINK THE SHIP.*'

'*Sink the ship?*' repeated Billy, in disbelief.

'Then it just says – *REPLY TO CONFIRM TIME*,' said Sophie. 'There's nothing else.'

For a long moment, no one said anything. In the silence, Sophie could hear the low, rapid ticking of the clock. None of them spoke, but she knew they were all thinking the same thing.

Forsyth wasn't only on board for the Almanac. The *Fraternitas* had sent him here to *sink* the *Thalassa* – and it was going to happen tonight.

CHAPTER THIRTEEN

Aboard the RMS *Thalassa*

In the First Class Entrance Hall, the ornamental clock chimed two o'clock in the morning, though no one was there to hear it. The passengers were sleeping peacefully, lulled by the gentle rocking of the ship.

But not quite everyone was asleep. In the deepest parts of the ship, the stokers and boiler-men were hard at work at the engines and furnaces, keeping the ship moving steadily onwards, through the night. In the galley, the night bakers were making fresh rolls for breakfast the following morning. On the navigation bridge, sailors were going about their duties under the careful supervision of First Officer Smith, the senior officer on watch. High above in the crow's nest, the ship's lookout stared out into a bitter cold night and a sky blazing with stars.

The sea was calm; the ship was surging serenely through the glassy black water. Having satisfied himself that all was peaceful, First Officer Smith began to wonder if it might be time for a warming cup of tea.

But elsewhere on the ship, things were beginning to happen. In First Class, there was the sound of footsteps and low voices in the passageway. In her bedroom, Princess Anna heard a door creak softly open. Someone was creeping into their suite. It couldn't be their steward – not now, not so secretly, in the middle of the night. *Who was out there?* For a minute, she flashed back to Wilderstein Castle, being woken suddenly in the dark, and realising that she was surrounded by enemies. Too frightened to move, she lay as if frozen, listening to the soft footsteps approach.

There were footsteps on the promenade too. Billy was racing along the empty deck, through the door, and down the spiral staircase towards the cargo holds, with Tilly close at his heels. He didn't slow his pace, not even for a moment. He knew there was no time to lose.

The instant that Sophie had finished reading the telegram, they'd realised what it meant. 'The device is in the cargo hold!' Billy had cried. '*That's* what Forsyth was doing down there.'

'It must be some sort of a bomb,' Tilly had said, grabbing the plan of the ship. 'It's been positioned so that when it goes off, it will damage the ship's hull and let water in.'

'But hasn't the *Thalassa* been designed to be unsinkable?'

'Not absolutely,' Mei had remembered, thinking of the

conversation at the dinner table. 'Perhaps not if it was deliberately sabotaged.'

Lil's face had paled. 'And what about the life boats? We heard Roberts say it himself this evening. There are only *half* the usual number on board! If the ship were to sink, there wouldn't be nearly enough for all the passengers and crew.'

For a moment they'd gaped at each other, horrorstruck. No one could survive for long in the Atlantic Ocean in the middle of the night, in water cold enough for icebergs to form. If the *Thalassa* were to sink, hundreds of people would be in terrible danger.

Then Lil had looked at Tilly. 'Can you stop this device? Dismantle it, or deactivate it?'

Tilly was already on her feet, racing to her room to grab tools from her carpet bag. 'I don't know, but I can try,' she'd said grimly. 'Billy – show me the way.'

Now, as they approached Cargo Hold 4, Billy's muscles were tense, every sense alert. Would they find Forsyth already there, activating the device? But the stairs and corridors were empty, and Cargo Hold 4 was dark and deserted. On the threshold, Billy took an electric torch from his pocket, and shone it cautiously towards the corner where he'd seen Forsyth.

'Look – there!' exclaimed Tilly, as the light glinted on something.

Hurrying over, they saw a small leather attaché case with

brass corners, not unlike Sophie's. It looked very ordinary and unimportant, lying in the corner, not at all like a device that could sabotage an immense ocean liner. For a split second, Billy wondered if they'd got it all wrong. Then he saw the luggage label attached to the handle with a piece of string. *Herr Fritzel, Cabin D56.*

Tilly was already on her knees beside the case. A moment later she had it open and Billy heard her gasp.

Peering over her shoulder, he saw that the case contained rows of narrow cylinders, wrapped in paper. They were tied together with twisted wires, which were in turn connected to what looked like a small alarm clock.

'What is it?' Billy whispered.

'Explosives. Dynamite, probably,' Tilly murmured back. 'Whatever it is, there's a lot of it. Enough to do serious damage.' She pointed to the clock. 'The alarm is set for three o'clock. When it goes off, it will close an electric battery circuit and set off the explosion. It'll blow a simply enormous hole in the hull. The ship won't stand a chance.'

Billy gaped at her and then at the hands of the clock, now pointing to quarter-to-three. 'Quickly!' he hissed. 'We have to stop it!'

Princess Anna crept out of bed. Her hands trembled as she pulled her dressing gown around her shoulders. Her heart was thumping so loudly that it almost deafened her, but she knew she had to act.

Someone was creeping around the suite. She'd heard the soft pad of their footsteps. Who was it, and what were they doing? She imagined a stealthy figure, sneaking in, opening cupboards and drawers. A thief, searching for money or jewels? She thought of Evangeline and Mr Van Bergen, and even poor Mademoiselle Esmé, sleeping comfortably in their beds with no idea what was happening.

Anna knew she couldn't stay cowering in her room. She was a princess. She was supposed to be brave. She remembered how Lil had rescued her and Alex at Wilderstein Castle, and she made herself go forward, towards the door.

She opened it a crack, hardly daring to breathe. Outside, the elegant sitting room was dark. There were no sounds but a gentle snoring, coming from Evangeline's room next door. Had she misheard those furtive little sounds? She stood still for a moment, listening. Nothing. Just to be sure, she reached out and turned on a small lamp – and then she almost screamed aloud.

The lamplight illuminated someone sitting in a chair by the door – someone who at first she thought was a complete stranger. Then she recognised the girl who'd sat opposite her at dinner. The girl who'd been wearing a pale-blue silk frock with puffed sleeves, and who'd seemed too shy to say more than a few words.

This person was nothing like that girl. She wore a dark jersey and skirt, her glossy black hair plaited efficiently back, her expression sharp and determined. The last word you'd use to describe her was *shy*.

And yet it *was* her, nonetheless. Anna's eyes widened in amazement as she whispered. '*Miss Zhang!*'

Across the passageway, Sophie and Lil stood by the door, watching and waiting. Sophie had a torch clenched in one hand, and her pistol in the other. She felt shivery with anticipation.

How strange it was to be here, knowing that around them the other passengers were sleeping, without the least idea that the immense ship was in peril! The clock showed that the time was now ten minutes to three. Would the others have reached the cargo hold yet? Would they have found the device? Would Tilly be able to deactivate it?

The Fraternitas *had sent Forsyth to sink the* Thalassa. It seemed so extraordinary. Now Sophie understood why Forsyth had been searching her cabin for the Almanac. The *Fraternitas* would not risk harm coming to their prized treasure – no doubt he'd been ordered to take it and keep it safe.

Standing in the dark, she began to make sense of it all. The *Fraternitas* were agents of chaos first and foremost. As long as she'd known them, they'd been plotting to stir up conflict, rebellion and disaster, planning to profit from the misfortune of others. Sinking the world's largest ocean liner was exactly the kind of thing they would do. And if the *Thalassa* sank, there would be far-reaching consequences. For one thing, no one would want to travel with the Atlantic Line after such a disaster. And without Mr Van Bergen at the helm, the company would surely flounder and collapse. Was that what the *Fraternitas* wanted to happen? Sophie remembered her conversation with Miss Russell, and what she'd said about *international collaboration*. That was the opposite of what the *Fraternitas* wanted. What they wanted was tension and discord – and to spark off a terrible war.

Beside her, she felt Lil shift restlessly. 'I wish we knew what was happening,' she muttered in Sophie's ear. 'I jolly well hope this works.'

Sophie hoped so too. They'd made their plan on the spur of the moment, while Tilly had raced off to the cargo hold with Billy. They'd guessed that after he'd activated his device, Forsyth would make for Sophie's cabin to find the Almanac. Of course, he wouldn't find it there. The Almanac was safely in the bag slung over her shoulder. But it *was* possible he would find the parcel that Sophie had planted. Would he be convinced by the decoy? Either way, his next destination would surely be the Van Bergen suite, to follow the chilling instruction *eliminate Van Bergen*. But if their plan worked, he'd come face-to-face with Sophie and Lil instead.

It had been quick work to switch the numbers on the doors of the two Deluxe Parlour suites. Now, when he came into what he thought was the Van Bergen suite, Forsyth would instead be entering Miss Zhang's suite – where they'd be waiting for him. They'd take him by surprise and capture him, while Mei stayed on watch to make sure the Van Bergens and Princess Anna were safe. Then they'd wake Mr Van Bergen and Captain Walker and tell them of their discoveries, with the decoded telegrams as evidence of a secret plot. Forsyth would be locked up in the brig, and she'd send a telegram to the Chief, who would make sure the American authorities were waiting for them on arrival in New York. At last, they'd have the Bureau's treacherous double agent under lock and key – and they could quiz him for answers about Joe.

But Forsyth still wasn't here. If he was due to complete the mission by three o'clock, they couldn't have much longer to wait. In the dim light, she saw the clock now showed five minutes to three. What was taking so long?

She began to wonder why Forsyth had been asked to specify the exact time he would complete his mission. Was it so they could predict exactly when the ship would begin sinking? Sophie had a vision of a roomful of financiers, gathered around a table in London or Paris or New York, smoking cigars and drinking brandy, waiting until exactly the right moment to sell their shares in the Atlantic Line before the crisis struck, their value plummeted and the company collapsed. Yes, that would be just like the *Fraternitas*.

But there was something else that was bothering her,

which didn't make sense. Why was Forsyth sabotaging a ship that *he himself was on*? Was he simply planning to take his chances in the lifeboats, counting on his boldness and daring to ensure he survived? She could see the *Fraternitas* taking that risk. But surely, after everything, they would not risk the safety of the Almanac?

'I can hear something!' murmured Lil, very low.

Sophie stiffened, hearing it too. Footsteps came down the corridor and stopped outside. For a moment there was silence, and then the door handle began to turn.

Beside her, Sophie could feel that Lil was poised, ready for action. The door opened without as much as a creak, just wide enough for a stealthy figure to slip inside, a revolver glinting in his hands. He closed the door softly behind him, but then as he turned, Sophie flashed the bright beam of an electric torch suddenly into his eyes – and Lil sprang.

She was tall and strong and she had the element of surprise on her side. What was more, she was furious. In barely a minute, she'd knocked the revolver from Forsyth's hand, sending it sliding across the room where Sophie raced to scoop it up.

But Forsyth recovered himself fast, and the revolver was not the only weapon he was carrying. The torchlight gleamed on the blade of a knife. Lil gasped as it came slashing towards her.

'Sophie – look out!' she cried, twisting away.

But Forsyth had already flung open the door, and raced out into the corridor, and away. Lil did not hesitate for a moment, but ran after him. Across the way, Mei opened the door of the Van Bergens' suite, her eyes wide and alarmed. Sophie took the opportunity to toss her Forsyth's revolver. 'Take this. Stay where you are – keep them safe!' she instructed breathlessly, before she dashed after Lil.

They raced through a door, then into the First Class Entrance Hall, where the hands of the ornamental clock now pointed to exactly three o'clock. Then they ran up and out on to the deck. Sophie expected to see Forsyth dart back through one of the other doors, trying to lose them in the maze of corridors, but instead he kept going straight ahead, running along the promenade.

All at once, he stopped still, close to the wooden balustrade. He turned back to look at them, still holding the knife. Sophie stopped short, her pistol in her hand, Lil standing firmly at her side.

This was a different Forsyth from the swaggering fellow they used to meet at the Bureau offices – or even from the smooth, confident villain she'd encountered in the Venetian tomb. His eyes seemed darker and wilder now, and there were new shadows under them. In the bitter cold night air, his breath puffed around him in ghostly clouds. Tiny splinters of ice hung in the air, fine as dust, glistening with bright colour when they were caught in the glow of the ship's lights.

'Give up, Forsyth!' yelled Lil. 'You can't get away from

us now!'

Forsyth glanced out at the water, and then a sudden, wolfish smile spread over his face. 'Oh, can't I?' he said, in his old jocular manner.

He reached into his pocket, and for a moment Sophie tensed, afraid he had another revolver. In fact, it was only a small parcel, wrapped in brown paper. Sophie recognised it as the decoy she'd left in her cabin.

'I've got it. There's nothing you can do now,' Forsyth gloated, grinning a little wider. 'The Almanac is *ours*.'

His expression was triumphant. Did he really believe she was idiotic enough to leave the Almanac unattended in her cabin, Sophie wondered?

'You never ought to have got involved in all this,' Forsyth went on, raising his voice above the sound of the waves and wind. 'I *warned* the Chief, but he didn't listen. Silly old fool. He's got no idea of the influence of the *Fraternitas*. Doesn't he realise it goes *right to the very top*? As if a couple of "young lady detectives" could ever contend with that!'

Sophie stared at him. What was he doing? Playing for time while he waited for the bomb to go off? But then, behind the whistle of the wind, she heard a peculiar sound – a twanging noise, followed by a dull *thunk*, as if something had hit the edge of the balustrade close to where Forsyth was standing.

'What was that?' she whispered to Lil.

But before Lil could answer, Forsyth did something that

neither of them could possibly have anticipated. He put one hand on the edge of the balustrade and lightly vaulted over it. For a moment, he stood balanced on the outside edge, directly above the water, and grinned.

'Good night, young ladies,' he said, before turning and diving away from them, vanishing suddenly out of sight.

'He'll be killed!' Lil gasped.

Together, they raced to the edge of the balustrade where a moment earlier Forsyth had been standing. Sophie's heart was beating furiously. Had Forsyth really thrown himself into the icy water?

But when they looked over the edge, they realised the astounding truth. Forsyth was skimming along a wire, which stretched from the edge of the ship down to a small dark craft that could barely be seen above the waves. It was so low in the black water that it would have been quite invisible, were it not for the light spilling from a single round hatch. Forsyth landed neatly beside the hatch, and almost before they'd had the chance to blink, he'd unfastened the wire, and then vanished through the hatch, which immediately closed behind him. A second later the vessel had disappeared beneath the water as if it had never been there at all.

'A *submarine* . . .' Sophie breathed.

The water below them was empty now. For a moment, there was a faint gleam beneath the waves – a periscope perhaps – and then that too was gone, as if the whole thing had been a dream.

But as they stared speechlessly out into the night, Sophie saw something else directly ahead of them, even darker than the darkness, growing larger and larger. Surely it couldn't possibly be . . .?

At her side, Lil had seen it too, and she was in no doubt. 'It's an *iceberg!*' she yelled.

In Cargo Hold 4, the alarm clock had begun to tinkle. But Tilly had already unclipped the wires. The bomb was deactivated. 'Let's get this out of here,' she said, dusting off her hands and getting to her feet.

But high above them, a bell was ringing in the crow's nest. Three times – the signal for danger. The lookout had been startled by someone shouting, down on the promenade deck, and then he'd seen it, looming out of the dark.

Now the telephone on the bridge was shrilling too. First Officer Smith jumped and almost spilled his tea, sending the cup rattling in its saucer. The voice on the other end of the receiver was loud and clear. 'Iceberg! Iceberg right ahead!'

Everything seemed to happen at once. Dashing for the wheelhouse, First Officer Smith was yelling: 'Turn to starboard!' Wheels turned, bells clanged, lights shone out into the darkness.

'The ship's slowing!' gasped Sophie at the balustrade.

'Are we stopping?'

'No,' said Lil. 'We're *turning*! Look!'

Very slowly, the great ship was beginning to change course. Ahead of them in the water was the vast shape of the enormous iceberg, wet and glistening, like a mountain emerging out of the dark.

'It's not enough – we're going to hit it!' cried Sophie, as they braced themselves for the crash.

But the crash never came. Instead, the bow of the ship began to swing to port, and the iceberg glided past on the starboard side. Slowly, slowly, the great ship went by, missing it by what seemed like only a matter of yards – until it vanished again, into the dark.

CHAPTER FOURTEEN

Aboard the RMS *Thalassa*

Anna knew she would never forget that night. How odd it seemed to be awake at three o'clock in the morning, while Miss Zhang – or Mei, as she had told Anna to call her – related a story of codes, a bomb and a secret book! At first, she'd tried to convince Anna to go back to her bedroom out of harm's way, but Anna had refused. She could scarcely just *go to sleep* knowing that there was a bomb aboard the ship, and they were all in grave danger. What was more, she would not leave Mei out here alone, to face a sinister secret agent who might come creeping in at any moment, intending to murder Mr Van Bergen. She was a princess, and she would be brave.

As they sat talking in low voices so as not to wake the others, they'd felt the ship shift beneath them, and they'd stared at each other, in horror – for a moment wondering if that strange movement they'd felt could be the bomb going off in the cargo hold below. Yet before they could do much more than rise to their feet, there were three taps at the door and Lil appeared, pink cheeked and a little breathless.

'It's all right. Forsyth's gone – escaped, if you can believe it. It's safe.' She looked over at Anna and smiled. 'Oh – you're here too, are you?' she added, not sounding particularly surprised.

'What about the bomb?' asked Mei, as they followed Lil out into the passageway.

'Tilly made short work of it,' said a fair-haired young man, dressed as a steward.

Tilly, the lady's maid, was shrugging on an outdoor coat. 'It's at the bottom of the ocean now. We threw it overboard, to be absolutely safe.' She saw Anna standing behind Mei and gave her a little smile. 'Hello,' she said with a nod, as if this was all very much in an ordinary day's work.

'That wasn't our only narrow escape,' said another young woman, whom Anna felt she dimly recognised. She wore a warm coat and had a bag slung over her shoulder, and was in the process of wrapping a scarf around her neck.

'What do you mean?' Mei asked her.

'Come and look,' said the young man. 'We're all going up on deck. Just wait until you see it out there.'

Anna looked at Lil, her face eager.

'Oh, come on, then,' said Lil. 'But you'd better put a coat on so you don't catch cold.' Then she shook her head. 'Gosh, hark at me talking about *catching cold*! I think I've been playing the governess for too long.'

The promenade deck, where she had recently watched Vera Lennox posing for photographs, was empty now – and freezing cold. In spite of her coat, Anna was shivering. But as they leaned against the balustrade, she saw that the sun was beginning to creep over the horizon, and the waves were turning silver and gold. In the pale light of dawn, she saw the shapes of immense icebergs glowing in the distance. They glittered in the first rays of the sun – pink and white, purple and blue. It was the most beautiful thing that Anna had ever seen, and she stood at the balustrade between Mei and Lil, gazing as if she would never stop.

'What a night!' exclaimed Lil. 'But at least the ship and everyone in it are safe.'

'Safe from icebergs . . . and suitcases full of dynamite . . . and undercover assassins in submarines,' said the young man, whose name was Billy. 'I can still hardly believe Forsyth escaped in a submarine. If I put that in a story, people would think it was too silly for words!'

'I do wish we'd caught him,' said Lil. 'Or at least that he hadn't looked so awfully *smug* about escaping. It was lucky you had the pistol, Sophie. It made me jolly well want to shoot him – again.'

'You *shot* him?' exclaimed Anna, turning to stare at Lil. 'Captain Forsyth?'

'Oh, that was ages ago,' said Lil with a shrug. 'And I only shot him a *bit*.'

'Well, I'm certain the *Fraternitas* won't be at all happy

with him when they realise that his mission failed and that he hasn't got the Almanac after all,' said Sophie, patting the bag slung over her shoulder.

'As if you'd really just leave it lying about in your cabin, so he could help himself!' Lil snorted. 'Honestly – what a juggins!'

'So what do we do now?' asked Billy. 'Ought we to tell the Captain?'

'I'm not sure what good it would do,' Sophie said. 'The danger is over now. And we aren't here as Bureau agents, remember. We're supposed to be ordinary passengers.'

'But we should notify the Chief,' said Lil. 'We could send him a telegram. After all, perhaps *this* was the big *Fraternitas* plot he talked about.'

'Yes, though of course we don't have any real evidence that the *Fraternitas* were involved,' Sophie pointed out.

'What about the telegrams? We've got those,' said Billy.

'But there's no mention of the *Fraternitas* in them, is there?' remembered Mei. 'Nor the Almanac. There's only a mention of a *book*.'

Sophie nodded. 'And *we* know that *Red* stands for *Red Dragon*, but really that could mean anything. The telegrams are a useful clue, but that's all they are for now. They only prove that someone called Florence Andrews at the Waldorf-Astoria Hotel in New York sent a coded message to someone else called Fritzel on the *Thalassa* to try and sabotage the ship.'

'And murder Van Bergen,' Mei reminded her. Anna gave a slight shiver at the words.

'Well, we know where to start in New York,' said Lil, bracingly. 'Florence Andrews at the Waldorf-Astoria. We'll jolly well have to find some evidence to prove the *Fraternitas* were behind all this. The likes of Forsyth simply cannot be allowed to go about trying to blow up ships, and that's all there is to it.'

Billy was looking out at the sky, and the rising sun. He gave Sophie a little nudge. 'We ought to go,' he said. 'It's getting late. Time we went back to where we belong, before anyone wonders what a couple of humble Second and Third Class passengers are doing on the swanky First Class promenade.'

'Good plan. I wouldn't put it past Roberta Russell to be up already, nosing about.' Sophie smiled at the others. 'See you in New York,' she said softly. A moment later, she and Billy had vanished.

Mei and Tilly disappeared just afterwards, going back inside together. Then only Anna and Lil were left, leaning on the balustrade, looking out across the pink-and-gold sea.

'I'm sorry you got mixed up in all this,' said Lil. 'I don't think His Majesty would be very pleased with me. You're supposed to be kept safe from assassins and bombs – not plunged right into the midst of them.'

'That was hardly your fault!' Anna protested. 'Anyway, I did say I wanted to see everything that was going on aboard this ship – and I rather think I have now.' She paused for a moment, thinking how funny it was that the First Class passengers would now be waking up in their comfortable beds, without the least idea of the dangers of the night.

'We'd better go. We don't want to be late for breakfast!' said Lil. As they walked together across the deck, she added. 'You won't say a word about any of this to Evangeline, will you? You know it's most awfully important, strictly confidential government business. . ?'

'Of course not!' exclaimed Anna at once. 'I can keep a secret. But what shall I say if she noticed that I was gone from my room?'

'Tell her the truth – that you went for a walk on deck, to watch the morning sunrise,' Lil suggested, with a smile.

In fact, Eva was still asleep when Anna let herself into the suite, shutting the door softly behind her. An hour later, they were all sitting together in the restaurant for breakfast, surrounded by the polite hum of conversation, while the waiters offered them a choice of tea, coffee or hot chocolate, poured from silver pots.

Anna watched Lil across the table. She was sitting very straight in her chair, her hair neatly pinned, her collar tidily buttoned, her spectacles firmly on her nose. Her eyes were bright and clear as if she'd slept for eight restful hours, and she was reminding Miss Zhang to eat her grapefruit. She looked like the last person who'd ever shoot anyone – even if it was only a bit.

As for Mei, she *was* Miss Zhang again, shy and timid, in her frilly silk frock, her hair fastened with an enormous bow. Anna blinked. Surely she could not possibly be the same girl who'd been in their suite in the middle of the night with a revolver in her hand?

Eva nudged her. 'What's the matter? You look awfully funny.'

Anna stifled a yawn behind her hand. 'Oh – er – I didn't sleep well, that's all.'

'Ah! There was a little disturbance in the night, I believe,' said Mr Van Bergen. 'Apparently we passed close to an iceberg. Probably the movement of the ship changing course was what disturbed you.'

They were not the only ones discussing the iceberg. 'A near miss!' exclaimed Vera Lennox, who was sitting just behind them. 'I suppose we should count ourselves lucky!'

'Oh, I don't know,' said Miss Beauville. 'Just think, Vera, dear, what escaping in a lifeboat could do for your career! I can see the film version now . . . *Miss Vera Lennox stars in "Saved from the Waves"*!'

At the next table, Colonel Wentworth was scolding his wife. 'Nearly drowned indeed... stuff and nonsense! Icebergs are perfectly common in the Atlantic at this time of year. You heard the Captain say so himself.'

News of the iceberg had also reached Second Class, where Sophie was having breakfast with Roberta Russell and Charlie Walters.

'Gosh, I'm sorry I missed it!' Walters was saying. 'Imagine the pictures I could have got! The majestic beauty of the iceberg shimmering out of the waves . . . the *Thalassa*'s near miss! To think I slept through the whole thing!'

'Cheer up, Charlie,' said Miss Russell bracingly. 'It's rotten luck we missed seeing it for ourselves, but we can still make a splendid story out of it. What *I* want to know is why didn't they spot the iceberg sooner? And exactly *how* close did we come?'

She carried on talking, but Sophie was only half-listening. She was still thinking of the dark shape of the submarine, vanishing beneath the water. By now, Forsyth would have told the *Fraternitas* that she and Lil were both aboard, she realised. They would know that she had not followed their instructions. What might that mean for Joe?

It was not a comfortable thought. Of course they still had the Almanac, and they could use it to bargain with. But Sophie felt more worried and uncertain than ever about what might lie in wait for them in New York.

'A narrow escape from disaster on the *Thalassa*'s maiden voyage is a much more interesting story than celebrity passengers,' Miss Russell was saying, tucking into her breakfast egg with enthusiasm. 'Moorhouse and Sir Chester will be delighted. Even better than royalty – or German spies. But you're very quiet, Miss Taylor. Don't tell me *you're* unnerved by a near miss.'

Sophie shook her head. 'Not in the least. It's just that I had a bad night's sleep.'

In fact she'd had no sleep at all, and she had a great deal to think about. In her pocket was the paper label Billy had taken from the case of dynamite. It was marked clearly with the name of Forsyth's alter ego, Herr Fritzel, and his cabin number, D56. As Miss Russell and Walters went on talking, wondering if their story about the *Thalassa* might now make the front page, Sophie found herself contemplating something quite different.

Why exactly would Forsyth leave the label on the case for anyone to see? It was true that Forsyth sometimes slipped up – just look at the way he'd been tricked by the decoy Almanac. But just the same, he was an experienced spy. There was something that didn't add up about it all: the peculiar coded telegrams delivered to his cabin, the label on the suitcase marked with that ridiculous name he'd used, *Herr Fritz Fritzel*. An obviously German name. The more Sophie thought about it, the more she saw that he'd left a whole trail of clues, quite as if he'd been doing it on purpose. Now, as if Miss Russell's chance remark about *German spies* had unlocked something in her mind, she began to wonder. Could it be that he had deliberately planned those clues, setting it up so the sabotage would look like the work of a German agent?

Two days later, the *Thalassa* steamed into New York.

On the First Class promenade, Anna stood with Evangeline and Mademoiselle Esmé - recovered from her seasickness now land was once again in sight - all of them well wrapped-up in coats with fur collars, watching the city grow larger out of the mist.

It was evening and New York City seemed to glitter with thousands of electric lights. Ahead of them was the immense figure of the Statue of Liberty, holding her torch high, while small tugs and ferry boats circled around her. As they drew closer, Anna noticed Lil, leaning against the balustrade, staring out at the city, her face set with a strange determination.

Sophie was watching the city too. From her position in Second Class, she glanced down at the Third Class promenade, and realised she could see Billy there, among a throng of people. He looked excited, and was saying something over his shoulder to a young fellow in spectacles who appeared to be pointing things out to him on the skyline. He caught Sophie's eye for a moment, and they gave each other a quick, barely noticeable smile.

As the tug-boats drew the *Thalassa* closer to the pier, Sophie saw that there was quite a crowd waiting for them. In all the excitement, she'd almost forgotten this was the maiden voyage of the largest ocean liner in the world: an event in itself. It was no wonder so many people had turned out to see the great ship arrive into port. But how different all this might have been if Forsyth's sabotage had succeeded!

She wished he had not escaped, but just the same she felt a surge of pride, knowing that once again they had taken on the *Fraternitas* and stopped them in their tracks. Now it was time to follow the clues they had left behind, and set out into the glittering city that lay ahead.

By the time the *Thalassa* finally nosed her way gently into the dock, it was quite dark and it had begun to rain. There was a tremendous hustle and bustle, as passengers got ready to depart in a flurry of raincoats and umbrellas. Everyone seemed to want to leave all at once, and Sophie found herself squashed uncomfortably amongst a crowd of Second Class passengers, all clutching their hand baggage, trying to stay dry and to disembark as quickly as possible.

Below them, the dockside was thronged with people and camera bulbs popped and flashed in the dark. Sophie stood with her suitcase at her side, her umbrella in one hand and the attaché case held tightly in the other – the Almanac once more hidden in the secret compartment, in case of baggage checks on arrival. Standing on her tiptoes, she saw that people were beginning to leave the ship, walking down the long gangway – though, of course, it was the First Class passengers who were first to disembark.

As they waited, the Second Class passengers grew more impatient. Beside Sophie, a couple of young men were leaning precariously over the railing, trying to catch the attention of someone below. As they jostled for position,

Sophie was pushed back further, squeezed beside a young woman not much older than herself, who was struggling to look after a baby, a toddling little girl and a large bag. 'I'm sorry,' said Sophie apologetically, trying to make room for her, and the young woman gave her a harassed but understanding smile.

It was cold and wet and uncomfortable, and Sophie began to wish heartily she was on dry land. Just then, she heard an insistent voice from somewhere behind her. 'Excuse me! I'm a reporter – *The Daily Picture*. I must get through at once. Excuse me! We're members of the press.'

It was Roberta Russell again. Charlie Walters was following her, lugging his bulky camera equipment. As people moved out of their way, Sophie and the young woman with the children were shoved back, further against the railing.

It was then that everything went wrong. Knocked off balance, the little girl stumbled. In one horrified moment, Sophie realised that she could easily slip beneath the railing, and down into the dark water below. Without a moment's thought she dropped her attaché case and umbrella and reached out, snatching up the little girl in one swift movement. Startled, the child began to cry.

The child's mother had seen what had almost happened and looked like she was about to burst into tears herself. A uniformed crew member had seen it too, and now he came hurrying forward. 'Step back, please – make room!' he ordered the jostling crowd. 'It looks like you're in need of assistance, ma'am,' he said to the young woman, in a different, much more kindly tone. He took her bag from her. 'Second Class passengers are disembarking now. Let's get you out of this throng.'

Sophie handed the little girl to her mother, who threw her a grateful smile and muttered her thanks, as she disappeared into the crowd. Wiping the rain off her face, Sophie bent down to pick up her attaché case.

But all at once, a wave of horror washed over her.

There was nothing there.

PART III

CHAPTER FIFTEEN

Coney Island
Brooklyn, New York City

'Night, fellas. Night, Ruby.'

'See you tomorrow.'

The last few customers were leaving – stepping outside into the blue night. The bell jangled as the door closed, leaving the three of them alone. Ruby, counting the day's takings; Leon, putting chairs on the tables; and Joey, wiping down glasses with a cloth.

They called him Joey here. He'd been called that once before, a long time ago. He hadn't liked it then, but it sounded different when Leon and Ruby said it, in their American accents.

'Not a bad night, considering the season ain't started yet,' Ruby said now. Her gold tooth glinted in the lamplight when she smiled.

'Don't get too excited. Molloy will be calling tomorrow

to collect his cut,' said Eddie gloomily, as he came stumping up the stairs from the basement. He slumped down on one of the tall stools at the bar. 'Pour me a drink, will you? I'm done in.'

Joe reached for a bottle, wincing a little as he did so. His shoulder was giving him trouble, as it often did at this time of night.

Ruby noticed the wince. She had sharp eyes and, in spite of her tough reputation, she was kind. 'You should hit the hay, Joey. You too, Leon. It's been a long day.'

They slept above the bar. Ruby had an apartment on the first floor; Leon and Joe each had a tiny room above. Now, as they went up the stairs, they could hear Ruby and Eddie talking together in low confidential voices: the clink of glasses, a few words floating up.

'. . . Molloy's getting out of hand. We can't go on like this.'

'Patty and Tony were saying the same. But what're we gonna do? No one dares go against him when he's got those heavies hanging round the whole time.'

'Not to mention the money. Where d'you suppose he's getting it all from? We're talking a *lot* of cash, Eddie . . .'

Joe pricked up his ears, interested. But Leon was jingling a couple of coins in his palm, and the sound masked the conversation.

'I'm going to put five cents on the numbers game tomorrow. I've got a good feeling about this one,' he announced.

Joe shook his head. 'You shouldn't waste your money on that stuff,' he said. 'The numbers game is a racket.'

But Leon only grinned at him. 'You'll change your tune when I win. Had a dream about the Brooklyn Bridge last night, and you know what dreaming about a bridge means? *Success in business*. It says so in the *Hand of Fate* dream book. I only wish I had more to bet. Maybe I could win myself a fortune.'

'And then what?' asked Joe.

'Oh, I'd be out of here,' said Leon, promptly. 'Farewell Coney Island! Farewell, dirty glasses and ash trays! I'd move up to Manhattan, get an apartment in one of those swanky new buildings, a sharp suit, shiny shoes. Find a job playing piano in a dance hall, or a movie house, or a Broadway theatre . . .' He looked so pleased with this vision that Joe couldn't help laughing.

'What about you?' Leon asked. 'What would you do if *you* won the numbers?'

What would he do? For a moment, Joe paused – but it was no good thinking about it. Instead, he shook his head at Leon. 'I wouldn't, because I don't play the numbers. It's a racket, remember?'

'Have it your way, pal,' said Leon easily. 'Night, Joey. See you in the morning.'

Joe said goodnight, and went into his room. It was small and bare – only a narrow bed, a crooked chest of drawers and an old chair – but he was grateful for it. He'd had plenty worse in his time.

The door closed behind him, and then came the familiar clunk of the key turning in the lock. Joe sighed. The sound was a reminder of something that he mostly tried to forget. Leon wasn't really his friend or his colleague, but his guard. And Ruby wasn't really his boss. She was keeping him prisoner here.

It was an odd kind of imprisonment. It wasn't as if he couldn't escape if he tried. He was quick and quiet, and he knew he could be out of the window, over the roof and away, before Leon or Ruby had even noticed he'd gone. It was what he'd do *after* that which was the problem. He'd be alone on the streets of Coney Island, without identity papers, or even so much as a cent in his pocket. What was more, he'd have to contend with Molloy.

Joe might be on the other side of the ocean, but in a strange way, New York wasn't so different to the East End of London. There were gangs here too – in fact, the whole city was run by them. The Monk Eastmans in the Bowery and their sworn enemies, the Five Pointers; the Morello gang in Harlem and the Bronx; the Black Hand in Little Italy; and the rival Tongs of Chinatown. And here, in Coney Island, there was Molloy.

Molloy had Coney Island in his pocket. He had his men all over these streets. If Joe wanted to get away, he'd have to outrun them – and he wasn't sure he could do that any longer. He didn't move as fast as he used to. He probably wouldn't make it to the end of the street before the men in the bowler hats caught him, and then what? He certainly didn't want to chance his luck with another bullet.

Anyway, Ruby would suffer if he tried to escape. When he'd first come here, still hazy with the pain of the gunshot wound and a broken shoulder, she'd been good to him in her brisk, no-nonsense way, setting him to work in the back room.

'Leon will show you how things work around here,' she'd said, nodding to a tall, thin boy who was busy washing glasses. Before she'd bustled back to the bar, she'd added quietly: 'A word to the wise. Don't get ideas about *trying* anything. Those fellows in the bowler hats? You don't want to mess with them.'

Joe hadn't needed telling twice. There was something about Ruby that made you listen to her. She was a tall, dignified woman whose age was hard to guess – she could have been twenty-five or fifty. There was a lot about Ruby that was mysterious. No one seemed to quite know where she'd come from: some said she was Cuban or Mexican, others that she was the daughter of a down-and-out musician from Harlem who'd taken up with the daughter of one of New York's fanciest upper-crust families. Whatever her real story was, people respected her. The shopkeepers, the vaudeville crowd, the barkers and sideshow folk, they all said: 'Afternoon, Miss Ruby,' with an extra tip of the hat.

Ruby's place might be a little down-at-heel, but thanks to Ruby, it had a certain flair. Perhaps that was why everyone seemed to come here – to drink beer or Coca-Cola, to eat peanuts and play cards, to pass the time of day or to call on Eddie who ran 'the numbers game' in an office down in the basement. You found people from all over at Ruby's: born-and-bred New Yorkers and new arrivals fresh off the boat; Germans and Italians; Irish and Polish; West Indians; even the occasional Chinese fellow. You could hear a dozen different languages spoken in a single evening. Joe had learned enough about New York to know that this was unusual. The city was full of immigrants from all over the world, but most of the time they didn't mix.

But this was Coney Island, where the ordinary rules did not apply. This was where the city folk came on weekends and holidays to enjoy themselves. Leon had told him that in summer the place would be crowded with people, arriving by trolley-car and train and ferry-boat, looking to enjoy the dance halls and vaudeville theatres, the beach and the bathing huts, the boardwalk and the big amusement parks – like Dreamland, Molloy's empire, which stood only a short distance from Ruby's place, and which he could see from his skylight window.

Now, he opened the window a little way, taking in a breath of night air. It smelled of rain and smoke and the salt-scent of the ocean. He left the window ajar as he unbuttoned his shirt, hanging it carefully over the back of the chair. In the cracked mirror on the wall, he could see the round scar the bullet had left on his shoulder. He'd thought he knew something about pain – after all, he was no stranger to fists, or boots, or even the sharpness of a knife. But when he'd been shot by Forsyth in a Shoreditch alleyway, it had been unlike anything he'd ever experienced before.

He didn't remember much about what had happened between that moment in the dark and arriving here – strong-armed out of a motor car by Molloy's bowler hats. Perhaps the pain had wiped it out. All that was left were a few hazy fragments – a doctor with rough hands, the sound of seagulls, the bitter taste of medicine. Lying in a narrow bed in a windowless room, while everything seemed to move up and down. He realised now he'd been on a ship. After the shooting, they'd patched him up and brought him here, to New York.

Why they'd done it, instead of leaving him to bleed in the alleyway, or dumping him in the Thames, he still didn't know. They wanted him for something. He just didn't know what it was.

Now, the memory of the pain was fading, though the scar would be there forever – like the thin white line on his arm that had once been left by Jem's knife. He touched each of his scars gently with a fingertip, and then wriggled his shoulder. It still ached badly, especially when he was tired. It was only in stories that the heroes could recover from a gunshot wound in five minutes, he thought.

In the distance, the lights of the big hotels on the other side of the beach were shimmering in the dark. He could hear the patter of rain on the roof, and the sound of the ocean. Impossible as it seemed, somewhere on the other side of that ocean, was London. Somewhere was the East End, with its docks and old inns and dark little streets. Somewhere was Piccadilly, with its red omnibuses, and crowds of shoppers. Somewhere, there was Sinclair's, with its glittering windows, its uniformed doormen, its customers in fur coats and feathered hats. And upstairs on the first floor was the office of Taylor & Rose Detectives.

As he often did, he tried to picture it. Mei, sitting behind the reception desk, her appointment book open in front of her. Sophie, examining the day's newspapers, or pacing up and down the office as she puzzled out a problem. Billy, tapping away at the typewriter, with Daisy and Lucky snoozing at his feet. Lil.

Did she ever think of him? Did she miss him? Would he ever see her again?

Joe shook the thoughts away. It was no good thinking about it. This was all there was now – Ruby's, Coney Island, New York. He took one last breath of damp salt-scented air, and then shut the window and headed for bed.

He didn't know it, but at that very moment, the RMS *Thalassa* was steaming into New York harbour.

CHAPTER SIXTEEN

Chelsea Piers
New York City

Sophie pushed her way along the crowded dockside. There were people everywhere – passengers, newsboys, street vendors, port officials, curious gawkers. Voices came at her from all directions.

'Tell us – what was it like being aboard the world's largest liner?' a journalist called out.

'Daddy! *Daddy!*' yelled a child, jumping up and down in excitement.

'Annabella?' cried out a woman, elbowing her way through the crowd. 'Where is Annabella?'

'Is it true that the *Thalassa* had a near miss with an iceberg?' shouted another journalist, actually reaching forward to grasp at her sleeve.

Sophie shook him off, and kept on driving forward, holding her suitcase before her like a shield. All around her was a clamour of noise – the shouting voices, the roar of engines, the hooting of horns – and yet she heard none of it, not really. The only thing she could hear was the painful thud of her heart.

The attaché case was gone. She'd lost everything: her money, her papers, her pistol. The coded telegrams that were the only evidence of the *Fraternitas* plot. And worst of all, far worse than anything else, the Draco Almanac.

In those terrible first moments, she'd searched desperately around, hoping against hope that her case had simply been lost underfoot. But it was nowhere to be seen, and as the passengers began to disembark, she'd been swept along amongst them, carried down the gangway and out on to the busy dock.

Now, she felt sick to her stomach. Had it all been a trick? The helpless young mother, the men who had jostled her, the little girl too close to the railing? Had someone been watching her, waiting for that split-second moment to pounce?

How could she have been so stupid? After everything she'd said, after all she'd told the Chief, the Almanac was gone. It could even now be in the hands of the *Fraternitas*. She thought of Joe, and an awful wave of black dread swept over her.

She was vaguely aware that a man was trying to get her attention – no doubt another journalist, or someone trying to sell something. She ignored him and pushed on, but behind her the voice called out insistently: 'Hey – miss – stop!'

Sophie went faster, not really knowing where she was going, conscious only of wanting to get away. Then someone touched her arm, and all her anger and fear seemed to surge up inside her, and she struck out.

'Get off! Leave me alone!' she cried furiously.

'Whoa!' cried the young man, letting go at once. 'Ouch! Hey, look, wait a second, miss. I just wanted to give these back to you – you dropped them back there.'

Sophie stopped in her tracks as she saw that the young man was holding out a pair of gloves – her own dark blue gloves with three little buttons. They must have fallen out of her pocket when she'd been struggling through the crowd.

She looked up sharply at the man who was holding them out to her. He looked like a perfectly ordinary, pleasant young fellow, wearing spectacles and a warm overcoat, the collar turned up against the cold and rain. A satchel was slung across his shoulders and he had a suitcase at his side. He was looking at her with an expression that blended interest and curiosity, and what might even have been a twinkle of amusement – but Sophie felt suddenly cold. *She couldn't trust anyone.*

'It's all right,' said the young man. He was still holding out her gloves. 'I'm not one of those leeches,' he went on, nodding at the journalists.

There was something familiar about his face. Sophie had seen him before – but where? The thought made her feel even colder. Was this some new plot of the *Fraternitas*? But what could they possibly want with her now? They already had what they wanted.

'I'm sorry I startled you. My name's Quinn – Daniel Quinn. I'm a passenger – straight off the ship, just like you.'

All at once, Sophie remembered where she'd seen this young man. He was surely the same fellow who she'd noticed chatting to Billy on deck, as New York had come into view. But if he was travelling Third Class, how had he managed to leave the ship already, with the First and Second Class passengers? She felt more suspicious than ever.

Daniel Quinn was looking at her keenly. 'Say, are you all right?' He waved a hand around as if to indicate everything – the darkness, the rain, the hubbub. 'This is no place for a lady, even one with a right hook as good as yours,' he said with a rueful grin. 'It's no place for anyone, come to that.'

'I'm sorry if I hurt you,' said Sophie, pulling herself together and accepting the gloves. 'I'm afraid I'm rather jumpy. I was robbed just as I was getting off the ship. My attaché case was stolen.'

She looked intently at the fellow from under her eyelashes as she spoke, watching for the slightest flicker that might indicate he already knew about the case and what was inside it. But his face showed nothing but concern. 'You were *robbed*? Did you see who it was? Did you go to the police, or the dock officials?'

Sophie shook her head. 'No. There didn't seem much point. I couldn't find an official in all that chaos, and anyway, I didn't see who it was. Not even a glimpse. They were too quick.'

'Anything important in it?'

Sophie made a face. 'All the money I had with me, for one thing.' Daniel Quinn looked horrified and sympathetic, but before he could say anything in response, she went on: 'It's not the end of the world. I'll go to a bank tomorrow and make some arrangements. Besides, it was my own fault. I was careless. But I hope you'll understand why I wasn't feeling very friendly.'

The young man looked at her with keener interest than before. 'You're, er – quite an unusual young lady, Miss, er . . .'

'Taylor,' she said crisply, once again looking for any flicker of recognition. But the young man only looked earnestly at her.

'Say, let me help you, Miss Taylor.'

'It's very kind of you, Mr Quinn, but –'

'Just call me Danny. Everyone does.'

'I'm really all right. All I need is a taxi.'

'You and everyone else here,' said Danny. As they'd been talking the crowd had swept them towards the street, where damp and bedraggled passengers were trying to get themselves and their suitcases into motor-taxis. 'C'mon, let me find you a cab – and carry your case.' Seeing she was about to protest he waved a hand at her. 'I'd feel like a real heel if I went off and left you here.'

Relenting, Sophie let him take the suitcase. After all, even if he did run off with it, what did it matter? All that was in it were frocks and petticoats. Her mother's necklace was fastened around her neck, and everything else important had already gone.

Danny whistled, managing to attract the attention of a motor-taxi. He opened the door and put her suitcase inside. 'Which hotel?' he asked as she climbed in out of the rain.

'The Westwood,' Sophie said, remembering the hotel where Carruthers had recommended she take a room.

Danny wrinkled up his face at once. '*That* drab old place? Full of doddery old men and stuffed shirts. And the food isn't worth eating. Look here – move over, won't you?'

Before Sophie could do anything to stop him, Danny had squashed into the back seat of the motor-taxi beside her and slammed the door. 'The Maple Hotel, please,' he told the driver.

'What *do* you think you're doing?' demanded Sophie, astonished.

'I'm taking you somewhere better,' said Danny. 'Only a couple blocks from the Westwood so it's the same neighbourhood, but altogether different. The Maple is a grand little place – kind of old-fashioned, but with lots of charm. And the breakfast is tip-top. It's the kind of place I'd want my sister to be staying, if she was by herself in the city, y'know.'

Sophie stared at him in annoyance and disbelief, and Danny grinned. 'Look, you can stop worrying. I promise you, I'm not some conman. This isn't a ruse.'

'Oh, really?' said Sophie. 'So I suppose you'd feel absolutely fine about a strange young man suddenly jumping into your sister's motor-taxi and whisking her off to a totally unknown hotel, would you?'

Danny burst out laughing. 'All right, you've got me there. But the thing is, I think you'll find you need me.'

'I definitely do *not* need you, Mr Quinn,' said Sophie.

Danny smiled wider. 'Oh, yes, you do. You just told me – you lost all your money. So how else are you going to pay for the cab?'

'I won't take no for an answer!' Mr Van Bergen insisted, as Mei, Lil and Tilly were ushered down the gangway, carefully sheltered from the rain by stewards holding umbrellas. 'Can't have Miss Zhang waiting about in all this rain. I insist you take one of my cars. Where are you staying?'

'Er – the Waldorf-Astoria,' Lil improvised quickly. Sophie had said it was very grand – so surely it would be the right kind of place for an immensely wealthy businessman like the fictional Mr Zhang?

It certainly seemed to satisfy Van Bergen. He nodded

and a moment later, they found themselves being helped into a large cream-coloured motor-car, their baggage stowed efficiently into what Van Bergen called 'the trunk'. Anna was lingering beside the car window.

'Come on, Anna! Our motor's waiting!' Evangeline called. But Anna stayed where she was, looking uncertain. Mei could guess why. It was a peculiar feeling to find yourself suddenly in a dark, strange city on the other side of the world. Mei felt it herself, and she had Lil and Tilly by her side. Until recently, Princess Anna had barely left Arnovia – and now here she was in New York, about to go off and stay in an unknown house, knowing all the time that her kindly host had recently been the target of a *Fraternitas* assassin.

'Will you come and see us tomorrow?' Anna asked suddenly.

'Oh – of course, if you like – though I'm not sure if . . .' Lil replied uncertainly, flashing a quick look at Mr Van Bergen and Evangeline.

But Mr Van Bergen bounded in enthusiastically. 'A splendid idea! Mother will want to thank you for taking such good care of the young ladies. Come tomorrow – I'll have a car collect you from your hotel.'

The motor rumbled away. The three of them did not talk much on the journey, not wanting to give anything away before the chauffeur. But when they pulled up at the hotel entrance, Mei and Tilly could not help exchanging a quick, awed glance.

Through the dark and rain, a vast building loomed above them, with rows and rows of brightly-lit windows. A doorman, dressed in a uniform trimmed with gold braid, whisked the door open, and a moment later they were standing in a huge, glittering entrance hall. It was like being on the *Thalassa* all over again, Mei thought – except this was on an even larger scale.

Lil was already sweeping over to the concierge, undaunted, the heels of her boots tapping briskly across the marble floor.

'Good evening. I would like to engage rooms, for myself and my pupil, Miss Zhang – and her maid, of course,' she announced in her most dignified voice, as if taking rooms at grand hotels was something she did every day. 'We have just arrived from England on the *Thalassa*,' she added.

The concierge nodded at once. Seeing the grand motor car at the door, and the chauffeur helping to unload several large steamer trunks, he was quick to help them. Before more than a few minutes had passed, the three of them were alone at last in an enormous, luxurious hotel suite.

Lil flopped down on a sofa with a sigh of relief. Beside her, Mei was staring around. 'This is going to cost us a *fortune!*' she exclaimed. 'Don't forget that Taylor & Rose are footing the bill for this trip, not the Bureau!'

'Well, I didn't really have much of a choice,' said Lil. 'I couldn't give Van Bergen the address of Jack's friend's apartment, could I? I hardly think the likes of Miss Zhang would be staying in an artist's studio in Greenwich Village!'

Tilly had dropped into an armchair, and was now running a hand through her curly hair to loosen the tight bun. 'Besides, it might be useful,' she added. 'We know "Florence Andrews" sent the telegram to Forsyth from here. Perhaps she's still here at the hotel? We could try and track her down. Anyway, it's only for one night – until you go to visit the Van Bergens tomorrow.'

'I s'pose we'll have to carry on being Miss Zhang and Miss Carter for a little while longer,' said Lil, kicking up her feet on the arm of the sofa in a very un-governess-like way. 'Gosh – and I *was* looking forward to getting out of these frightful clothes!' But after a moment she added, 'Though actually, I think it's rather a good thing. Now that we know Van Bergen is a *Fraternitas* target, we ought to stick close to him.'

'Do you think they might come after him again?' asked Tilly.

Lil shrugged. 'Who knows *what* they might do. That's what we have to find out.'

Mei looked thoughtful. 'We know the Van Bergens are wealthy society people. Evangeline is always saying that her grandmother knows *anyone who's anyone* in New York. Perhaps she might know where we can find Mrs Davenport.'

Tilly nodded. 'She might. And if we can find Mrs Davenport . . .'

She didn't finish the sentence, but she didn't really need to. *If they could find the Black Dragon, they might be able to find Joe.*

Lil got up from the sofa and went over to the window, sliding back the heavy curtain. Down below, she saw the night-time city – shimmering street-lamps, glowing windows, the beam of headlamps going by as cars swished past on the wet road.

Behind her, Tilly and Mei were still talking and making plans, but Lil did not really hear them. Leaning her face against the cold glass of the window pane, she stood watching the rain fall – and wondering whether somewhere in this huge unknown city, Joe could be watching it too.

CHAPTER SEVENTEEN

Fifth Avenue
New York City

The rain had stopped when Van Bergen's car came to call for them at half-past nine the following morning. It seemed rather early for a social call – but, perhaps, Lil thought, things were different in New York?

As the motor rolled northwards, Lil watched, fascinated, as the city unfolded. There were squat brick buildings and tall stately ones, jostling side-by-side. There was traffic everywhere: motor cars honking horns, rattling horse-drawn carts, trams running on rails, and high above everything, an elevated railway line where trains rushed noisily by, giving off smoke and steam. Then there were people: office workers, shoppers, newsboys hawking papers, shoe-shine boys polishing the city boots of businessmen until they gleamed. Beyond was a cityscape of cranes and spires and skyscrapers, glittering glass and steel. It was noisy and lively and thrilling, and Lil was entranced by its jangle and clatter.

But as they drove on, the streets became quieter, the buildings more solemn and sedate. They passed Central Park, and Lil stared out at the vast stretch of greenery – far larger than a London park. The trees were pink with spring blossom, spotting the ground with fallen petals. As for the houses facing the park, they were not like ordinary houses at all, but more like mansions. Some had ornate turrets, others columns, and one especially grand edifice looked like a vast French chateau that had sprouted up unexpectedly on a New York street.

It was outside this immense building that the motor drew to a halt. The street was still and quiet, and Lil realised she had been right – this was not the usual hour for paying calls. But, as the chauffeur helped them out of the motor, she saw that the door of the Van Bergens' mansion had opened, and a very dignified butler had appeared to welcome them inside.

With a great deal of ceremony, he ushered them through a magnificent hallway, into a splendid drawing room. A stately-looking elderly lady was sitting in a high-backed chair, her hair elaborately curled, a pearl necklace gleaming at her throat. Evidently this was the famous Mrs Alma Van Bergen.

'Miss Zhang and Miss Carter, ma'am,' intoned the butler.

'Please, come in and sit down,' said Mrs Van Bergen,

without getting up. She gestured regally towards some chairs at a little distance from her. 'I am Mrs Van Bergen – Evangeline is my granddaughter. The young ladies will be down any moment. I know Her Royal Highness will be glad to see you.'

As she spoke the words *Her Royal Highness*, Mrs Van Bergen's cold expression transformed into a rather awed look. Lil found herself wanting to giggle, for at that moment, Anna and Evangeline came into the room, Anna looking every bit an ordinary schoolgirl, from the toes of her boots to the ribbons on her sensible plaits. Mrs Van Bergen, however, looked rather as though she might drop a curtsey at the very sight of her.

'Hello!' exclaimed Anna, obviously delighted to see them. Evangeline seemed keen to welcome them too, though Lil couldn't help suspecting that was partly because she was eager to show off her grandmother and her magnificent home.

'My son Theodore has told me all about you, Miss Carter,' said Mrs Van Bergen, unbending a little now that Anna was here. 'You used to be Her Royal Highness's governess, I understand?'

'Yes, before she went to school,' said Lil rather vaguely, hoping Mrs Van Bergen would not press her for details.

'Most fortunate that you were aboard the *Thalassa*! I'm afraid the governess we appointed was a failure. *Seasickness*, indeed!' she added, with an annoyed tut.

'It couldn't be helped,' said Lil. 'Seasickness can be, er – very unpleasant, I believe.'

'Well, we certainly shall not be engaging her in future,' said Mrs Van Bergen, primming up her mouth in disapproval. 'I am most grateful for your care of Evangeline and Her Royal Highness.'

Yet though her words were appreciative, her tone remained cool and formal. Lil had spent enough time in polite London society to understand that while Mrs Van Bergen might be glad that her granddaughter and important guest had been well taken care of aboard the *Thalassa*, she was not keen to continue the relationship here in New York. Indeed, if it were not for Anna's sudden invitation last night, Lil did not think that a governess, even a Royal one – nor a young Chinese girl, no matter how immensely wealthy – would ever have been invited to drink tea in Mrs Van Bergen's drawing room.

'It was my pleasure,' she said politely, wondering if Mrs Van Bergen might have been friendlier had she known that they'd saved the *Thalassa* from disaster – and her son from an assassin's plot.

Evangeline was keen to tell them all about their plans for their time in New York, including shopping, concerts and the theatre. 'Then next week, Uncle Teddy is taking us to stay at Manhattan Beach.'

Mrs Van Bergen looked disapproving. 'Normally at this time of year we'd go to Long Island, but my son has taken a fancy to the idea of Manhattan Beach instead. He plans to take the young ladies on a tour of his Brooklyn shipyards and the new houses he is building for the workers – which will no doubt be *instructive*,' she said, as if that was about the best she could say for the idea. 'Of course, it will be good for them to be beside the ocean. The sea air is very healthful.'

While Lil was conversing with Mrs Van Bergen about the benefits of healthful sea air, Mei took the opportunity to speak quietly to Anna. 'We won't be at the Waldorf-Astoria much longer,' she said in a low voice. 'But this is where you can reach us, if you need us.' She deftly slipped a piece of folded paper into Anna's hand unseen, as Lil changed the subject.

'I wonder if you might be able to help me with something, Mrs Van Bergen. A small matter of business.'

'*Business?*' said Mrs Van Bergen. She looked affronted by the idea of such a thing, and Lil hurried to explain.

'A former employer of mine, the Countess of Alconborough, has asked me to deliver some important papers to a distant family connection of hers – a Mrs Viola Davenport,' she invented – guessing that the Countess's name would impress Mrs Van Bergen. 'I believe Mrs Davenport came to New York from London a year or two ago, but the Countess has lost touch with her. I thought perhaps you might know of her?'

'Mrs *Davenport?*' Mrs Van Bergen repeated in a sharp

voice. 'Why – yes. I have heard of someone of that name. I believe she has a suite at your hotel – the Waldorf-Astoria. You ought to be able to find her there,' she said tersely.

Lil detected disapproval. In Venice, Mrs Davenport had been part of an unconventional artistic set, throwing wild parties in a crumbling old palazzo. Perhaps her bohemian ways were frowned upon here, amongst genteel New York high society?

'Thank you, that is most helpful,' she said, putting down her teacup. 'It has been a pleasure to meet you, Mrs Van Bergen. But now Miss Zhang and I must be on our way.'

It was true in more ways than one, Lil reflected, as they said their goodbyes to Anna. Her conversation with Mrs Van Bergen had made up her mind: the prim governess and her wealthy pupil had served their purpose. If they were going to track down Mrs Davenport, it was time to try a different approach.

A short time later, they were back at the Waldorf-Astoria, in the hotel's famous 'Peacock Alley'. The grand corridor, faced with amber marble, was a place where society ladies met to parade in their newest and most stylish gowns. Today, several pairs and small groups could be seen strolling along, or sitting talking over the latest news – whether it was the likely winner of the Presidential Election, the astonishing new Maison Chevalier pantaloons that Diana

Beaufort had brought back from her trip to Paris, or the rumours that Mrs Alma Van Bergen was currently playing host to a genuine European princess.

A little away from the others in a corner with a good view of Peacock Alley and the vast expanse of hotel foyer, two young ladies were sitting together on a low seat as though whispering secrets to each other. They made a glamorous pair, both wearing smart little hats with feathered plumes, fashionably slim kimono-style frocks and bold crimson lip-rouge. One of them was holding a little gold powder compact.

'No doubt some of those *film actresses*,' a passing lady whispered to her companion, who shuddered. 'Powdering their noses in public! Quite shameless. I declare, the Waldorf-Astoria is *not* what it used to be.'

'Now *this* is more like it,' said Lil, her eyes glinting with amusement as she used the compact mirror to survey the view behind her. 'I was tired of being a prim and proper governess. Being a disreputable film actress is *much* more my kind of thing.'

'Don't you think we're attracting a bit too much attention?' asked Mei in a low voice, as one of the women tossed an especially contemptuous glance in her direction.

'Absolutely not!' said Lil. 'They'll be so busy being scandalised by us that I'll bet they would never suspect what we're really doing here.'

'I suppose no one would expect girls who look like *this*

to be detectives,' Mei reflected.

'Exactly,' said Lil. 'Frightfully idiotic. As if the way you *look* has anything to do with your *brains*. Now – what's our next move?'

'I was wondering if we could get a look at the hotel register,' Mei suggested, thinking of her own careful records of appointments and clients at Taylor & Rose. 'We could find out which suite is Mrs Davenport's – and whether Florence Andrews is still staying here.'

But Lil was frowning across the foyer. 'Mei!' she hissed suddenly. 'I think that's her!'

'Who? Florence Andrews?' said Mei, in surprise.

'No! *Mrs Davenport!*' Lil flipped open a copy of *Vogue* to hide her face, while Mei – who had never met Mrs Davenport, and so was less likely to be recognised – looked across the lobby to see a woman gliding towards the door. In spite of the warm spring weather, she wore a long fur coat with a wide-brimmed hat and a veil, which partly concealed her face.

'She's going out,' Mei whispered. 'I think she's getting into a motor.'

Lil dropped *Vogue* at once. 'Let's go!' was all she said.

Outside in the street, they found two or three motor-taxis waiting for any hotel guests who might require them.

'Oh, sir,' said Lil, rather breathlessly, to the driver as they piled inside. 'Would you please follow that car just ahead? Our dear friend Viola left her address book behind and I know she'll be absolutely lost without it, if she's to send out the invitations for her luncheon party! We simply must catch her up!'

From the back seat, they watched Mrs Davenport's car, moving slowly through the traffic up busy Fifth Avenue. But after only ten minutes had passed, they saw it come slowly to a halt, on the edge of Central Park.

'Stop here, please!' said Lil at once. Their own taxi pulled up a short way behind.

'Are you ladies getting out?' asked their driver.

But neither Lil nor Mei answered him. They were watching as three figures appeared from beneath the trees. There was a shorter man, and just behind him, two taller ones, both wearing bowler hats. As they watched, the shorter man walked rapidly across to Mrs Davenport's motor and leaned in at the open window to speak to her.

Lil and Mei exchanged a glance. The man was not at all the sort of person they'd expected Mrs Davenport to meet – certainly not the sort of gentleman that could be found at the Waldorf-Astoria.

'Er . . . are you getting out?' the driver tried again, sounding irritated now.

The man said a few final words to Mrs Davenport, then turned away, as the car began to move off again.

Lil made up her mind quickly. 'Yes – I'll get out here!' she said with a meaningful glance at Mei. 'You carry on. I'll meet you later.'

And before Mei had chance to reply, Lil had slipped out of the taxi and was gone.

As the taxi door closed behind her, Lil felt a sudden burst of excitement. Here she was in a new place, doing what she did best – going undercover, on the trail of a mystery. And this time it wasn't just any mystery. This time she was finding Joe.

Tilting her hat to the most stylish angle, she set out confidently, as if she knew exactly where she was going. She followed the man, as he walked back towards his companions. They were both big, hulking, heavy-set fellows, and there was something about the way they stood waiting that Lil found distinctly menacing.

As the three men walked off together, she continued behind – staying far away enough that she would not be noticed, but close enough that she wouldn't lose sight of them. But after a few minutes had passed, the shorter man stopped abruptly beside a park bench, to light a cigarette. As he did so, he wheeled around and stared behind him – looking directly at Lil.

Lil tried to keep her own expression quite calm. She walked on, as if she were not very interested in the man, humming 'The Fairest of them All' quietly to herself. Yet her heart was beginning to beat faster. There was something about the way the man was looking at her that she did not like – his hard expression and his cold, appraising eyes.

'Say, Molloy, are you coming?' called one of the men from a little way ahead. From the way he spoke, Lil could tell immediately that *Molloy* was the man in charge.

Molloy gave her one last cool look, and then turned away. As he did so, he let his used match and empty cardboard matchbook fall carelessly to the ground.

Lil did not dare follow the men any further. Instead, she walked as far as the park bench, and then sat down – as if this had been her intended destination all along. As she had done at the hotel, she took her compact out of her bag, and opened it, apparently examining her face in the mirror, but really using it to look ahead, along the path. The three men had now almost vanished out of sight.

She felt a stab of disappointment. But she had learned *something* useful, she realised, as she clicked the compact shut and dropped it into her bag. That man was important, she felt sure of it. And now she knew his name – *Molloy*.

On the ground before her, beside the toe of her boot, she saw the matchbook he had dropped, lying among the damp pink petals from the blossoming trees. Once she was sure that the three men had gone, she bent down and picked it up between her gloved fingers. Printed on it in bold letters was a single word.

DREAMLAND.

CHAPTER EIGHTEEN

The Upper East Side
New York City

Sophie woke with a start. For the first few moments, she knew nothing except that sunlight was slipping through the curtains, and that outside she could hear the hum of traffic. Comfortable as her cabin had been, it was pleasant to be sleeping in a proper bedroom on land once more. The bed was soft and warm, and she felt very snug indeed.

But then, in a nightmare flash, it all came rushing back. The *Thalassa* arriving into the docks. The crowds and rain. Dread swept over her. *The Almanac was gone.*

For a minute or two, she stayed where she was, remembering the night before. Driving through the streets of New York, with the dark and wind and rain outside. The tall shapes of buildings, the neon glitter of electric lights, steam rising from a vent in the yellow glare of a street lamp.

Danny Quinn had talked for most of the journey, pointing things out to her. This way was Little Italy, that way was Chinatown, that enormous building covered all over with a criss-crossing mesh of scaffolding was the Woolworth Building, going up on Broadway. 'It'll be the tallest building in the world,' Danny had told her. 'New York's *all* about being the tallest – or the biggest, or the fastest.'

Sophie had stared out at the buildings towering above them. 'It's very impressive,' she'd murmured.

Danny had nodded. 'But for every grand new apartment block, there's a rotten old tenement where families are living squashed up together, without water or proper ventilation. And for every shiny new skyscraper there's a sweatshop where kids are working for a pittance,' he'd sighed.

Sophie had looked at him, a little surprised. 'You could probably say the same for London,' she'd observed. 'Or Paris – or St Petersburg.'

It had been Danny's turn to look surprised. He'd already told Sophie that he'd been away for a while, travelling in Europe. 'Kind of like what they call the Grand Tour, I guess – except there wasn't so much of the *grand* about it. Mostly I was working.' But he evidently hadn't guessed that Sophie had experienced something of a Grand Tour herself.

'Maybe,' he'd agreed. 'Anyway, it's home.' He'd fallen silent then, gazing out of the window with a look on his face that Sophie had recognised. She'd seen that New York was Danny Quinn's city in the same way that London was her own. For a brief moment, she'd forgotten about the Almanac, and felt a spark of excitement at the prospect of exploring it for herself.

'You must be eager to get home. It's kind of you to help me.'

But Danny had just shrugged. 'It's nothing. It's on my way, anyhow.'

He'd pointed out the Maple Hotel as they turned a corner, but against his advice, Sophie had stuck to her plan of going to the Westwood – a large, grey, sombre-looking place. As she'd clambered out of the taxi, Danny had handed her a card with his name and address.

'I know you can look after yourself, Miss Taylor – but if you want a tour guide, or someone to show you where you get the best pastrami sandwiches, or you know, a punchbag, this is where you can find me.'

'Thank you,' Sophie had said politely.

But he hadn't finished. 'It's just that – well, you're all by yourself,' he'd continued, a little awkwardly. 'And I wouldn't want –'

'I know, I know,' Sophie had interrupted. 'You wouldn't want your sister to be here in the city all by herself, *et cetera*.' She'd known she sounded rude but she couldn't help it. No doubt Danny Quinn was trying to be chivalrous, but she found it so irritating that just because she was young and female, people assumed she was helpless, when in fact she could manage perfectly well by herself.

Though, of course, she *hadn't* managed by herself, a small voice had whispered to her grimly. As a matter of fact, she'd failed.

Danny had been looking at her with a slightly odd expression on his face. 'You know, I don't actually have a sister,' he'd said.

'You don't?'

He'd laughed. 'I suppose I meant a sort of *hypothetical* sister. The truth is, I'm all alone in the world. No sisters – no brothers – no parents living. It's just me.'

'Me too,' Sophie had said, without thinking. Immediately she'd regretted it. The friendlier he'd been, the more she'd felt sure she shouldn't trust him. It was all too likely that he'd been sent by the *Fraternitas*. Just the same, after his taxi had disappeared into the night, she'd felt unexpectedly sorry to see him go.

Inside, the empty lobby of the Westwood Hotel had been as large and grey and unappealing as the outside. A young man behind the desk had greeted her in a hushed voice, which became very chilly indeed when he understood that she was alone.

'It's *very late*,' he said. 'I don't believe we have *any* rooms available.'

Sophie had realised that what he really meant was that they did not have any rooms available for a young woman travelling by herself – which as far as he was concerned, was not a respectable thing to do.

'I'll need to check,' he'd continued. 'Wait here, please.'

'Don't trouble yourself,' Sophie had snapped, and without hesitation, she'd swept out again – going back into the rainy night, in the direction of the Maple Hotel.

Now, as she looked around her room, she reflected that, much as she hated to admit it, Danny had been right. The Maple was more like a pleasant private home than a hotel. But no amount of cosy comfort could make up for the sick feeling in her stomach.

She saw from the clock beside the bed that she'd slept late. She had no appetite, but she knew she ought to go down to breakfast. Her fingers fumbled as she did up the little buttons on her blouse. Keep your head, she reminded herself, straightening her collar. She had to face up to things: go downstairs, have breakfast, make a plan.

Not that there was much planning to be done. There was only one thing she could do now – go to the others and tell them that she'd let them all down.

Breakfast was served in a sunny dining room, full of the fragrances of hot coffee and cinnamon – which would have been delicious if Sophie had felt in the least like eating. A girl and a lady who Sophie guessed was her mother were sitting at the next table, talking companionably. They smiled and nodded, wishing her a friendly 'good morning'. Almost at once, a waitress appeared at her side to fill her coffee cup.

'Miss Taylor?' she asked. 'This has just come for you.'

She held out an envelope and Sophie took it, surprised and a little confused. It couldn't be from Lil or Billy – they had no idea she was here. Then for a split second, her thoughts jumped to Danny Quinn. Had he guessed she'd end up here after all?

But when she turned over the envelope, she saw that on the reverse, was the familiar, twisting shape of a black dragon.

To Miss Taylor and Miss Rose —

NO MORE TRICKS.

This is your final chance. Deliver the Almanac to us, or your friend will suffer the consequences. You have been warned.

Brooklyn Bridge. Midnight tomorrow.

Come alone and leave the Almanac by our symbol.

-- The Black Dragon

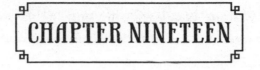

CHAPTER NINETEEN

Chinatown and Greenwich Village New York City

Mei watched from the taxi window as the streets grew darker and narrower. Men loitered in doorways, or hawked their wares from push-carts. Women sat on doorsteps, or went by with baskets over their arms. What was Mrs Davenport doing in this part of the city, so far from the elegant Waldorf-Astoria, and the dignified streets around Central Park?

They drove along a crooked thoroughfare, going uphill, and then downhill. At last, Mei saw Mrs Davenport's car pull up on a street lined with shabby buildings, criss-crossed by rickety iron balconies and fire escapes.

Mrs Davenport's car had parked directly beneath a sign indicating this was *Pell St.* As Mei watched, Mrs Davenport went up the steps of a building, her sumptuous fur coat trailing behind. The door opened a crack, and Mrs Davenport disappeared inside.

'I'll get out here,' said Mei hurriedly to the driver.

He grunted in reply, accepting the fare she handed him. As the taxi drove away, leaving her alone on the pavement, she wondered if she'd done the right thing. Now she was alone, and not entirely sure where she was. What's more, she looked as out of place here as Mrs Davenport. The glamorous clothes that had worked at the Waldorf-Astoria were all wrong on a street like this.

She glanced up at the tall, dark building before her. The ground floor looked like a shop, but the windows were dark and shuttered, and the sign above the door was too faded to read. She knew she couldn't just stand here staring – already a man had emerged from a doorway and had given her an odd look. For a moment, she wasn't sure what to do. But then she caught a delicious and distinctly familiar fragrance in the air. The smell transported her straight home to Limehouse, to her father's grocery shop, and her brother Song making dumplings in the kitchen.

Turning around, she realised that a short distance away was a little eating house with steamed-up windows. A string of coloured paper lanterns fluttered outside, and the sign, written in both English and Chinese characters, read *TEA HOUSE*. Mei sniffed again, recognising the delicious savoury smell of roast pork – and then pushed open the door.

The eating house was small and cosy. There were only a few diners, most of whom appeared to be Chinese. They barely looked up from their bowls of noodles as Mei slipped in, and she was glad of it. Ever since they'd left London, she'd felt so conspicuous – whether in her frilly frocks on the *Thalassa*, or her stylish outfit at the Waldorf-Astoria. However she'd been dressed, it had been hard to forget that she was travelling to a country where people like her were unwelcome. But here, as she settled herself at a table by the window, affording a good view of Mrs Davenport's car and the building across the way, she felt really comfortable in New York for the first time.

A waitress greeted her and brought tea – hot, fragrant and delicious. Mei sipped it gladly and ordered some dumplings which came served in a round basket, giving out savoury-smelling steam. They tasted exactly like home.

She ate them slowly, savouring each mouthful, her eyes fixed on the house across the street. But everything remained perfectly still. After a while, a little group of boys came running along the street and stopped to admire Mrs Davenport's smart motor, exactly like Mei's little brothers would have done, back at home. The driver got out and waved them away.

When the waitress came back to fill her teacup, Mei dared to ask a question. 'What's that shop over there?'

'That's Mr Kee's,' said the waitress. 'He's an importer of Chinese fancy goods, but he's away just now, so the shop's closed.'

Mei sipped her tea. 'And above the shop?' she asked casually, trying to sound no more than idly curious.

'The offices of Mr Kee – and of *Sai Wing Mock*,' said the waitress. She spoke in a meaningful whisper, as if Mei would understand who she was talking about – though in fact she'd never heard the name in her life.

'Sai Wing Mock?' she repeated uncertainly.

'Of the *Hip Sings*,' the waitress added, in an even lower whisper. But before Mei could ask any more, she hurried away into the kitchen, as if she'd already said too much.

'There . . . *Dreamland*! I knew I'd seen it somewhere before,' said Billy, pointing at the poster on the corner of the street.

'It's a funfair!' exclaimed Lil in surprise. It was difficult to imagine any connection between the Black Dragon and a *funfair*. The grim-looking man she had seen earlier that morning did not look much like someone you could imagine at a fun-fair either.

Tilly was studying the address at the bottom of the poster. 'It's in Brooklyn – and it's opening on Saturday.'

At their feet, Lucky tugged on her lead. She was thrilled by the sights and sounds of Greenwich Village – and most especially by its fascinating smells of woodsmoke and oil paint and motor-engines. A wonderful garlic aroma drifted from the window of a small Italian restaurant; the door of a shabby café let out a fragrance of coffee and warm bread; and beside a rubbish bin, someone had dropped the corner of what smelled like a most interesting sandwich. Lucky wriggled her tail joyfully, excited to investigate, but

to her enormous annoyance, Billy picked her up and tucked her firmly under his arm.

'There were a couple of fellows I met on the ship who were moving to Brooklyn to live with an aunt and uncle,' he mused. 'They were from Ireland – and Molloy is an Irish name, isn't it?'

'Let's pay them a visit,' said Lil promptly. 'Even if they've never heard of Molloy, they might be able to tell us more about this Dreamland place.' She paused, glancing in at the window of a bakery. 'Doesn't that smell heavenly? I'll go in and get some doughnuts. Investigating always makes me awfully hungry.'

As they walked back with the bag of doughnuts, Lucky began giving out little yaps of welcome, and they saw that Mei was hurrying towards them, still dressed in her film-actress finery. She was pink-cheeked and a little out of breath, but excited to tell them what she'd learned in Chinatown.

'Sai Wing Mock, of the Hip Sings?' repeated Billy. 'What does that mean?'

'Sai Wing Mock is a gangster,' said Mei promptly. After she'd left the eating house, she'd tracked down the boys she'd seen admiring Mrs Davenport's car. A shiny five-cent piece had been quite enough to persuade them to provide the information she'd been looking for. 'He's the leader of the Hip Sings – one of the most powerful Chinatown gangs.'

'I say, that's rather interesting,' said Lil.

'And that's not all,' continued Mei. 'I got a clue too.'

From her pocket, she produced a coloured postcard with a picture of the Statue of Liberty on it. On the back, a message had been scrawled:

POSTCARD

Everything tip-top for Saturday.
Charlton is just the fellow!
Don't fuss — I'll see to all the
arrangements. You can count on me to
make sure it all goes with a bang!
— R

Mrs Davenport.
Waldorf-Astoria
Hotel. Fifth Avenue.
New York City

'It came from Mrs Davenport's handbag,' said Mei, rather proudly.

'Her *handbag?*' repeated Billy. 'How on earth did you manage that?'

'With a Chinatown gang of my own,' said Mei, with a grin. Seeing that the others looked baffled, she explained. 'The boys. When Mrs Davenport came out of the shop, I had two of them begin fiddling with her motor car. While the driver was shooing them away, and she was distracted, the other boy swiped this from her bag. It cost me fifty cents and some buns from the bakery to get them to do it, but I'd say it was well worth the investment.'

'I say! This is a fine clue!' exclaimed Lil. 'I wonder what it means? Who's *Charlton* – and who's *R*?'

'*R* for Red – as in the *Red Dragon*?' suggested Tilly.

'It does sound rather like Forsyth,' agreed Lil, as they turned inside the doorway of a small shop, a sign above the door reading MOONRISE BOOKSTORE and then in smaller letters underneath: *Proprietor: Flora Cardell-Ree.*

Inside, the shop was painted a rich orange and lined with bookshelves overflowing with books. Between the shelves were paintings, prints and even a few small sculptures. Posters advertised a poetry reading, a series of lectures and a women's suffrage march. Two ladies were examining a stack of books, while the shop's owner Flora was wrapping a painting for another. She waved a hand as they passed, heading for the narrow stairs, but paid them little attention. The Moonrise Bookstore had all sorts of eccentric people coming and going: Flora was not likely to turn a hair at the sight of four young people and one small dog.

It had been Lil's brother, Jack, who had arranged the apartment for them. It belonged to one of his artist friends, a young American who was travelling in Europe and had been only too delighted to lend it to them as a headquarters. Tucked above the Moonrise Bookstore in the middle of Greenwich Village, it was made up of four roughly furnished little rooms: a small kitchen, two tiny bedrooms, and a sitting room which had mostly been used as a painting studio and was still cluttered with canvases and easels, smelling strongly of paint and turpentine.

'I'm glad we've got something to eat while we make our next plan,' Lil was saying as she came through the door, brandishing her bag of doughnuts. 'I do think to make a good plan, you need a really decent snack and – oh!' She stopped suddenly in her tracks. In the middle of the sitting room, perched on the edge of the chair beside a large half-finished canvas daubed with a smudgy New York street-scene, was Sophie. She looked pale and she was holding an envelope in her hand.

'A message – from the Black Dragon?' asked Billy eagerly.

But Lil had already hurried to Sophie's side, the doughnuts forgotten. She'd seen at once that something was wrong. 'What is it?' she said.

Sophie looked up at her. 'I've got something perfectly dreadful to tell you,' she said, trying to keep her voice steady. 'It's the Almanac. It's *gone*.'

For a few moments, no one said anything. Sophie could hear the traffic outside and some snuffly noises from Lucky, who had found the bag of doughnuts and was busy trying to get inside it. Then Billy and Mei both spoke at once:

'*Gone*? It can't be!'

187

'What do you mean, *gone?*'

Tilly just stared at her, frowning.

'It happened yesterday, as I was leaving the ship,' Sophie explained grimly. 'There was a child in trouble – I thought she was going to slip over the edge. So I put the attaché case down, to help her. It was only for a moment. But that was all it took. I didn't even see it happen.'

She looked around at their shocked faces, but her eyes kept returning to Lil, who was sitting on the arm of her chair. 'It must have been a trick. I ought to have known. I ought to have been more careful. I'm so terribly sorry.'

'It's not as bad as you think,' said Tilly, all of a sudden.

'I don't see how it could possibly be any worse!' Sophie exclaimed.

Tilly seemed about to speak again, but Sophie cut her off. 'No – please, don't sugarcoat it. The *Fraternitas* have the Almanac. They're probably working out how to make the secret weapon as we speak. And now we have nothing to exchange for Joe – and who knows what will happen to him – and it's all my fault.' Her voice wobbled as she said Joe's name.

Billy and Mei looked horrorstruck; Tilly was still frowning, but now Lil spoke. Sophie could see that she too was shaken, but her voice was clear and steady.

'Don't be a duffer. You had to help someone in trouble. You couldn't have done anything else! And if it was a trick, then all I can say is, it must have been a jolly brilliant one, if it fooled *you*.' She reached out for Sophie's hand and gave it a firm squeeze. 'Don't forget, we *all* made this plan. If it's not worked out, we're *all* responsible, not just you. All right, so the *Fraternitas* have the Almanac. Well then, we'll get it back – and get some evidence for the Chief into the bargain. Now, do buck up, Sophie, because we've got a lot to do and we need to make a plan.'

Sophie was lost for words. She found she had tears in her eyes. In all the time they'd been friends, Lil had never stopped surprising her. And yet in a way, it wasn't a surprise at all. If there was one thing you could be sure of, it was that when you needed her most, you could count on Lil to be a jolly good friend.

The others were nodding too. Billy's face was full of sympathy; he gave her arm a little pat, while Lucky tried to scramble up on to her knee, making friendly and interested whining noises. But there was one thing that was still bothering her.

'What about *Joe*?' she whispered.

Lil took a deep breath. 'We may not have admitted it, even to ourselves, but we all know jolly well that Joe may not be here at all. It may just be a ruse cooked up by the Black Dragon to get us to do what she wants,' she said, in the same steady voice. 'But if he is here in New York, we *will* find him.'

Billy was looking at the new letter from the Black Dragon, his face grave. 'We'll have to be quick about it.

189

They're proposing that the handover takes place tomorrow.'
He read the letter aloud. '_NO MORE TRICKS._ _This is your_
final chance. Deliver the Almanac to us, or your friend will suffer
the consequences. You have been warned. Brooklyn Bridge.
Midnight tomorrow. Come alone and leave the Almanac by our
symbol.'

'But – it doesn't make any sense!' exclaimed Mei.

'I know,' said Sophie. 'I don't understand it either.'

'If the _Fraternitas_ already _have_ the Almanac, why do they
want us to deliver it to them tomorrow?' Mei wondered.

'Because they _don't_ have the Almanac,' said Tilly
suddenly, in a rather strangled voice. As they all turned to
look at her in surprise, she lifted her chin and added: 'I
do.'

Coney Island
New York City

Lunchtime at Ruby's, and the place was full of tobacco smoke and conversation. From his place behind the bar, Joe could see the usual gang of old-timers sitting around the stove, exchanging stories. Not far away were a group of workmen from Dreamland – decorators, carpenters and mechanics, still in their dusty or greasy overalls. At a corner table, Miss Patty from the vaudeville theatre was talking over plans for the new season show with two of her dancers, calling over at regular intervals for 'More coffee, please, honey.' Tony, who ran an ice-cream cart on the corner, was leaning against the bar chatting with the white-haired old fellow that everyone called 'Grandpops'.

Nearby, Leon was at the piano, playing quietly. He had a way of picking out a melody, mixing it up with something else, and turning it into a new invention of his own. Joe found himself tapping his toe to the music and thought –

not for the first time – that if Leon had a half-decent piano, he'd be as good as the fellows who played in the Marble Court Restaurant at Sinclair's.

Not that there was much chance of Leon getting to play anything but Ruby's rickety upright any time soon. Now, he broke into a syrupy, sentimental little tune – one that he'd learned from Joe himself, who whistled it occasionally, usually without realising he was doing it. It was called 'The Fairest of them All' and Lil had sung it, back when she'd been in the chorus at The Fortune Theatre. Of all the songs in a rather silly show, 'The Fairest of them All' was certainly the silliest, with lyrics Lil had declared 'perfectly idiotic!' But the tune was catchy, and for some reason, it had stuck.

Now, Joe remembered how Lil had often trilled a bit of 'The Fairest of them All' when she was in an especially exuberant mood. Secretly, he'd always rather liked the song, because he always thought of Lil as 'the fairest of them all' herself. Did she still sing it, he wondered? Or had she forgotten all about the song – and him?

'Joey – hey, Joey?' Tony waved a hand, and Joe realised that he'd been trying to get his attention.

'Sorry,' he said, with a smile. 'I was miles away.' Literally miles away, across the ocean in London. 'Did you want another drink?'

At the piano, Leon had changed the melody, turning it into a snappy ragtime tune.

'That's more like it,' said Ruby, swinging her shoulders

in time to the rhythm.

The bell over the door jangled, and Eddie came in, looking flustered. He nodded around to Miss Patty, to Tony and Grandpops and then made straight for Joe.

'Molloy wants to see you.' He jerked his head at the door. 'Come on.'

He spoke quietly, but suddenly it was as if everyone in the place was listening. Grandpops broke off, mid-sentence. Miss Patty stopped talking and at the piano, Leon stopped playing.

'What's this all about, Eddie?' asked Ruby, before Joe could speak.

Eddie looked away as if he did not want to meet her eyes. He shrugged. 'Don't know. Molloy wants to see him, right away. That's it.'

'He can't just take my bartender when he feels like it,' declared Ruby, folding her arms. 'I need Joey here. Look how busy we are! It's the lunchtime rush.'

Eddie shook his head. 'Get Charley to pour the drinks, then. Or pour 'em yourself. Come on, kid. He doesn't like to be kept waiting.'

'Well, if he wants to see Joey – then I'll come along too,' said Ruby. 'I've had just about enough of him throwing his weight around like this.'

Eddie gave her a long look. 'C'mon, Ruby. Don't be stupid,' he said, his voice dropping to a whisper.

'It's all right,' Joe said, putting down his cloth. 'I'll go.'

He gave Ruby a small smile and then nodded to Leon. 'See you later.'

But as he followed Eddie out of the bar, conscious that everyone was watching, he felt fear spreading over him. He'd always known this moment would come. You didn't kidnap someone from the East End, smuggle them across an ocean, put them to work in a Coney Island bar and then just . . . forget about them. Molloy wanted him for a reason. He'd always known that – and based on what he knew about Molloy, it wasn't likely to be anything good.

Outside, it was a beautiful day. The sky was high and blue and the air rang with the clanging and hammering of the work going on at Dreamland. He'd expected they'd go over there to see Molloy, but instead, a motor car was waiting. The bowler hats were leaning against it. Joe felt his stomach lurch, and he cast a glance back towards Ruby's, but it was too late. With a nod to Eddie, the bowler hats pushed him roughly into the back seat.

'Sorry, kid,' said Eddie through the window.

'Where are they taking me?' Joe managed to ask.

'To Molloy. Look – just tell him whatever you know, all right? It'll be better for you that way.'

Joe sat silently as they drove away from the ocean. He was turning over Eddie's words in his mind. *Tell him whatever you know.* But what *did* he know? Only what had happened in London – his investigations into the double agent at the Bureau, which had led him to Norton

Newspapers and, in the end, to Forsyth. But that had been months ago, and London was so far away. What could a man like Molloy have to do with the British Secret Service Bureau, or a fellow like Forsyth? Yet there *must* be a connection, Joe thought, as they rumbled through the streets of Brooklyn. Otherwise he wouldn't be here at all.

The car slowed, and he glanced out of the window to see that they were turning through the gates of a large building with tall chimneys. It looked like a factory, and Joe caught sight of a sign on the gate reading: *BROOKLYN PICKLE WORKS*.

The car halted in a yard, and a moment later, Joe was hustled out. The bowler hats were not gentle about it, wrenching his bad shoulder and making him yelp with pain. One of them smirked as the other opened a door and pushed him up a flight of steps.

Joe's mouth was dry and his heart was beating fast now, but though he was afraid, he knew better than to show it. That was an old instinct. Instead, he kept his head up as they hurried him up the stairs, keeping his eyes open for any hint of a way out.

Through one door, he glimpsed a big room where men in overalls were shifting crates and boxes. Through another, he saw a brightly lit space where several people in white coats were working at long metal benches. A science laboratory, Joe realised, remembering the university labs he'd once visited with Tilly. Strange machinery gleamed, cold and sinister. Whatever was going on in there, he was pretty sure it wasn't anything to do with *pickles*.

The bowler hats shoved him through another door into a rough kind of office. There was a table, covered in papers, and two chairs. Sitting in one of them, smoking a cigarette, was Molloy. Joe recognised him at once – his small, hard eyes, and the low, gravelly sound of his voice as he spoke.

'Sit down,' he said, waving his cigarette at the chair opposite him.

Joe didn't have any choice in the matter. The bowler hats pushed him into the chair, and then retreated, standing by the door with their arms folded.

'You been at Ruby's – what – six months now?' said Molloy, looking keenly at Joe. 'You're a good worker, I hear. I like good workers.'

Joe felt baffled. Surely Molloy hadn't dragged him all the way here to compliment him on his work as a bartender?

Molloy stubbed out his cigarette in an already overflowing ashtray. 'Shame we can't keep you around. But – that's how it goes.'

Joe's stomach twisted, although he stayed sitting up straight in his chair, keeping his face carefully calm.

Just then, the door banged open and another man strode in. He was dark-skinned, his black hair untidy and his fingers covered in ink stains. Like the others Joe had seen in the laboratory, he wore a white overall.

'Is that him?' he demanded. His voice was absolutely

English. What was more, Joe thought he sounded educated – like Leo, or Jack, or their university friends.

'That's him,' said Molloy.

The man frowned at Joe, who felt his skin prickle. Suddenly he felt sure he *knew* this fellow, though he couldn't have said how. An image flashed briefly into his mind of the East End docks in the dark.

'Now, look here, boy,' said the man, still frowning at Joe. 'Tell me everything you know about the Draco Almanac.'

Joe stared back at him, confused. 'The . . . what?'

'The *Almanac*, boy. Don't trifle with me. Have you seen it?'

'I don't know what you're talking about,' said Joe truthfully. 'What's an almanac?'

The man gave a snort of irritation. 'The *book*! The ancient book of the *Fraternitas*, written by the dragons of old. Containing all their secrets, including the instructions for making their greatest weapon: the legendary sky fire, *feu du ciel*. It's no use pretending. We know they found it – the girl, Taylor, and her friend.'

'A *weapon*?' Joe repeated. He was beginning to understand now. When he'd left London, Sophie had been in Russia on the trail of a dangerous secret weapon. But this was the first time he'd heard anything about a book.

'Yes! The weapon!' the man repeated impatiently. 'Are you an imbecile? That's what I just said!'

'Take it easy, Snow,' said Molloy.

Snow. Somehow that name was familiar too.

'All I need to know is whether you've *seen* the book. Can you remember anything that's inside it?' Snow went on. 'I've been working for so long to try to replicate the sky fire. I've carried out the tests – my formula is so close – and yet its power is still so frustratingly limited! If I only had the instructions from the Almanac – if I knew the lost secrets of the dragons! The sky fire must be ready for the presentation.' He stared at Joe, wildness in his eyes. 'If there's anything you can remember about the book, anything at all –'

But Joe could only shake his head. 'I don't know anything,' he said in a quiet, even voice. 'I can't help you. I've never seen any book. I didn't know it existed until just now. The last I heard, Sophie was in St Petersburg, on the trail of the Count von Wilderstein. I know he was supposed to have some information about a secret weapon, and I guess that's this sky fire you're talking about. But I don't know if she ever tracked him down. How could I? I've been here in New York the whole time.'

He glanced at Molloy as he spoke, who nodded to Snow, as if to confirm it was true.

But Snow could not seem to accept this. He ran his hands through his hair, making it untidier than ever, and began rattling off questions muddled with scientific terms and words in other languages that Joe couldn't even begin to understand. In the end, he had to hold up his hands. 'I can't help you,' he said again. 'I don't know anything about this. Even if I *had* seen this book, I wouldn't be able to tell you what's in it. How could I? I'm no scholar. I don't know a thing about science, or Latin, or French, or anything like that.'

Seeing that Snow was about to begin all over again, Molloy intervened. 'Give it a rest. It's obvious he doesn't know.'

Snow groaned. 'It's hopeless! I'll never be ready for the presentation!' He looked from Molloy to Joe, and then stalked out of the room, slamming the door behind him.

Joe's mind was racing, trying to piece together all he'd heard, but he couldn't think fast enough to make sense of it. Already, Molloy was talking again:

'I think you've been honest with us, kid. And I can usually tell. I've got a feeling for it.' He lit another cigarette. 'But the thing is, I can't afford to rely on *feelings*. I need to be sure you aren't holding out on us. Keeping anything important back.'

Joe stared at him, not understanding what he meant. Then Molloy nodded to the bowler hats, standing by the door. One of them gave Joe a mean little grin.

'Over to you, boys,' said Molloy, with a wave of his cigarette. 'Make sure he isn't keeping any secrets. And try not to make too much of a mess in here, won't you?'

One of the fellows cracked his knuckles. The other one chuckled. Then together, they made straight for Joe.

CHAPTER TWENTY-ONE

The Moonrise Bookstore
Greenwich Village
New York City

Sophie stared down at the book in Tilly's outstretched hand, hardly able to believe her own eyes.

It was unmistakably the Draco Almanac. There was the golden eye, gleaming on the cover. But how *could* it be?

'I took it from the safe at the office before we left,' Tilly explained. 'I swapped it for another book – a decoy. I guessed that you wouldn't look at it too closely.'

Sophie remembered the morning she'd left Taylor & Rose – quickly bundling the wrapped Almanac into her case without a second glance. Tilly had been right, and now her cheeks burned. How stupid she'd been.

'But *why?*' demanded Lil, from where she was still sitting, perched on the arm of Sophie's chair.

But Sophie already knew the answer to that. 'Because you wanted to look at it. I said no, but you decided to do it anyway,' she said.

Tilly nodded. She looked ashamed – but only a little. 'I know I oughtn't to have gone behind your back, and I'm sorry. But I'm not going to apologise for wanting to look at the Almanac. I couldn't let something like that be destroyed, without studying it first. It would have been all wrong.'

'And so you took it, and brought it with you, to New York?' Billy said incredulously.

Tilly nodded. 'I thought it over, and I came to the conclusion that it might actually be safer. No one knew I had it – not even any of you. No one knew I was coming to New York. The *Fraternitas* were never going to look twice at a lady's maid. I was careful never to let the Almanac out of my sight – in fact, I spent most of the voyage studying it. It's written partly in French and partly in Latin, and partly in code made up of symbols. It isn't at all easy to understand.'

'So that's what you had in your bag,' said Mei. '*The Almanac*! And *that's* why you spent so much time in your room.'

'And how you came up with the idea that I should leave a decoy in my cabin to dupe Forsyth,' Sophie said softly. 'You'd already used the same trick to fool me. I was carrying a decoy for the whole voyage. What was it?'

'An old book of fairy tales,' Tilly admitted. 'I found it in a shop on the Charing Cross Road. It's about the same size and has a similar gold design on the cover.'

Sophie didn't know what to say. She felt as if the whole

world had turned upside down. She stared at Tilly – *Tilly*, who had been with her on her assignment in Paris, who was one of the most sensible and dependable people Sophie knew.

'I'm sorry I tricked you,' Tilly said, looking around at them all, her gaze level. 'I hope you'll forgive me for that. Especially you, Sophie. I know you were doing what you felt was right, and I hope you'll understand that I had to do the same.'

'*Forgive* you?' Sophie said. She blew out a long breath. She hated the thought that Tilly had deceived her. The fact that she'd been tricked as easily as Forsyth stung worst of all. She was hurt and angry and ashamed – and yet she could see quite clearly *why* Tilly had done it. Tilly believed that knowledge mattered, more than almost anything else. And who was to say that she was wrong? Sophie had always felt so firm in her ideas about *doing the right thing*, but now that solid ground seemed shaky. 'If it wasn't for you, the *Fraternitas* would have the Almanac,' she said at last.

'Will you let me tell you what I've found out about it?' Tilly asked. 'I think it might come in useful now.'

Sophie and Lil exchanged a quick glance, and then Lil nodded. Seeing that they were all listening, Tilly folded her hands solemnly and cleared her throat, in the manner of an elderly professor giving a lecture.

'There's no doubt that the Almanac is hundreds of years old, though precisely *when* it was written, I'm still not sure. It collects together the most important secrets of the original *Fraternitas* – secrets they believed that future generations could use in order to herald an Age of Dragons, in which the *Fraternitas* would reign supreme.'

'What are the secrets?' asked Billy at once.

'All sorts of things,' said Tilly. 'There are rituals and ceremonies. Secret codes and symbols they used to communicate. And instructions for making various substances – including something called *feu du ciel*, or in English, sky fire.'

Tilly flipped open the book to show the images that had so horrified Sophie when she'd first seen them by lamplight in the darkness of an underground tomb. Even here, on a bright spring morning, they made everyone wince. The sky blazing with fiery stars, flames raining down on to rooftops, screaming people with their hair aflame.

'Secret knowledge. Obscure rituals. Codes and symbols. Instructions for brewing up peculiar substances. Do you see?' Tilly asked eagerly. She turned to Sophie. 'The clue was there right at the beginning, when we were in Paris – remember? *The Fraternitas Draconum was originally a society of alchemists.* The Draco Almanac is a book of alchemy!'

Tilly looked around at them triumphantly, as if it explained everything. But the others were confused.

'What's *alchemy?*' asked Lil, frowning.

Sophie tried to remember what she knew, which wasn't much. A young man from the Sorbonne university in Paris had explained it to her once, but she'd been trying to solve a murder at the time so she hadn't given him her full attention. 'The alchemists were a cross between early chemists and magicians,' she recalled. 'They tried to find ways to turn ordinary metals, like lead, into gold – and to make an elixir of life that would enable them to live forever. They hid their knowledge in secret books, full of strange symbols and images. . .'

Tilly beamed, looking as if she wanted to send Sophie straight to the top of the class. 'Exactly! *Symbols. Images.* Just like these – the green lion, the black sun, the hand with five fingers, the eye . . .' She flicked through the pages of the Almanac, pointing to the pictures as she spoke.

'But no one could really turn lead into gold, could they? And there's no such thing as an elixir of life – or at least, only in stories,' said Mei, frowning.

'Precisely!' said Tilly. 'As it turns out, using a book of fairy tales as a decoy wasn't too far off the mark. There's all sorts of things mixed up in here – myths and legends, astrology, magic. Really, the Almanac is really more like a spell-book than a science book.'

'It sounds *fascinating*,' said Billy, staring down at the strange diagrams on the pages.

'Oh, it's tremendously interesting,' agreed Tilly in a matter-of-fact voice. 'And rather horrible. Some of these rituals are enough to give you nightmares.'

'So what about the sky fire?' Lil wanted to know.

'Well, it's taken me a long time to decipher it,' said Tilly. 'I've never seen anything at all like it before. I'm not even certain it would actually work, not without testing it anyway.' Seeing Sophie's horrified face, she added hurriedly: 'Which *of course* I would never do. But studying it has given me an idea for how we could follow the Black Dragon's instructions.'

'Follow them? What do you mean?' asked Billy.

Tilly took a pencil from the table. 'The instructions for making the sky fire are written using old alchemical symbols,' she explained. She drew a small circle with a cross above it, in the margin of Lil's *Vogue* magazine. 'This is the symbol for *antimony*. It's a semi-metallic chemical element, which – well, never mind that. It's not really important. However, if I were to put a line across the circle, like this, it becomes the symbol for *cinnabar*, an ore of mercury.' Next, Tilly drew a triangle. 'This symbol represents *sulphur*. But if I put an extra line *here*, it would instead be the symbol for *phosphorous*. Do you see?'

'You mean we could amend the Almanac before we give it to them?' said Mei, realising what she was suggesting.

'We'd only need to make tiny changes to make the instructions quite different,' said Tilly. 'The marks we'd make would be so small, I don't think they'd be able to tell we'd interfered. Not unless they already suspected it, anyway.'

'They won't suspect,' said Sophie. It was quite clear to her that no one would imagine that *they* could decipher the Almanac – not without the help of the Bureau and the Chief's experts. Decoding ancient books and deciphering alchemical symbols was simply not the kind of thing anyone expected of young ladies – and certainly not a young lady like Tilly. Really, she was rather an extraordinary person, Sophie thought.

The others were exchanging excited glances. Lil was on

her feet, her eyes sparkling. 'Do it. Make the changes,' she told Tilly. 'The rest of us will keep investigating. Then, tomorrow night, we'll hand over the book.'

There was a sudden burst of eager, breathless conversation as they began to talk it over. But Sophie's attention kept being drawn back to the Draco Almanac, lying on the table, beside the bag of doughnuts.

She knew Tilly's plan was a good one. Yet she still felt uneasy. Even without the proper instructions for making the weapon, could they really just hand over the Almanac to the *Fraternitas*? She couldn't help thinking of the warning Carruthers had given her. What would happen if they did not deliver it back to the Bureau? What would the Chief say when they told him the book they'd worked so hard to obtain had been given away?

But what troubled her still more was her instinct about the Almanac itself. She thought again of those horrifying illustrations, and remembered what Tilly had said about *nightmares*, and her skin prickled.

Sophie did not believe in alchemy, or magic spells. Yet as she looked at the Almanac, her unease seemed to grow, spreading like a dark shadow. There was no doubt about it: the book had power. And now they were proposing to put it straight into the hands of their enemy, the Black Dragon.

CHAPTER TWENTY-TWO

Williamsburg
Brooklyn
New York City

Billy sniffed appreciatively as they stepped into the shop. A young woman in a brown apron was serving customers at a long wooden counter, while another weighed out coffee beans, and a third worked a large hand-turned grinder. Shelves lined the walls, reaching up to the ceiling, filled with containers labelled in neat handwriting: *Brazilian, Turkish, Java. Orange Pekoe, Black China. Jasmine, Oolong, Irish Tea.* A rich, delicious coffee smell fragranced the air.

It had been easier to track down Pat and Jimmy O'Hara than either Billy or Lil had expected. Although Billy did not know exactly where their aunt and uncle lived, he knew they ran a shop in a district of Brooklyn called Williamsburg. After taking the train there, they'd begun exploring, walking down streets lined with shops and tenement buildings. This part of New York was quite different to the wide tree-lined streets around Central Park, and Billy had stared around him at horse-drawn carts and rattling milk-wagons, bakeries and barber shops, dime stores and a hardware shop with brooms and buckets and birdcages hanging up outside. It was clear this was a neighbourhood where ordinary people lived: down side streets lines of white washing were strung between buildings, and children played skipping games. While he'd been taking it all in, Lil had spotted the gaily painted shop sign reading O'HARA'S TEA AND COFFEE PROVISIONS.

As soon as Billy explained who he was to the young woman behind the counter, they were bustled through to the back of the shop, and ensconced in a parlour with dark green wallpaper and lace curtains. A moment later, Pat and Jimmy came rushing in.

'Bill!' exclaimed Jimmy, clapping him on the back, quite as if he was greeting a long-lost relation. 'This is grand! We said you should come and look us up, but we never thought you'd come so soon.'

'Hope you're feeling better now you're on dry land?' said Pat with a grin. He turned to the pleasant-looking woman who'd come into the room behind them, bearing a tray of tea and sticky slabs of fruitcake. 'Poor Bill had the most terrible seasickness on the crossing, Auntie Mary. Never seen anyone look so green in my life.'

'Sick as a dog he was,' said Jimmy, nodding in agreement. Then seeing Lil, his expression changed. 'Er – oh – good morning, miss,' he said, suddenly polite.

Billy had forgotten that Lil's appearance could have a powerful effect on people, and for a moment wished she hadn't come at all. It would be a great deal easier to find out what they wanted to know if Pat and Jimmy weren't both staring at her, tongue-tied, as if a film star had suddenly materialised in their aunt's front parlour.

But Lil soon set them at their ease, shaking hands in her friendliest and most ordinary manner. 'I'm Lil – well, Lilian Rose, if you want to be proper. I'm a friend of Bill's, from London,' she said cheerfully. 'Thanks awfully for having us. This tea is perfectly splendid, Mrs O'Hara. Not that I'm surprised, when you have such a marvellous shop!'

Mrs O'Hara looked pleased. 'We've had the place going on for ten years now. It's a family business, but it's grown too much for me and the girls to manage by ourselves. That's why we're so pleased Pat and Jim could come out to join us. And America's a fine place for young people.'

'What brings *you* here?' Pat asked Lil with interest. 'Do you work for Mr Sinclair too?'

'That's right,' said Lil vaguely, accepting a slice of cake. 'Thanks most awfully – how delicious. But actually, Bill and I are having a day out. We're on our way to Coney Island. We thought we might visit Dreamland.'

Mrs O'Hara looked surprised. 'Dreamland? You won't find much to see there today. It doesn't open for the summer season until Saturday.'

'Dreamland?' asked Jimmy, intrigued by the name. 'What's that?'

'It's an amusement park,' explained Mrs O'Hara. 'There are a few of them down at Coney Island – by the beach. Dreamland is the biggest and fanciest of the lot. Or it *was*, up until last summer, when the place burned to the ground. An accident – or so they *said*.'

'I say – what really happened?' asked Lil.

'I oughtn't to spread about gossip,' said Mrs O'Hara. But seeing they were all listening intently, she couldn't resist carrying on. 'Some said that fire was no accident at all, but set on purpose. The place had been worth hundreds of thousands of dollars. After the fire it was sold off for next to nothing. Not the first time that kind of thing has happened round these parts.'

Billy and Lil exchanged a look. 'But it's reopening this weekend?' Billy prompted.

'Yes. The new owner has been rebuilding the place over the winter. They say it'll be bigger and better than ever. There's to be a grand opening on Saturday with free admission for all, and fireworks in the evening. We'll go along of course, along with half of Brooklyn, I daresay. Perhaps we'll even be able to tear your Uncle John away from the shipyard for an hour, to have a look,' she suggested to Pat and Jimmy. To Lil and Billy she explained, 'My husband John's not really a fellow for amusement parks. He usually works on Saturdays, but I reckon even he'd take some time off to give Dreamland a once-over. He's a carpenter up at the Atlantic Line shipyard. That's how we were able to get the boys passage over on the *Thalassa*,' she added rather proudly.

'Oh! He works for Theodore Van Bergen, then?' asked Lil with interest.

Mrs O'Hara laughed. 'I suppose he does, in a way! They don't see much of him at the shipyard. Though I may say, Tom speaks very well of the fellow. Sees to it his workers are treated properly and paid a fair wage. He's been building new houses for them nearby, clean and comfortable and a price they can afford. There's to be a hospital too, and a school for the children. That's a lot more than many would do – more than most, I'd say.' Mrs O'Hara glanced at the clock. 'Mercy me – I've been sitting here gabbing away for too long. I ought to be getting back to the shop.'

'It's been lovely to meet you, Mrs O'Hara,' said Lil – at her warmest and most charming. 'Before you go, even if Dreamland is closed, is there anything else we might see at Coney Island?'

Mrs O'Hara considered this. 'Well, there's Madame Olga's Museum of Curiosities. I don't care for that sort of thing myself, but the girls like it. And you could look for Tony's cart – he does the best ice creams in Coney Island.'

Billy gave Lil a quick glance and then added, 'Actually, there is someone we're hoping to look for while we're there. A man called Molloy. I don't s'pose you know anyone by that name?'

His casual remark had an extraordinary effect on Mrs O'Hara. Her pleasant face suddenly turned wary, and she put down her cup.

'Molloy? What do you want with Molloy?' she demanded.

'Oh, er – we heard that a friend of ours is working for him,' Billy improvised. 'We don't know exactly where he's living, but we thought if we tracked down Molloy we might be able to find him.'

Mrs O'Hara got to her feet. All her friendliness had disappeared. 'I'm sorry, I can't help you. I'll be getting back to work now. You too, boys. There's all those deliveries to be unpacked. Nice to have met you both,' she added, nodding to Lil and Billy with a fixed smile – sounding all at once as if she didn't think it had been *nice* in the least.

Lil reached out and touched Mrs O'Hara's arm. 'You *do* know who this Molloy is, don't you? Can't you tell us who he is?' she asked earnestly. 'We're new here, and we don't know anyone. But we really want to find our friend. We think – well, we think he might be in trouble. And this is the best clue we have.'

Mrs O'Hara looked at her hopeful face for a long moment, and then sighed. 'You seem like decent young folks, so I'll give it to you straight. If you know what's good for you, you'll stay away from Molloy. And if this friend you're looking for really is working for him, you're better off staying clear of him too.'

'But *why?* Who *is* Molloy?' asked Lil.

'We don't know anything about him, only his name,' Billy added.

Mrs O'Hara sat back down, and lowered her voice, rather as if she thought someone might be listening – even though there was no one in the parlour but themselves. 'He calls himself a businessman. Hmph! I could think of other names. A couple of years ago he was just a small-time crook. But now, he's got Coney Island in the palm of his hand. The sideshows, the penny arcades, the theatres – he owns half of them, and bullies the rest. He's got a couple of nasty thugs that do his bidding, and woe betide anyone that doesn't fall in line. Washed up in the Hudson – and that's if they're lucky. He's not a man you want to have anything to do with, if you can help it. Especially a pair of youngsters fresh off the boat.'

Jimmy and Pat were listening, eyes wide, but Lil and Billy exchanged a swift glance. They might be on the other side of the Atlantic, but Molloy's methods were quite familiar to them. Nasty thugs, bodies in the river . . . they'd encountered all this before.

'*Molloy* is the new owner of Dreamland,' Mrs O'Hara went on. 'People are saying he's got a rich backer, someone putting up the money for redeveloping the place. And that's not all. He's been expanding, moving further north, buying up factories and who knows what else.' She looked at them both earnestly. 'You go along and enjoy your day out at Coney Island – and maybe we'll see you at Dreamland on Saturday for the grand opening. But if you listen to me, that's as close to Molloy as you want to get.'

'Thank you for telling us,' said Lil. 'We're awfully grateful.'

Mrs O'Hara nodded. She had thawed now that she understood they had no real connection to Molloy. Billy and Lil got up to go, saying farewell to Jimmy and Pat, and promising to call again soon.

But at the shop door, Mrs O'Hara paused. 'If you really want to find your friend, you could try Ruby's,' she said suddenly.

'Ruby's?' Billy repeated. 'Where's that?'

'It's a Coney Island bar. If your friend is there, then Ruby's bound to have seen him. She knows everyone.'

'Marvellous!' exclaimed Lil. 'Thank you!'

But Mrs O'Hara frowned anxiously. 'You take care now. Don't go poking about Coney Island asking lots of questions. Watch your backs – and stay away from Molloy.'

CHAPTER TWENTY-THREE

The Waldorf-Astoria
New York City

Across the water in Manhattan, on the Upper East Side, Sophie was crossing the vast entrance hall of the Waldorf-Astoria, with Lucky at her side.

In many ways, she thought it was very like the grand hotels of Paris or London. Here were the marble floors and uniformed porters; here were the chandeliers and fashionably dressed guests. But there was something that seemed different about the Waldorf-Astoria. Perhaps because it was built on such a huge scale. It was even bigger and more luxurious, as everything in New York seemed to be.

She was glad she'd put on her most stylish hat, and that Lucky was at her side, glossy black coat gleaming. A well-groomed pedigree lapdog seemed exactly the right accessory for a smart young lady visiting a top New York hotel. What was more, there was something reassuring about the dog's presence: the friendly sound of her pattering paws, and her beady black eyes looking around eagerly, as she sniffed about her, excited by a new place to explore.

Sophie was grateful for the company. She was still reeling from everything that had happened since they'd left London – and worried about what lay ahead. Now, after a restless night, with her anxieties dancing about her head, she felt unsettled.

As she passed Peacock Alley, where elegant ladies were strolling, her attention was caught by a young man, hurrying across the foyer towards the door. In a flash, she thought she recognised him as Daniel Quinn. But a moment later he was away, into the street outside, leaving Sophie frowning after him. Had she been mistaken? Could the smart young-man-about-town she'd just glimpsed possibly be the same bespectacled fellow with the overcoat and satchel she'd met on the dockside? And if so, what could he be doing at the Waldorf-Astoria? Perhaps she had imagined it – and yet she found herself glancing about uneasily as she entered the restaurant.

Mei was waiting for her at a table in the corner. It was a well-chosen spot, with a clear view across the expanse of restaurant and beyond, but screened from sight by a large potted palm. Mei had a pot of tea at her side, and a newspaper spread before her. She looked relaxed and composed – but at the same time alert and intent. She clearly had lots to say, because she started talking almost before Sophie had taken her seat.

'I've been watching all morning – and I've found out where Mrs Davenport is staying. She's in the Josephine Suite, on the second floor,' Mei began in a low voice, as Sophie looked around, taking in the gleaming silverware, snowy-white napkins and menu card listing all kinds of splendid, unfamiliar things like *lobster cocktail, clam chowder, raspberry water-ice* and *peach ice-cream*. At her feet, Lucky sniffed about, hoping to discover the crumbs of a caviar sandwich, or some morsels of French cheese.

'She breakfasted there this morning – coffee and boiled eggs,' Mei went on. 'Then, her dressmaker visited at eleven, and stayed for about half an hour.' She broke off as a man in a white jacket and gloves passed their table. Mei caught his attention with the slightest gesture of her hand. 'Excuse me – could you bring another cup for my friend?'

'Of course, ma'am,' said the head waiter.

Sophie looked across the table at Mei. It was hard to believe that the girl who'd once been frightened by the prospect of taking an omnibus across London was the same poised, elegant person who sat opposite her, looking quite at home in one of the finest hotels in America. 'I must say, you've got very good at going undercover,' she observed. 'I think the New York high life suits you.'

Mei blushed. 'I s'pose I've learned a bit, from watching Lil.' She pushed her copy of the *New York Evening Telegram* across the table, leafing past the front page with the bold headline *THALASSA'S NEAR MISS! ATLANTIC LINE*

FLAGSHIP ESCAPES ICEBERG COLLISION! 'There's something I want to show you. Look at the piece here, about the opening of Dreamland.'

Sophie scanned the newspaper article. '"After a devastating fire last year, the entire park was destroyed,"' she read aloud. '"Shortly afterwards the site was purchased by Coney Island Holdings Ltd, who have since undertaken extensive work to rebuild and refurbish Dreamland, at a reputed cost of $500,000." That's a tremendous amount of money.' She read on: '"Planned entertainments for the opening day will include an evening firework display, and a demonstration from prize-winning aerialist Mr G. Charlton,"' she finished in surprise. She knew Charlton. He was a young British pilot whom she'd encountered when she'd flown in the Grand Aerial Tour of Europe with her friend Captain Nakamura.

'Remember the postcard?' Mei went on eagerly. 'It mentioned *Charlton* and *Saturday*! Surely *this* is what it was talking about?'

Just then the head waiter appeared with Sophie's teacup and saucer, and they had to break off their conversation. As he poured tea into Sophie's cup, a younger waiter came scurrying over. 'Miss Andrews has arrived, sir, with the rest of the luncheon party,' he said.

Mei's eyes widened, as the head waiter finished pouring Sophie's tea, and bowed politely to them both. As he moved away, they saw him glancing over to a long table set for a large party. 'Everything's ready – I will show them directly to their table,' he said.

'Miss Andrews!' Mei whispered excitedly.

But Sophie was already looking across the room. 'Oh no!' she groaned, grabbing for Mei's newspaper to hide her face.

The head waiter was ushering in a party of diners – and right at the front of the group was Miss Roberta Russell.

'Again?' muttered Sophie, peeping out from behind the newspaper. 'Why does she always seem to follow me wherever I go? Look – there's Charlie Walters too. And goodness, I think that's Sir Chester Norton himself!'

Sophie had met the owner of Norton Newspapers once before, in Paris. He was a shrewd-looking gentleman in his fifties with greying hair and an intelligent expression. With him was a man of a similar age, who wore gold-rimmed spectacles and a green silk necktie. 'I think that might be Albert Moorhouse – the editor of *The Daily Picture*,' murmured Sophie. 'Miss Russell did say he was in New York with Norton.'

'This way, Miss Andrews,' they heard the head waiter say, addressing the woman who had walked into the restaurant beside Roberta Russell. She appeared to be about thirty, very neat and trim in a well-cut dark suit. She carried a small leather case, and looked extremely efficient. Could this be the woman who had sent the telegram to Forsyth?

But before Sophie had more than an instant to wonder,

something else happened that took her completely by surprise. While Miss Andrews and the rest settled themselves around the table, another guest strolled into the restaurant. She wore a boldly printed tea-gown and a feathered turban, and as she reached the long table, she greeted the whole party as if they were old friends.

'It's Mrs Davenport!' squeaked Mei.

There seemed to be an atmosphere of celebration in the air. Sir Chester ordered some drinks, and as the head waiter hurried past their table once more, they heard him say: 'Bring the '89 champagne, Maurice. But have the bartender mix a dry martini for Mrs Davenport. You know how particular she is.'

Seated beside Albert Moorhouse, Mrs Davenport was now leaning across the table to speak to Miss Russell. Sophie could see only the back of her head, but across the table, Roberta's face was animated, almost awed. Suddenly, she recalled her own first encounter with Mrs Davenport, at a country house party. She'd been called Lady Tremayne then, but she'd made just the same effort to be charming to the young people present, including Sophie herself.

The champagne arrived and Sir Chester lifted his glass to make a toast, speaking loudly in order to reach everyone along the table. From their corner, Sophie and Mei could hear every word.

'I'm delighted that Norton Newspapers will be expanding to New York, and even more delighted to welcome Mrs Davenport as a partner in this new venture. To the successful acquisition of the *New York Evening Telegram!*'

Everyone raised their glasses. Sophie could see Roberta smiling as Charlie Walters tapped his glass against hers. Mrs Davenport inclined her head graciously, then turned to murmur something to Moorhouse, who laughed as if entertained. The whole party looked bright and happy, yet Sophie felt a sudden darkness invade the white-and-gold restaurant. The shadow of the *Fraternitas* seemed to sweep over the glittering chandeliers, the fizzy champagne.

Did anyone at that table have the slightest idea that Mrs Davenport was not merely a glamorous New York socialite – or now it seemed, a businesswoman – but one of the leaders of a criminal organisation? They could not know that the woman sitting amongst them was, in fact, a murderer.

In Venice, Mrs Davenport had poisoned an innocent old lady who had threatened the success of her schemes. She'd sent Forsyth to trick Sophie, and leave her shut up in an underground tomb to die. She had plotted to sabotage the *Thalassa*, putting thousands of lives in danger. And now here she was, coolly sipping her martini at the Waldorf-Astoria, as if all that meant nothing at all.

On the other side of the table, Mei wasn't looking at Mrs Davenport. She was still staring at Florence Andrews, who was sitting on Mrs Davenport's other side.

'*It's her . . .*' Mei breathed.

'She's the one who sent the telegram,' agreed Sophie. 'She must be working with Mrs Davenport.'

'No – well, yes – but it's more than that!' Mei's eyes were very wide. 'Sophie, I think she's *the smart woman*. The one that we saw at the offices of Norton Newspapers!'

Sophie sat back in her chair, trying to take it in. *The smart woman*. Could it be that the woman at Mrs Davenport's side was the same woman Joe had seen collecting stolen secrets from the Bureau? The one who was working hand-in-glove with Forsyth – and who, together with Mrs Davenport, was surely responsible for Joe's disappearance?

All at once, she got to her feet. The confusion and uncertainty she'd been feeling seemed to vanish like a cloud rolling away, leaving clear skies.

'What *are* you doing?' hissed Mei, looking up at her in alarm.

'Stay here,' said Sophie. 'Keep watching and listening. Don't let Roberta Russell see you.'

'Where are *you* going?' demanded Mei in a whisper.

But Sophie had already gone.

CHAPTER TWENTY-FOUR

Coney Island
Brooklyn
New York City

'**S**o this is Coney Island,' said Lil. She shaded her eyes with her hand as she gazed out over a wide expanse of sand, sky and shimmering ocean. She'd expected a seaside town, somewhere rather like Brighton, but Coney Island wasn't a bit like anywhere in England. The light was pale and clear; the sky seemed to stretch out very high above them; and the air smelled of salt and seaweed. There were boats dotted across the horizon, and on the sand, a couple of children were digging for clams. Mud seeped from between the wooden slats on the sidewalk beneath their feet.

Together, she and Billy walked along streets called Surf Avenue and Sea Beach Walk, peeping into the windows of shops and restaurants. Unlike in Williamsburg, many of the windows were dark and dim. Most of the booths and huts along the boardwalk were still shuttered for the winter, their windows boarded up against salt-spray and wind. Only a handful were open for business, with signs advertising *Pretzels* or *Candy*, and the smell of fried food in the air. Yet there was a certain buzz of anticipation. Here and there workers were making repairs or touching up paintwork. A man was pasting a poster to a wall, advertising *The Circus of Marvels World Tour: Coming Soon to Coney Island!* in bold scarlet printing. Lil stopped in her tracks to stare at it. 'Golly! Look at that!' she exclaimed.

But Billy was staring up at a white tower, strung with electric lights. 'This is it,' he said. 'This is Dreamland!'

The name was written in tall letters across a gateway, beyond which they could see glimpses of a fairy-tale scene – turrets, spires and towers. Yet as they peered through the gate, Lil saw that the fantastical constructions were nothing but papier mâché and gold paint. 'Like an enormous theatre set,' she said.

And just like backstage in a theatre during rehearsals, Dreamland was full of activity. There were workmen painting and hammering, or going by with wheelbarrows, and electricians fixing up strings of lights. Huge posters advertised *Grand Reopening Saturday – Admission Free! Spectacular Aerial Display! Firework extravaganza!* Others listed the attractions to be found in the park: *Travel the Alps of Switzerland! Take a gondola through the Canals of Venice! Descend into the terrifying depths of Hell-Gate!* For now though, the gates were fastened shut.

Dreamland had been easy to find, but tracking down Ruby's was more difficult. They passed a vaudeville theatre, a shooting gallery, and a dozen different bars and restaurants – but not one of them was called *Ruby's*. In the end, Lil stopped to ask a workman, who was hand-painting a sign reading *Popcorn* in curly scarlet letters, a pipe clenched between his teeth. He was not very friendly, only jerking a thumb in the direction of a place they'd walked past twice already – a narrow brick building, with a faded striped canopy. A shabby sign was printed with the words: *FLYNN'S BAR.*

'Old Flynn's place, it used to be,' growled the man, without taking his pipe out of his mouth. 'Everyone calls it Ruby's now.'

They walked towards it, exchanging uncertain glances. It had a down-at-heel look that was not very appealing. But if this was where Joe's trail led, then Lil was adamant this was where they must go.

Inside, they found themselves in a large room with wooden tables. There was sawdust on the floor but it was not as grubby as Lil had expected. Instead, it was cosy and comfortable, in a rough-and-ready kind of way. In one corner, a young fellow was tinkling softly at the keys of an old upright piano; in another, a few men gathered round a stove, nursing mugs of ale. The walls were hung with intriguing things: paintings of steamboats, old theatre programmes, autographed photographs of vaudeville dancers and seashells displayed in a glass-fronted case.

An old fellow at the bar was holding forth, saying in a quavery but persistent voice: 'And her husband died, you know – from the bite of a lizard, in Cuba –'

As Lil and Billy stepped in, he stopped talking and the bar became suddenly quiet. Lil did not usually mind being the centre of attention, but now she did not like the feeling of so many eyes swivelling to look at them. Perhaps if it had been the middle of a sunny day in high summer, when Coney Island would no doubt be full of visitors, things would have been different. But now, they stood out. The bartender frowned, his expression hostile.

'Gee, I'm awfully tired, Wally,' Lil said to Billy. She spoke brightly, in an American accent. 'We've walked so far, I reckon my feet might just about drop off. Let's sit down and order some lemonade.'

For a moment, Billy looked awkward. But he'd been a Taylor & Rose detective for far too long to be thrown off by one of Lil's spontaneous undercover performances. 'All right,' he muttered, following her over to a small table, close enough to the bar that they'd have a chance of hearing what was going on.

'What are you up to?' he demanded in a low voice. 'Why the accent? And why am I called *Wally*? It sounds ridiculous.'

'This is Molloy's patch. If he's working with Mrs Davenport and he hears two young English people have been nosing around asking questions, he might get suspicious,' Lil explained with a shrug. 'I thought we'd

227

better pretend to be Americans. *Wally* is the sort of thing American boys are called,' she said, indicating a faded tobacco advertisement on the wall featuring a baseball player named Walter Johnson. 'Look, you can give *me* a name if you like.'

This idea cheered Billy up at once. 'All right . . . *Gladys*,' he said with relish. 'You go and get us some drinks. That fellow's giving us an awfully funny look.'

Sure enough, as Lil went up to the bar, she saw that the bartender was scowling at them. She glanced around, looking for someone who might be the Ruby Mrs O'Hara had spoken of, but there wasn't another woman in the place. Was that why the bartender was looking at her so suspiciously? Perhaps American girls didn't go into bars like this.

Just the same, she asked for two lemonades, smiling at the bartender and trying to make a little polite conversation – about the weather, and the new Dreamland amusement park. 'It sure looks like it will be quite a place!' she exclaimed in her very best American drawl. The bartender only grunted, as he took out two lemonade bottles.

'Ignore him, sweetheart,' said the old man with a long white moustache, who was sitting at the bar eating his way through a bowl of peanuts. 'Charley ain't got no manners. That's why normally Miss Ruby don't let him serve the drinks.'

'Where's the other bartender today, Grandpops?' asked a man who was sitting a little further down the bar. 'The young fellow. Nice kid.'

228

'Gone off,' said the old man briefly.

'Ah, it's about time he got a day off,' said the other man, with a chuckle. 'I didn't think Ruby ever let him out. Don't reckon he's been anywhere but behind that bar since Christmas.'

'It wasn't any *day off*,' said Grandpops, adding in a lower voice. 'He got a summons. From *Molloy*.'

Lil listened intently as she handed over a few coins to the bartender. The other man shook his head gravely. 'Poor kid. I hope he ain't got himself into trouble.'

Grandpops nodded. 'Now that kid, Joey, *he* has manners all right. Listens to us old-timers gabbing away, just as if we were saying something worth hearing. I guess that's how they make 'em in England.' He smiled at Lil vaguely, as she picked up the lemonades to carry back to Billy, fighting to stop her hands from trembling.

She saw from Billy's face that he too had heard what the old man had said. They were both battling to keep their expressions perfectly calm and unconcerned, but then, as she passed the piano, the piano-player broke into a new tune, and Lil faltered.

The bottles of lemonade slipped from her hands and crashed to the ground, but she barely even noticed them.

If she'd been unsure before, she was certain now.

For she had known the tune at once – there was no mistaking it. In this funny old bar in Coney Island, the pianist was playing 'The Fairest of Them All'.

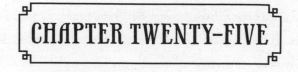

CHAPTER TWENTY-FIVE

The Waldorf-Astoria
New York City

S ophie went swiftly up a wide carpeted staircase and along a corridor, looking all about her for the Josephine Suite. She hadn't reckoned with just how large the Waldorf-Astoria was – two huge buildings, connected by miles of corridors. She knew she did not have much time, but she tried to walk calmly. If she was not going to draw attention to herself, she knew she needed to look as if she were 'going to do something perfectly dull and ordinary – like buying postage stamps', as Lil had once said.

But it was difficult to seem perfectly dull and ordinary, like a person thinking only about postage-stamps, when you were *actually* going to do something not only risky, but certainly illegal. Sophie knew she did not have the Bureau to get her out of trouble, and she knew she could not afford to make any more mistakes.

At last, she reached the door marked *Josephine Suite*.

Although she knew Mrs Davenport was downstairs in the restaurant, she paused outside, listening for sounds within. Then she tapped briskly on the door, and listened again. When there was no answer, and she was quite satisfied there was no one inside, she slipped a couple of pins from her hair, and began picking the lock. Even without her lock-picks, she was an old hand at this, and it was only seconds before the lock clicked open and she was inside Mrs Davenport's suite.

It was a splendid place, full of sumptuous fabrics and costly furniture. There were paintings on the walls, curios littered about on side tables, and several books left scattered across the rug, but Sophie did not stop to look at them. She did not have time for that. Instead, she quickly scanned the room, and then went through a door, into a lavish bedroom, full of the heady smell of a rich, spicy perfume.

Here was what she'd been looking for – a small writing desk, scattered with letters and papers. Amongst the papers were a cup half-full of black coffee, thick and bitter-smelling, a jewel box, a cigarette case and several bottles of French perfume, all of them almost empty.

Sophie pulled on a pair of gloves and went to work, swift but methodical. The writing desk might look like a mess, but that did not mean Mrs Davenport didn't know exactly where everything was. Carefully, she examined each item and replaced it: an invitation to an exhibition of new European paintings at a gallery on Lexington Street;

a programme from a production of the opera *La Bohème*. A receipt from Cartier for a pair of diamond and pearl lavalier earrings had been used as a bookmark inside a leather-bound copy of Henry James's *The Wings of the Dove*. There were one or two letters, which Sophie scrutinised intently, but there was not a single dragon symbol to be seen. Instead they were mostly bills from grand shops like Bergdorf Goodman or Tiffany's.

Surely there must be *something* here to prove Mrs Davenport's connection to the *Fraternitas*? Sophie turned to the desk drawers. In one, she found a handful of papers, and realised that each of them was either a property deed or a bill of sale. Each related to a different New York property – apartment buildings, factories and office blocks. A number of them were in Brooklyn, and each of these was owned by the same company – *Coney Island Holdings Ltd*. It caught her eye at once – it was the company that owned Dreamland! Taking a pencil and paper from her pocket, Sophie jotted down the key details from each paper, before reordering them and returning them to the drawer exactly as she'd found them.

In the second drawer of the desk, she found a black leather appointment book with gold-tipped pages. As she took it out and flipped open the cover, several photographs slipped out from where they'd been tucked inside. Sophie frowned. These were family photographs — and she recognised the girl in the first picture at once. It was unmistakably Leo, at perhaps nine or ten years old. She had a bow in her hair and was frowning at the camera as if she did not want to be photographed at all.

Sophie paused, intrigued. She knew Mrs Davenport had once been very fond of Leo, but she'd never expected her to keep her picture like this. Leo was one of the Loyal Order of Lions now, and the last time her godmother had seen her, she'd been spying on the secret meeting of the *Fraternitas* in Venice. And yet here was her photograph, tucked carefully away for safekeeping. There was another picture of Leo too, looking a little older, standing awkwardly with her mother and father and her brother Vincent. Then came several pictures of people Sophie did not recognise, and two of a grand country house. The last photograph showed a girl of around her own age, standing beside a young man. They were posed stiffly, dressed in old-fashioned clothes, their expressions serious. The picture was soft with age, curling slightly at the edges, but the inscription on the back was still legible: *John and Viola, 1884.*

A sudden noise from the sitting room made her start up. It was the sound of the door handle turning. Sophie dashed across the room towards a large mahogany wardrobe. She had no time to look for a better hiding place. Still holding the appointment book, she flung herself inside.

She found herself standing amongst Mrs Davenport's clothes, surrounded by furs and brocades, the soft brush of velvet, the slippery touch of satin. She pressed herself back as far as she could into the darkest, most shadowy corner of the wardrobe, while outside, footsteps padded across the room. The spicy smell of Mrs Davenport's scent tickled her throat, and for a horrible moment, she thought she was going to cough.

Swallowing down the tickle, she stayed perfectly still, listening. Was Mrs Davenport back from the restaurant already? Then she heard the distinctive rattle of a dustpan and bucket, and let out a long breath of relief. It was a hotel chambermaid, who had come to clean her rooms.

Of course, being stuck inside the wardrobe with a chambermaid outside was very far from ideal. But there was nothing she could do about it now. She'd have to hold her nerve and wait until the chambermaid had finished her work – hoping that she would leave before Mrs Davenport returned.

At least she had the appointment book. That would give her something to occupy her while she waited. Careful not to make even the smallest noise, she opened it, flicking through the pages in the light that filtered through the wardrobe doors. As the chambermaid moved about outside – humming to herself as she swept the rugs, made the bed and collected the coffee cup – Sophie found today's date:

18 MON

19 TUESDAY — 11.30am - M - Central Park
12 noon - Pell St

20 WEDNESDAY — 11am - Dress fitting
2pm Luncheon party (GOLD)

21 THURSDAY — 3pm - Hairdresser
6pm - Private view, Stieglitz Gallery

22 FRIDAY — 8pm - Dinner Delmonico's

23 SATURDAY — 4pm - Presentation -
Ocean View Suite,
Orient Hotel

SUNDAY

From where she crouched uncomfortably in the back of the wardrobe, Sophie stared down at the page. There it was - the single word GOLD, seeming to flash and glitter before her eyes.

Now she understood exactly why she'd felt the dark shadow of the *Fraternitas* downstairs in the Waldorf-Astoria's restaurant.

It wasn't only the Black Dragon who had been there.

The Gold Dragon had been there too.

CHAPTER TWENTY-SIX

The Brooklyn Bridge
New York City

Night was falling in New York. The city glittered, neon-bright, sprinkled with sparkling lights. As Sophie crossed the foyer of the Maple Hotel, she saw that the other guests were heading out for dinner, or the opera, or the theatre. 'We're off to see Mr Ziegfeld's new show, and I can't wait!' said a friendly girl, as her party waited for a motor-taxi. 'It's supposed to be simply marvellous! Isn't New York splendid?'

Sophie nodded and agreed that it was, before she slipped away quietly, unnoticed amongst the evening gowns and dinner jackets. She wore a plain, dark coat, which would keep her warm at midnight, and boots that she could run in, if she had to. Her pistol was gone, but she still wore her mother's green necklace for luck.

Out in the street, she paced in the direction of Greenwich Village. It was a long walk, but she didn't mind. Walking helped her think, and there was no doubt that she had a great deal to think about.

After what Billy and Lil had discovered in Coney Island, earlier that day, Sophie knew that they had no choice but to hand over the Almanac. Joe really *could* be here – and they could not afford to risk his safety. *No more tricks.* If there was even the smallest chance they could get him back, they must take it.

Yet the idea of giving the Almanac to the Black Dragon still felt wrong – especially after all she'd learned at the Waldorf-Astoria. She'd had to wait for nearly half an hour, cramped up in the back of the wardrobe, until the chambermaid had finished her work. Once she'd gone, Sophie had slipped out of the wardrobe, quickly replacing the appointment book and making her escape. So much time had already passed that she knew she could not risk investigating any further. One narrow escape had been more than enough.

Now, she turned it over in her mind, remembering what she'd seen in the restaurant. Miss Florence Andrews, the smart woman – sender of coded telegrams, organiser of luncheon parties, receiver of secret information. Albert Moorhouse – editor of *The Daily Picture*. And sitting between them, Mrs Davenport. The Black Dragon herself, looking absolutely as if she belonged.

Could Moorhouse be the Gold Dragon? He fitted Leo's description to perfection: the grey hair, the smart clothes, the businesslike manner. Of course, there had been two or three other gentlemen at the table who matched it too, including Sir Chester Norton himself. But it was *Moorhouse* who had sat beside Mrs Davenport. *Moorhouse* into whose ear she had whispered. *Moorhouse* who had printed story after story in *The Daily Picture* about German spies.

In Venice, Leo had heard Gold talking of *stirring up spy fever* in Britain – and who could be better placed to do that than the editor of a newspaper? Roberta Russell had told her Moorhouse was *obsessed with spies*. He was the one who'd called for the changes to Billy's detective yarns, adding in references to German secret agents. He'd even appointed a spy editor.

As she walked, she began to stitch it together. If Moorhouse was Gold, then Florence Andrews was likely his secretary, working with him at the office of *The Daily Picture*, and travelling alongside him to New York. She must know the secrets of the *Fraternitas*. Perhaps she even hoped to be able to join herself one day, as Mrs Davenport had done.

But what about the others at the luncheon table? Sophie felt a sudden jolt as she remembered Roberta Russell's eager conversation with Mrs Davenport. Sophie had never been very fond of Miss Russell, but the thought that she might be mixed up with the *Fraternitas* was horribly disconcerting.

No, Miss Russell could not know about the dragons, she decided. The young journalist might be ambitious, but

Sophie felt certain she'd have no interest whatsoever in an ancient society of wealthy and pompous middle-aged men. In spite of everything, the thought of it made her smile. Yet there was something else too, and for a moment she felt like she was clutching at the thread of a clue, something important she'd missed. But almost at once, it slipped away again, and she found that she was already approaching the Moonrise Bookstore.

Though it was long after closing time, the lights were still on. Inside, Flora was tidying up, moving around cardboard boxes piled high with printed magazines. As Sophie came in, a box burst, scattering magazines everywhere. Sophie hastened to help pick them up.

'Thanks,' said Flora breathlessly, as Sophie efficiently stacked up the magazines again. As she did so, her eye was caught by the magazine's title – *LUNA* – and the publisher, the Moonrise Bookstore itself.

Flora followed her gaze. 'An experiment in publishing,' she explained with a sigh, heaving the cardboard box into an untidy corner behind the counter. 'But not a very successful one. I had an idea of publishing a magazine with contributions from some of New York's most interesting female writers and artists. There's some terrific content – essays, political pieces, stories, poetry. But I've had no luck getting it out there. Unless they're Edith Wharton, no one seems very interested in reading what New York women have to say.' Flora gave a disappointed shrug. 'Now I've got dozens of magazines leftover that no one wants. *Not* my most sensible business idea,' she concluded.

But Sophie was thinking. Flora's words had reminded her of Roberta Russell again. There was something she'd said when they'd been talking on the *Thalassa*. '*Moorhouse will want the piece to be all about celebrities and fashions. That's all he thinks lady journalists are capable of writing.*' It had been only a passing remark, but suddenly, Sophie felt quite sure it was important.

Just then, she heard feet on the stairs and looked up to see the others coming down towards her. They were all dressed as she was, in dark, practical clothes – and they looked ready for anything.

There was Mei, her hair plaited back, her face set. There was Tilly, carrying the brown paper parcel that contained the Almanac, her shoulders squared and her expression serious. There was Billy, looking a little nervous but immensely determined, with Lucky tucked under his arm. 'She wouldn't be left behind,' he explained. But somehow it seemed right to have Lucky with them too.

Leading the way was Lil, looking for all the world like a commanding officer leading her troops into battle. Her head was high and her eyes were blazing.

Sophie looked up at them and felt a surge of pride. This was as it should be, just as they'd planned it. The whole Taylor & Rose team, together, ready to face whatever lay ahead.

'Going out for the evening?' said Flora, so engrossed with her books and boxes that she'd barely noticed their appearance. 'Do have a nice time!'

But the door had closed: the agents of Taylor & Rose were already gone.

Night on Brooklyn Bridge. Far below, the water glittered darkly, stirred by the wind. Ahead of them, the bridge stretched, misty and deserted. In the distance, Lil could hear the hum of the city – a discordant melody of rumbling traffic, tooting horns, the clatter of a train flashing by over the bridge and disappearing into the night. She had the feeling of being at the centre of everything: the midpoint of a great web of crisscrossing streets and tunnels, waterways and bridges, railway lines and electric lights, shimmering in the dark.

They'd left Billy, Mei and Tilly waiting at the far end of the bridge. The Black Dragon's letter had been addressed to Sophie and Lil alone, and this time, they meant to follow the instructions absolutely. Now, they walked across the bridge together. It looked empty and strange, lit at regular intervals by lamps, but with pools of deep darkness in between. Lil was glad of their electric torch, but gladder still that Sophie was carrying it. No matter how hard she tried to keep them steady, her own hands had begun to tremble.

Ever since the visit to Ruby's, she had felt stretched

tight, as if every muscle in her body was tensed. Hoping, yet hardly daring to hope at the same time. This was why they'd come here, what it had all been for.

Beside her, she heard Sophie gasp. The beam of the torch had illuminated something ahead of them on the wooden boards. In the yellow circle of light, they both saw it – a crude chalk drawing of a twisting shape that they knew was meant to be a dragon.

Lil's stomach lurched. This was it. It was really happening. Beside her, Sophie looked across the empty stretch of bridge ahead of them, and then back the way they had come, to where they knew the others would be waiting anxiously. Then she looked at Lil. The wind blew wisps of hair across her pale face as she reached inside her bag and took out the Almanac. For a moment she weighed it in her hand, and then suddenly, she ripped off the brown paper covering. 'Better not leave them in any doubt it's the real thing this time,' she said. Then, taking a deep breath as if steeling herself, she placed the Almanac on top of the chalk dragon.

They looked at it, and then at each other. 'What now?' said Sophie.

Lil glanced around. A short distance away, she saw a wrought-iron bench, placed so that people could stop and rest as they crossed the bridge, or sit to admire the view. She jerked her head towards it. 'Now we watch and wait,' she said.

On the other side of the bridge, Billy and Mei exchanged worried glances, as the time drew closer to midnight. Tilly was along the bridge in the darkness that lay beyond. She knew she couldn't possibly see what was happening, but just the same, her gaze remained fixed on the distant point where Sophie and Lil must be. Beside her, Billy twitched from one foot to another. 'Come on, Joe,' he murmured.

On the bench, Lil took out her watch and glanced at it. Five minutes to midnight. Beside her, Sophie did not take her eyes from the small, dark shape of the Almanac, lying on the ground. The street lamp caught the gold eye on the cover, making it glitter. Any moment now, they'd learn whether the Black Dragon was telling the truth, and whether Joe was still alive.

An English bartender called Joey. Sophie felt a flare of hope, and then almost as quickly, it faded. Even if it had been Joe, they didn't know what had become of him. He'd been *summoned by Molloy,* which didn't sound good. If it was Joe, he'd been in trouble with someone very dangerous. So where was he now? Was it really possible they would get him back? Or had they made the wrong choice? Were they about to lose the Almanac for nothing?

A train clattered by in a rush of wind, and all of a sudden, Sophie was somewhere else altogether. She was no longer on the Brooklyn Bridge but in the leafy Summer Gardens of St Petersburg, where she'd once shared pastries with the Count Von Wilderstein and promised him she'd destroy the book. Then she was in the cosy secret room in Soho, beside a blazing fire – hot buttered-toast and the smell of the Chief's pipe. He'd trusted her with the Almanac. He was expecting her to return it. And then she was back at Taylor & Rose, Carruthers leaning forward, gripping her hand, urging her to promise she'd bring it safely back. *You'll be in fearful trouble if you don't.*

Finally, and most unexpectedly, there was Papa, in her childhood bedroom. Sitting at the end of her bed in the candlelight, telling her one of his endless stories. Tales in which the virtuous heroes always did the right thing and won the day – and the dastardly villains were always punished. She looked at the Almanac lying on the ground and then squeezed her eyes shut, trying to swallow down the feeling that this was *all wrong*.

The truth was she was not so certain what was *right* and what was *wrong* any longer. She'd always done her best to live up to Papa's stories, to make him proud of her. *Keep your chin up, keep your head,* and *do the right thing.* But what if there wasn't one simple *right thing to do?* It was funny how none of Papa's stories had ever mentioned that.

Beside her, she felt Lil stiffen. Looking across the bridge through the fog, she saw something – a flicker of movement. She stared. *Someone was coming.*

She almost expected to see the dramatic figure of the Black Dragon herself, gliding across the bridge, her long fur coat sweeping behind her. She almost expected to see Forsyth, swaggering towards them, full of bravado, delighted to have regained the upper hand and to be seizing his prize at last. But instead she could only see the vague outline of a group of men, making their way across the bridge. Through the dark and the mist, Sophie made out the shape of three – four – five of them?

They stopped some distance from where the Almanac lay, in a patch of shadow the lamplight did not reach. Lil and Sophie watched, hardly daring to move a muscle, though Sophie could feel Lil's hand clenching hers tightly.

One of the men detached himself from the group and moved forward, staying in the shadows. Sophie could see the flash of a revolver in his hand. He strode to the Almanac, picked it up, and gave it a quick, cursory glance. Then he looked over to the bench, where Sophie and Lil were sitting, and gave them a sharp look through hard, narrow eyes.

Neither of them moved. It was if they were fixed in position. The man stepped back, rejoining the others, and there was a mutter and flurry of sudden movement. One of the men had pushed himself forward to grab the Almanac and was leafing through it feverishly.

Where was Joe? Panic was rising in Sophie's chest. There was a dull thudding sound, as if someone had dropped a heavy bag on the wooden boards ahead of them. Then, as if it had been a signal, the group of men moved away across the bridge again, their dark coats flapping in the wind.

They did not look back at Sophie and Lil, frozen on the bench. They gave no message or sign. They simply disappeared into the dark, taking the Almanac with them. Sophie watched it vanish, the book she'd worked so long to find, that she'd promised she would destroy.

'They're leaving . . .' Lil whispered. Her voice was hoarse. She stared at Sophie dumbly, as if she couldn't believe it, and then leaned forward, covering her face with her hands.

But Sophie grabbed her arm. 'What was that?' she demanded, staring ahead into the darkness. She'd heard something – a small sound, like a little groan.

There was something lying on the boards, several yards away from them. As they watched, it moved slightly. This time, they both heard a groan.

That was all it took. Sophie and Lil raced forward across the bridge, hand in hand.

PART IV

CHAPTER TWENTY-SEVEN

Greenwich Village
New York City

It was just like Lil had imagined it – and yet it wasn't a bit like that at all.

It was early morning instead of afternoon. There was no rain against the window, and instead of tea and buns there was coffee and bagels from the bakery down the street. They certainly couldn't have been much further from the office of Taylor & Rose Detectives.

Yet, just as she had imagined, they were together at last.

Joe was lying on the sofa. His face was bruised and his shirt front was stained with blood, but he looked a great deal better than when they'd first brought him through the door. Lil couldn't stop looking at him. She felt as if she needed to make sure he was still there.

In some ways, it was like looking at a stranger. She'd forgotten how tall he was, or what his voice sounded like. He looked older – and different, somehow. Yet his hand when he squeezed hers felt just the same. Large and warm and familiar. A little clumsy, but very kind.

He'd always been shy about his feelings. Yet now it was he who murmured, 'I thought I'd never see you again,' as the others bustled about, bringing hot water and blankets. And for once, it was Lil who didn't have the words to reply. Instead, she squeezed his hand tightly in return.

'I do think you ought to go to bed,' said Tilly, coming over with some bandages.

Joe shook his head. 'No – no,' he insisted. 'It's been too long – I need to catch up. I don't want to miss any more.'

Mei made the coffee, while Tilly assessed Joe's injuries with her most professional air. 'There doesn't seem to be anything broken. I'd say you were jolly lucky,' she announced.

'Oh, it wasn't luck. They weren't aiming to do real damage,' said Joe wearily. 'Only to frighten me a bit.'

Sophie grimaced, and Lil knew she was thinking of the shadowy men on the bridge, swooping away into the dark like a flock of black birds. They had been more than a *bit* frightening.

'I wonder if this cut ought to have a stitch in it? I think I could probably manage that,' Tilly went on.

'Shouldn't we get a doctor?' said Sophie hurriedly.

Joe smiled at her and shook his head. 'No thanks, Soph. Definitely no doctors. They might ask questions and Molloy was pretty clear about *not talking*.' He nodded to

Tilly. 'Do what you have to do. Anything would be better than that doctor fellow last time.'

'Last time?' asked Billy eagerly. He was hovering close by, looking worried and excited and clearly in a great hurry to know everything.

'When I was shot by Forsyth,' said Joe. 'A bullet and a broken shoulder wasn't so nice. This is *nothing* compared to that.'

'Forsyth! That rotter!' exclaimed Lil angrily. 'I'm jolly well *glad* I shot him back!'

'You shot him back?' repeated Joe in surprise. Then he laughed – and winced with the pain of the sudden movement. He squeezed Lil's hand. 'Of *course* you did,' he said.

Sophie sat down in a chair on Joe's other side, wrapping her hands around her cup of coffee. 'Can you tell us what happened?' she asked. Like the others, her expression was still a little dazed, as if she could not quite believe this was really happening.

'It all started when I went to watch that woman from Norton Newspapers,' Joe began, frowning as he thought back to that drizzly autumn day on Fleet Street. 'The one I'd seen collecting the secret papers.'

'Florence Andrews,' said Mei, with a quick glance at Sophie.

'Is that her name? Well, I followed her from the offices right out to the East End, but the whole thing was a trap.

253

Forsyth was waiting for me. I knew then that *he* was the double agent. When I saw the gun, I thought I was a goner.' He paused for a moment, remembering. 'Anyway, he shot me. After that, things got blurry. They patched me up and brought me over here, but I don't remember much. Next thing I know, I'm in Coney Island, being set to work at this bar –'

'Ruby's,' supplied Billy.

Joe's eyes widened. 'How did you know that?'

'We went there yesterday – Billy and me. We were trying to track you down,' said Lil.

Joe grinned at them. 'Of *course* you were,' he said again.

'We heard them talking about an English fellow called Joey – and that's when we felt sure you had been there – and that you really were still alive.'

'We thought you were dead for months,' Billy explained. 'They found your cap in an alleyway in the East End – with blood all over it. If we'd known . . . if we'd had any idea where you were . . .' He shook his head, blowing out a long breath, lost for words.

Joe nodded. 'I know. You hadn't got a clue what had happened. It was the same for me. I didn't know if *you* knew Forsyth was the double agent, or what was happening to any of you. The last thing I heard Sophie was missing in St Petersburg and Lil had gone looking for her! I was thinking about you all the time, and wondering.' He looked around at them all. Lucky had wriggled up on to the sofa beside him, and he gave her ears a little stroke before he went on: 'Anyway, Ruby was good to me. Kept me busy, working in the kitchen or behind the bar. And Leon, the piano player – he was my friend. It wasn't so bad there; only of course, I couldn't leave. You see, Coney Island is run by this gangster, by the name of –'

'*Molloy*,' said Billy.

Joe nodded. 'Right again. Everyone does what he says – even Ruby. He used to be just a small-time crook, but then he got all this money from somewhere. Now he's running all kinds of shifty business: protection rackets, illegal gambling, opium lairs and the rest. It's making the Coney Island folk miserable, but they can't do anything about it. He's got these thugs who work for him, and – well, you can see the sort of thing *they* do.' He gestured ruefully to his face. 'No one wants to get on Molloy's bad side. *He* was the one who brought me to Ruby's and told her to keep me there. I didn't know what he could possibly want with me.'

Sophie was nibbling her bagel. Now she quickly explained that Molloy was working for the Black Dragon, head of the New York branch of the *Fraternitas*. 'She calls herself Mrs Davenport now, though you'll remember her as Lady Tremayne.'

'Lady Tremayne? What – the Baron's *sister*?' exclaimed Joe. He let out a low whistle. 'So *she's* Molloy's rich backer.'

'She used you as leverage, to get us to give up the Draco

Almanac,' said Sophie.

Joe looked at her solemnly. 'I can't believe that you handed it over to them. Did it really have the instructions for making this weapon – the *feu du* whatsit?'

'*Feu du ciel*,' said Tilly. 'It means sky fire. It did, but I made some adjustments. They won't be able to use the instructions now.'

'Good,' said Joe, settling back against his cushions with a sigh of relief. 'I didn't like the look of that laboratory place they have. Who knows *what* they might be cooking up there.'

'A laboratory?' repeated Tilly.

'That's where Henry Snow was working,' said Joe. Seeing the others staring in surprise, he added. 'Didn't you see him on the bridge? I s'pose you might not have recognised him in the dark. It took me a while to remember where I knew him from, but it came to me while Molloy's men were kicking me in the ribs.' He winced again at the memory.

'Henry Snow! Gosh!' exclaimed Lil.

'But who *is* Henry Snow?' asked Tilly. She'd never encountered the name before.

'A scientist. He used to work for the Baron, finding new ways to make weapons,' explained Joe. 'Now he's *here* in New York, doing the same thing. He's working out of an old pickle factory in Brooklyn. That's where they took me so Snow could question me. He's been experimenting with making a version of the sky fire. He wanted to find out if I knew anything about the Almanac.'

'*The Brooklyn Pickle Works!*' exclaimed Sophie. 'That was one of the names on the papers from Mrs Davenport's desk. I've started looking into the addresses I saw there,' she went on. 'Most of the properties have been bought within the last year by holding companies with very ordinary-sounding names. The Brooklyn Pickle Works is owned by a company called *Coney Island Holdings Ltd* – the same one that owns Dreamland. Several of these properties were sold very cheaply, because they'd recently *burned down* in peculiar circumstances.'

'Exactly like Dreamland!' exclaimed Billy.

'Yes. And look at this,' said Sophie. She took out the copy of the *New York Evening Telegram* that Mei had shown her at the Waldorf-Astoria, but this time she leafed past the article about Dreamland, to a smaller story on one of the back pages. '"*Investigations continue into the fire at a garment factory on Essex Street last month, which injured twelve workers. The Fire Marshal has concluded that the blaze originated on the roof of the factory,*"' she read aloud. '"*While initially believed to be an accident, evidence gathered at the scene now indicates that the fire was the result of an arson attack.*"'

'An arson attack . . . originating on the roof . . .!' murmured Mei. 'Do you suppose it's the sky fire?'

'Snow did talk about testing it out,' said Joe.

'And guess what I found in Mrs Davenport's desk?' said

Sophie. 'Papers pertaining to a factory on Essex Street – signed only last week!'

'Gosh!' exclaimed Lil. 'So you think she's targeting these properties, burning them down – and then buying them up cheaply?'

'That's it,' said Sophie. 'She uses these companies as a front, to make it all seem above board. But really, she's building her own empire here in New York, just like the Baron once did in the East End of London.'

'And Henry Snow is working for her, making weapons!' said Billy. 'She was helping the Baron before, wasn't she – with that factory in Silvertown, where he was manufacturing explosives. Perhaps she's picked up where he left off?'

Joe nodded slowly. 'That sounds about right. Snow kept going on about all the work he'd done, but how he still hadn't perfected the sky fire – it wasn't powerful enough. The legendary weapon of the dragons of old, or something rum like that. And something about a presentation? The fellow seems half-mad, if you ask me.'

'A *presentation*?' Sophie repeated. 'That's what Snow said?'

Joe nodded, and Sophie pushed her notebook into the middle of the table. 'Look. This is what I jotted down from the Black Dragon's diary,' she explained, pointing at the entry for Saturday.

Tuesday 19th April
11·30 – M –
Central Park
12 – Noon – Pell st

Wednesday 20th April
11am – Dress fitting
1pm – Luncheon Party
(GOLD)

Thursday 21st April
3pm – Hairdresser
6pm – Private view,
Stieglitz Gallery

Friday 22nd April
8 pm – Dinner
Delmonico's

Saturday 23rd
April.
4pm Presentation
– Ocean View Suite,
Orient Hotel

'*Presentation*,' read Lil aloud. 'I say! Do you suppose that's the same presentation Snow was talking about?'

'A presentation of the weapon,' mused Tilly. 'So he's going to show the Black Dragon what he's been working on?'

'Maybe not just her. Perhaps the Gold Dragon as well, while he's here in New York. That might explain why Snow was in such a hurry to have it ready,' suggested Sophie. She was already imagining Henry Snow proudly presenting his terrible creation to Moorhouse and Mrs Davenport, while

259

Florence Andrews sat to the side, making efficient notes.

But Lil's thoughts had moved in a different direction. 'Where's Manhattan Beach? I'm sure I've heard that name before.'

'Here,' said Billy, brandishing the map. 'Very close to Coney Island – just a mile or so along the shore.'

'Coney Island again – and *Saturday!*' said Mei. 'It's the opening day of Dreamland. And it was on that postcard I found, the one that mentioned Charlton.'

They stared at the jumble of evidence on the table, trying to make sense of it. Then Tilly put down her cup, sat back, and summarised what they knew. 'So the Black Dragon is following in the Baron's footsteps, here in New York. She's working with Molloy in Coney Island, and a gang leader in Chinatown and probably others too. She's got a scientist – Henry Snow – developing new weapons and testing them by setting buildings on fire whenever they feel like it.'

'And now the Gold Dragon has come to New York to see what she's been doing,' Sophie continued. 'No doubt they plan to sell the new weapons to make a profit, if there should be a war. They are certainly doing all they can to start one. I'm sure that's what was going on aboard the *Thalassa*. Forsyth posed as "Fritzel" so people would believe the bomb was planted by a German spy – a strike against Van Bergen's ship, and his international alliance.'

'So what do we do now?' asked Mei.

"Yes, what's the plan?" Tilly wanted to know.

'I don't know,' Sophie admitted. 'It's all very well to have worked it out, but the problem is we've got no evidence. Not even the smallest shred of proof.'

'What about this?' said Mei, pointing to Sophie's notes. 'The addresses – the buildings that burned down.'

'None of them have been bought in Mrs Davenport's name. And even if we could prove that she's behind the holding companies, there's nothing *wrong* in that. Buying up cheap property doesn't make her a criminal.'

Billy sighed. 'And the letter from the Black Dragon doesn't help either. We can't prove it came from Mrs Davenport.'

'She wasn't on the bridge – and I never saw her with Molloy, or in Coney Island, or even with Snow, come to that,' Joe pointed out.

'But we saw her talking to Molloy!' said Mei. 'And I saw her visiting Sai Wing Mock.'

'It still doesn't prove anything,' said Lil. 'She could have been . . . asking Molloy for directions. Or going to Mr Kee's shop to buy something. All we really have is Joe's story about being kidnapped and taken to Coney Island by Molloy.'

'Which sounds pretty outlandish,' said Joe. 'Anyway, there wouldn't be any use walking into a New York police station to accuse Molloy of a crime. Half of the police force are taking his bribes to look the other way. We'd only land ourselves in hot water. Molloy made it pretty clear what he expected us to do. Go back to London – *pronto*.'

'But we can't just leave!' exclaimed Mei.

Lil and Sophie exchanged thoughtful glances. 'Can't we?' Lil asked after a moment. 'We've done what we came to do.'

'We've found out what the *Fraternitas* are doing in New York. We know what they're working on, and who's involved. And I'm pretty sure I know who the Gold Dragon is – Albert Moorhouse,' said Sophie.

'And we've got Joe back,' added Lil softly.

'There's an Atlantic Line steamer leaving for Southampton tomorrow,' Sophie went on. 'We could book passage for us all today and be back in London this time next week.'

'Third Class this time, I think,' said Lil. 'More than good enough for the likes of us. And it will be jolly to travel all together.'

'Better company than the voyage last time, that's for sure,' said Joe, with a rueful smile.

'So we'll go back to London and report to the Chief?' said Billy.

Sophie nodded. 'And then start a new investigation focusing on Moorhouse. It'll be much easier to do that back in London.'

Mei and Tilly looked at each other, as if they couldn't quite believe their ears.

'But – you can't mean it?' protested Mei. 'We might never have another chance like this!'

'We know where both the Gold Dragon and the Black Dragon are going to be on Saturday afternoon,' said Tilly, jabbing a finger at Sophie's notes. 'Surely we have to stay until then – and at least *try* and see what they're up to?'

'Maybe we could even get the evidence for the Chief!' said Mei.

But Joe looked worried. 'Molloy said we weren't to go anywhere near Coney Island. Not Ruby's, not Dreamland, not anywhere in Brooklyn. Not just me – all of us. He said that if he found us back there, he wouldn't be handing out any second chances. Let's just say, I don't think it would only be a matter of his thugs *frightening* us next time.'

'But they wouldn't know me, or Mei,' Tilly pointed out. 'Why shouldn't we go and try and get some proof of what they're doing?'

'But what kind of proof?' asked Sophie. 'It's the same problem we always come back to. What caught out the Baron in the end was paperwork – accounts. Mrs Davenport is too clever for that. She's made sure the trail doesn't lead back to her.'

'And getting into that lab would be impossible,' said Joe. 'You should have seen the place. Great big gates, high walls, guards on duty.'

'They aren't going to be at the lab, though,' Mei pointed out. 'They're going to be at the Orient Hotel. Perhaps we could creep in and hide, to eavesdrop on this *presentation*?'

'But we still wouldn't have any real evidence,' said Sophie. 'If only there was some way to capture a conversation – not just write it down, but record the actual words, the way a photograph records a picture! Then we could *prove* what they'd said. But there isn't.' She shook her head. 'What's more, it would be very dangerous – and don't forget, we're alone here. No Bureau, no Scotland Yard. No help from the New York police. There's no one to back us up, if we need it.'

'Actually,' Billy spoke up suddenly, 'I was thinking about that and it's not strictly true, is it? I mean –'

Mei interrupted. 'So you really think we should just *give up* and *go home*? Just let the *Fraternitas* carry on?'

Her voice was disbelieving and her expression disappointed. Sophie looked at her sympathetically. Once, she'd have been just the same way – so determined and focused on *doing the right thing*. But now, sitting here beside Lil and Joe, she wondered if perhaps *doing the right thing* really meant keeping the people she loved most safe and happy.

Sophie reached up and touched her mother's necklace at her throat. All at once, she felt a longing to be back at Taylor & Rose, working on quite an ordinary sort of case. Recovering a lady's missing jewels, or reuniting long-lost relations, or trailing someone who the Chief suspected might be one of Ziegler's spies. She wanted to call in at the

Bureau for their instructions, and find Carruthers there, with his feet kicked up behind the desk, pretending he wasn't glad to see them. She wanted to walk along Piccadilly, looking at all the shop windows; to have tea and buns at Lyons' Corner House with Lil; or perhaps to go with Jack to the Café Royal wearing a new frock – though of course, he'd likely be inviting his new friend Ella to do such things with him now. The thought of that made her feel rather sad.

'But we're the *Loyal Order of Lions!*' Mei continued. 'We swore an oath to do everything we could to stop the *Fraternitas!*'

'We can't just leave,' Tilly said again. She turned to Sophie. 'What if there *was* a way to capture a conversation . . .' she began.

But just then there was a tap on the door, and Flora wandered in. 'Good morning,' she said, not in the least bit troubled by the tense atmosphere, nor the unfamiliar bandaged young man lying on the sofa. 'A note came for you. Oh – are those bagels?'

Billy handed her one wordlessly, while the others all stared at the envelope she'd passed to Mei. They were looking for the black dragon symbol – but it was not there. Instead, there was a monogram which Lil recognised immediately. The envelope was handwritten, addressed to *Miss Carter and Miss Zhang*.

Dear Mei and Lil,

I wanted to let you know we're headed to the Orient Hotel at the Manhattan Beach resort for the last week of our holiday. Mr Van Bergen will be taking us out on his yacht and on Saturday afternoon he has also arranged a tour of the Atlantic Line shipyard for us.

Perhaps you might come and see us at the Orient? It would be jolly to see you again before we leave.

With love from
Anna

'So the Van Bergens are staying at the Orient too – and they'll be there on Saturday!' exclaimed Lil.

'That seems like an awfully big coincidence,' said Mei.

She put the letter on the table, where they could all see it. As Sophie looked at it lying amongst the other papers – her notes, the newspaper articles, the map of New York, the postcard and the Dreamland match-book – something extraordinary happened.

It was as if everything had come together, like the shining coloured-pieces in a kaleidoscope, settling into place to form a perfect, glittering pattern. Princess Anna's letter, Dreamland, Charlton, Henry Snow, the Atlantic Line – everything they'd learned in New York and aboard the *Thalassa*. Everything she knew about the *Fraternitas*. At last she understood what the 'big plan' was that the Chief had talked about and now she felt as ice-cold as if she had been plunged into the freezing waters of the Atlantic.

She'd been quite wrong, she saw that now. People were in danger. They had to act: they had no choice.

'You're right,' she said, turning to Mei, and then to Tilly. 'You're absolutely right. I don't know what I was thinking. The presentation isn't simply about *showing* the Gold Dragon the weapon. It's about *demonstrating* it. Testing it. And we have to stop it.' She looked down at the now-empty bag of bagels on the table and then turned abruptly to Lil. 'Do you have any more of those doughnuts?' she asked urgently.

'Doughnuts?' repeated Lil, confused.

'Yes. Doughnuts!' exclaimed Sophie. 'Because we need to make a plan – and quickly. And it's going to have to be the best plan we've ever made.'

CHAPTER TWENTY-EIGHT

Coney Island
Brooklyn, New York City

'Ladies and gentlemen, welcome to Coney Island – America's playground! Roll up, roll up for Dreamland – truly the land of dreams. Grand opening today! Free admission for all!'

Voices boomed across the pier as people spilled from a ferry boat, dressed in their finest spring clothes. Delighted screams and shrieks of laughter mingled with the clatter of the rollercoasters. A fresh breeze blew from the ocean, sending flags and streamers waving, fluttering ribbons and skirts, sweeping a young man's straw hat from his head. People sailed by on bicycles as a band played, and children ran through the crowds with striped lollipops or puffs of cotton candy.

Above everything towered Dreamland – a fantasy of storybook temples, pagodas and castles, glittering with tinsel and gilt. People had been surging through the gates since early that morning, eager to take in the new and improved attractions – to admire the *Gondolas of Venice*, ride the *Shoot-the-Chute* waterslides, and venture into the sinister dark grotto, where the figure of an immense demon loomed over a sign reading, in bold red letters, *Hell-Gate*. Camera bulbs flashed as film actress Vera Lennox posed with a cone of popcorn. Dashing young aviator Mr Charlton found himself mobbed by a crowd of admiring fans, all keen to get his autograph or shake his hand.

Amongst the noise and excitement, nobody noticed the hard-faced man stalking through the crowds, or the fellows in bowler hats following him like a couple of black crows.

Nobody except the young lady watching them from beside the ice-cream cart. Dressed in a pretty blue frock and a straw hat with a ribbon bow, she looked like any other visitor as she strolled after them, strawberry ice in hand. As she walked on, past the coconut shies and the helter-skelter, she appeared to be simply enjoying herself, though really she was watching their every move.

After a while, she turned away, apparently satisfied – and instead moved towards the familiar figure of Miss Roberta Russell, who was standing beside a striped tent, making notes. Not far away from her, Charlie Walters was snapping pictures.

'Good afternoon,' said Sophie, with a smile.

Miss Russell started. 'Why, Miss Taylor! I did think I might run into you somewhere in New York, but I didn't think it would be here!' She took in Sophie's pretty frock and pink ice-cream in surprise. 'Are you . . . working?' she asked doubtfully.

'Even detectives need a day off every now and then. You ought to try it yourself sometime. But I suppose you're here writing about the opening of Dreamland?'

'Yes, for *The Daily Picture*. I must say, I was surprised. I didn't think an amusement park was quite to Moorhouse's tastes. Still, Charlie says it will photograph beautifully, and Norton is keen because Charlton is doing the aerial display this afternoon.'

'What about the *New York Evening Telegram*?' Sophie asked, casually. 'Is Norton going ahead with the acquisition?'

'Yes, and I'm jolly pleased about it. It should mean I get to spend more time here, and I rather like New York.' Miss Russell looked around, waving her pencil as if to encompass the lively activity around them. She caught the attention of Charlie Walters, who turned and adjusted his camera to snap a picture of the two of them standing together.

'Someone really ought to explain to Mr Walters that it's polite to *ask permission* before you go taking photographs of people,' Sophie observed. She paused and then added: 'Anyway, I thought you two would probably be at the Orient.'

'The Orient? That big hotel down the shore, at Manhattan Beach?' Miss Russell asked at once. 'Why?'

Sophie raised her eyebrows. 'Oh, didn't you hear the

rumour? By all accounts, there's a European princess staying there. Someone rather important. They've been trying to keep her visit hush-hush, but word got out, and now I daresay everyone will want pictures of a princess on holiday by the ocean. Just the sort of thing Mr Moorhouse would be interested in.'

Miss Russell's eyes lit up. 'A *princess*? Which princess?'

Sophie shrugged. 'I'm afraid I don't know,' she said, returning to her ice cream.

Mis Russell frowned. 'Why are you tipping me off about this?'

Sophie shrugged again. 'I thought about what you said on board the ship. *We working women should stick together.* You helped me, so I'm helping you. You'd better be quick though. Now word's got out, I don't suppose she'll be there much longer.'

And with that, she disappeared into the crowd, while Miss Russell cried out: 'Charlie! Pack up your camera! We've got to get over to the Orient Hotel – and fast!'

Not very far away, beside the tinkling carousel, two young people were strolling arm-in-arm. The young man – tall, handsome but walking a little stiffly – had a straw hat tilted over his eyes, partly concealing his face. The young lady wore a white frock with a cherry-coloured sash and a wide brimmed hat. She looked perfectly carefree, but her voice, when she spoke, was anxious.

'I wish you'd stayed behind,' Lil whispered. 'What if Molloy sees you?'

'You know I couldn't let the rest of you do this without me,' said Joe. 'I know how things work around here. And this is important. If the Black Dragon carries out what she's planning . . .' He shook his head, thinking back to what Sophie had told them, in the apartment in Greenwich Village.

'I couldn't see it at first, but now it's all quite clear,' she had said. 'Dreamland opens on Saturday, with an aerial display from Mr Charlton. We know from the postcard that Forsyth is planning something for Saturday which involves Charlton. At the same time, Snow is going to demonstrate the sky fire he's been working on, at nearby Manhattan Beach. Meanwhile Mr Van Bergen, a *Fraternitas* target, will be close at hand, visiting the Atlantic Line shipyard. Do you see?'

She'd stared around at them, but no one else, not even Lil, had been able to keep up with her. 'The Black Dragon is going to use Charlton's aerial display at Dreamland as cover, to drop sky fire from the plane on to the shipyard,' she'd explained. '*That's the presentation she's planning.* She'll take out Van Bergen, destroy the shipyard, and demonstrate the power of the weapon to Gold, all at the same time.'

'Destroy the shipyard?' Mei had murmured, horrorstruck. 'But would Snow's sky fire be powerful enough for that? Without the instructions from the Almanac?'

'Obviously it's already powerful enough to burn down a factory,' Tilly had said. 'With multiple firebombs, dropped directly on the target from the air, who knows what the damage could be. A shipyard is full of highly flammable and combustible materials. There could be explosions, and depending on weather conditions, the fire could easily spread out of control.'

'But all the workers!' Billy had exclaimed. 'And the people who live nearby, in Van Bergen's new houses – and the hospital, and schools!'

'Princess Anna will be there, with Mr Van Bergen and Evangeline,' Mei had realised, her face growing paler.

But Lil had already been looking at Sophie. 'We have to stop this,' she'd said. 'But how? What do we do?'

Joe had forgotten what it was like, being with the others puzzling out something like this. He'd marvelled at the way they'd pieced it all together. He'd found himself watching them as if he was seeing them for the first time. Billy asking questions. Lil tossing in ideas. Mei making connections, while Tilly figured out the details. Sophie, leading the way, always a few steps ahead of everyone else. Finally, they had put together a plan that just might work.

Joe knew it was a long shot. There had been so little time to prepare. It was by some measure the most difficult and complicated scheme they'd ever come up with, and there could be no second chances. There was so much risk, and there was a great deal that could go wrong. Now, in spite of his efforts to reassure Lil, he felt twitchy and nervous. His eyes kept darting through the crowds, expecting to see Molloy and his bowler hats striding towards them.

Lil gave him a little smile. Having her by his side like this still seemed like something from a dream. Now he was back here at Coney Island, he felt as if she might vanish at any moment, and the thought of that was worse than anything.

'Is that it?' she said, pointing towards the large building ahead.

'I reckon so,' said Joe. 'If he's anywhere about, that's where he'll be.'

Together they passed under an illuminated sign reading *Grand Palais de Danse*. Inside, couples swirled around the floor, while an orchestra played a waltz. Joe looked at them for a moment, wondering what it would be like if he and Lil were simply here to enjoy themselves – to go dancing, to eat ices, to walk by the ocean. But then he saw who they were looking for. 'Over there,' he murmured.

Lil looked across to the table where a young man was sitting close to the orchestra. He showed little interest in the dancers, but his attention was fixed on the musicians, his toe tapping in time to the melody. As they made their way over to him, he looked up, startled – but when he realised who it was, his face was transformed with delight.

'Joey!' exclaimed Leon. 'You're here! We thought . . .

well, you don't want to know *what* we thought when you didn't come back. Are you all right?'

'No thanks to Molloy, but yes, I'm all right,' said Joe. 'Come outside. We need to talk to you.'

'Ruby's mad as hops about what happened,' Leon said as they stepped back out into the sunshine. 'She's got the others riled up too. Tony, and Miss Patty, and even old Grandpops. They're all saying they've had enough of Molloy throwing his weight around. Not that there's much they can *do* about it, with those thugs of his backing him up, not to mention all the cash he's splashing about. But what happened to you? And how come you're all dressed up like a swell?'

Joe did not even try to answer his questions. 'Leon, this is someone I want you to meet. My, er – my friend, Lil.'

'Your *friend*?' asked Leon, a grin spreading over his face. 'Well! It's nice to meet you, Miss Lil.'

'Actually we've met before,' said Lil serenely. 'I nearly spilled lemonade on you at Ruby's the other day, when you were playing the piano. You're a jolly good musician.'

'And Lil ought to know. She's been on the stage herself,' said Joe, proudly.

'What, are you one of the new girls from Miss Patty's show, then?' asked Leon.

'No, more like the West End, actually,' said Lil. 'In London, you know. But never mind that now,' she went on, as Leon stared at her in astonishment. 'Joe tells me that you'd like a new piano. Well – I think we can help with that, if you can do something for *us*.'

'A new piano?' Leon laughed aloud at the very idea. 'What sort of something?'

Lil tucked her free arm through Leon's. 'Come with us and we'll tell you,' she told him. 'But we'll have to hurry. We don't have much time.'

'You are ready, Mr Charlton?'

The pilot gave the nose of his plane an affectionate pat. 'Yes, all shipshape! You know, we must have done twenty exhibition flights since winning the Grand Aerial Tour – and yet the old girl's still as reliable as ever.' He looked across the field, towards the turrets and spires of Dreamland. 'Tell you what, though, I've never flown her anywhere quite like this before. Jolly long way from Piccadilly Circus, what?' He gave a little chuckle. 'Though I don't s'pose that means much to you, eh?'

The man beside him shook his head politely. '*Nein*. Piccadilly Circus – this is in London, *ja*? Never haf I been there.'

His German accent really was unusual, Charlton thought. He'd got to know plenty of native German speakers during the Grand Aerial Tour, but he'd never encountered one who spoke quite like this. 'Where did you say you were from again, Fritzel?' he asked. 'Berlin, was it? What brings you here?'

276

'I come here for my work,' said Fritzel.

'You know about planes, I hear? Think you can handle co-piloting? I need someone to navigate for me – and to chuck out the leaflets to the crowds.' Charlton tugged on his moustache, feeling a little anxious. This Fritzel fellow seemed a decent enough chap, but there was something about him that was *off*. When you were up in an aeroplane, you needed a co-pilot you could count on.

'*Ja, ja,*' said Fritzel, nodding enthusiastically and gesturing to the bag at his side. 'I am ready. I know the route, and I haf the leaflets here.'

At that moment, a young fellow came running across the field towards them. 'Excuse me, Herr Fritzel, sir,' he stammered nervously. 'Mr Molloy sent me to fetch you.'

'Why?' snapped Fritzel, his voice no longer good-natured. 'It's time for take-off.'

'He says there's *trouble*. Urgent. Something to do with a couple of girls. I think he said their names were *Taylor and Rose?*'

Fritzel's face turned grim beneath his flying cap. '*Again.* Good heavens, will those accursed females never leave me alone?' he muttered, in a distinctly different voice. Then as if remembering himself: 'I come at once, *ja*. You will wait for me here, please, Mr Charlton.'

'Trouble with the ladies, eh?' said Charlton. 'No worries, old chap. You go. *Cherchez la femme*, or however the saying goes.'

Fritzel went hurrying off across the field after the young man. Left alone, Charlton turned back to his plane, giving her another little pat, making a few final adjustments, and polishing her to make sure she was sparkling clean.

'Good afternoon, Mr Charlton,' said a voice at his side.

Charlton looked down to see a young lady in a trim flying costume standing beside the plane.

'Good heavens – Miss Alice Grayson!' he exclaimed in astonishment. 'This is the last place I'd expect to – why, the last time we met it must have been –'

'In Zurich, when we celebrated your win of the Aerial Tour! Surely you haven't forgotten that night at the Grand Café Odeon?' Sophie said with a smile. Alice Grayson was the alias she'd used as Captain Nakamura's co-pilot.

'Most certainly not, Miss Grayson!' Charlton laughed. 'What a party that was. But what brings you to New York? Are you here with Nakamura?'

Sophie shook her head. 'No, he went back to Japan last year. It's just a coincidence I'm here, but Herr Fritzel asked me to step in, to co-pilot in his place. His business is going to take longer than he anticipated, you see.'

'Indeed? Well – I must say, I'm terrifically glad you can help, Miss Grayson,' said Charlton. 'I know I can count on *you* as a co-pilot.'

'As it happens, it's been a while since I've flown, but I'm sure it will soon come back to me,' said Sophie. She looked up at the sky. 'Flying conditions don't-look too bad, though these winds may give us a little trouble. Lucky we don't have far to go. Fritzel has given me the details of the route. Shall we be off?'

She swung herself lightly into the co-pilot's seat at the rear of the plane. Just then, the young man came running back again, carrying a bag. 'For you, ma'am,' he said.

'Oh – thank you,' she replied as she pulled her flying cap over her hair. 'We don't want to forget the leaflets, do we, Mr Charlton?'

'Absolutely not!' Charlton clambered into the front seat, settled himself and then waved a cheery hand to the men waiting on the field to help start the plane. All his uncertainty had gone as he turned and grinned at his co-pilot. 'Ready to go, Miss Grayson? Then up, up and away!'

Forsyth did not hear the roar of the aeroplane engine above the music and noise of Dreamland as he stormed out of the entrance towards Ruby's. He knew where the bar was, though he'd never been inside. These spit-and-sawdust saloons were not at all his kind of scene. He considered himself more of a martinis at the Waldorf-Astoria kind of a fellow.

'I thought Molloy said he'd dealt with them!' he muttered to himself as he crossed the street, all traces of Herr Fritzel's German accent gone. 'It's time I put a stop to this. After all I've done to win over Black – *and* impress Gold – I simply can't have a couple of *girls* mucking things up for me any longer.'

He banged open the door, making the bell jangle violently. Inside, the bar was almost empty. He saw that an odd-looking woman was alone behind the bar, talking in a low voice to a lone customer – an old fellow with white hair.

'Where's Molloy?' he rapped out shortly.

The woman smiled, flashing a gold tooth. 'In the basement with Eddie,' she said, jerking a thumb towards a narrow staircase behind the bar.

Forsyth pushed rudely past her and hurried down the stairs. He was meant to be in the air by now – he didn't have time to waste. Through a heavy door, he found a storeroom full of bottles and barrels, and a rough kind of office, but both of them were empty. No sign of Molloy, nor Miss Taylor and Miss Rose, nor even of this *Eddie* fellow, whoever he might be.

'Where is everyone?' he demanded.

Almost before the words were out of his mouth, the heavy door banged suddenly shut behind him.

Forsyth spun around. 'What's this? What the devil is going on?' He pushed at the door, but it wouldn't budge. 'Hey – let me out!' he yelled.

'Good afternoon, Captain Forsyth,' came a horribly familiar voice from the other side of the door. 'Though really I s'pose I should probably just call you *Forsyth* now. What do they call it when people are kicked out of the British Army – is it a *dishonourable discharge?*'

'What d'you think you're doing?' shouted Forsyth. He looked around wildly but there was no way out, not even a window. He thumped on the door again.

'Or perhaps I should call you *Herr Fritzel?*' Lil went on, sounding very sprightly. 'Though I must say, I think your German accent needs work. Maybe I could give you a few pointers?'

'You won't get away with this!' roared Forsyth, more furious by the minute. 'Don't you know this is Molloy's place?'

There was a pause and then he heard a male voice say thoughtfully: 'Funny you should say that. I'm not so sure it *is* Molloy's place any longer. Not like it was, anyway. Come on, Lil – don't waste your breath. Just leave him be.'

'All right,' agreed Lil, readily. 'Jolly appropriate to leave him, since it wasn't so long ago he tried to shut Sophie up in an underground tomb. This is *much* more comfortable, which is probably a good thing since who knows how long it might be before anyone comes to let him out? Oh, and Forsyth, *do* be careful of those bombs you've got with you. From what I hear they can be awfully dangerous, and you *really* wouldn't want to be trapped down here with them if they were to go off, would you?'

Forsyth looked in horror at the bag of firebombs at his side, and then began pummelling the door with his fists. 'Molloy! *Molloy!*' he yelled desperately.

'You can shout as much as you like. No one's going to

hear you,' said Lil. 'A few of the regulars are upstairs, having a sing-song.'

Forsyth sank down on the floor of the cellar, his head in his hands, as at the piano upstairs, Leon began to play the opening notes of 'The Fairest of Them All'.

Outside Ruby's, the tune floated out on to the sidewalk, while high above, Mr Charlton's plane swooped across the blue sky. People had stopped in their tracks to watch, forgetting their ice creams as they stared at the plane rising high in the air and then pirouetting down in a series of daring spiral dives and steep turns above the ocean.

From where he stood, surveying the crowds, Molloy watched too. He watched – and he waited. But after a few minutes had passed he began to frown. Why weren't they taking the route he'd given Forsyth?

The spectators gasped and clapped in dazzled admiration as the plane circled back over the beach and bathing huts, skimming over the rooftops of the grand hotels at Manhattan Beach, swooping over the tenements and factories of Brooklyn, and then coming towards Coney Island once more.

'What's he doing?' muttered Molloy, as all around him, people shaded their eyes with their hands to get a better look, or waved their handkerchiefs into the sky.

'Isn't Mr Charlton *marvellous?*' exclaimed someone in the crowd.

'What a fellow! Just look at him go!' gasped someone else.

The plane sailed directly over their heads, and the co-pilot leaned out, scattering a handful of something bright and glittering into the crowd. Horrified, Molloy flung himself backwards – but it was only coloured confetti, fluttering over his head like snowflakes. There were candies wrapped in shiny paper too, and a handful of printed leaflets. The watching people grabbed for them in delighted excitement.

One of the leaflets landed at Molloy's feet. He picked it up and saw it was a printed magazine. Underneath the title LUNA was a heading; *POETRY. POLITICS. LITERATURE AND ART BY THE WOMEN OF NEW YORK.*

Molloy's hard face creased into a scowl. 'What's Forsyth playing at?' he murmured.

One of the bowler hats looked puzzled. 'Forsyth? You mean the English guy? He's over at Ruby's.'

'*Ruby's?*' Molloy looked startled. 'He's supposed to be up *there* in the darn *aeroplane*. Not drinking at the bar!'

'He can't be in the aeroplane, boss. Saw him go over there only five minutes ago.'

'Dammit!' exclaimed Molloy. For a minute it seemed he would stride off in the direction of the bar, but then he paused and frowned harder. While all around him clapped and waved, he stared up at the plane, sweeping back down

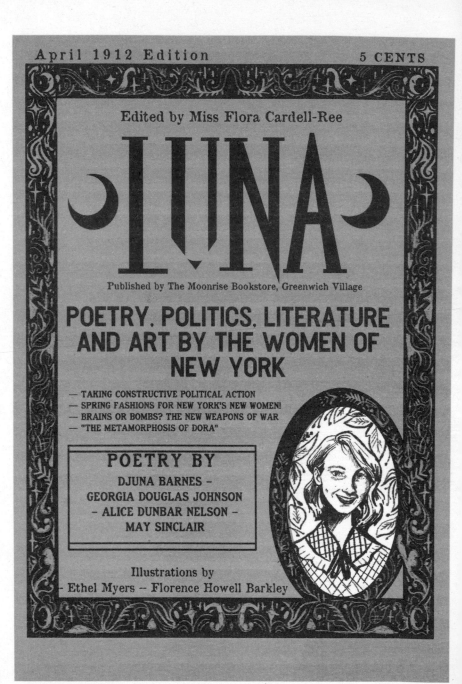

Edited by Miss Flora Cardell-Ree

LUNA

Published by The Moonrise Bookstore, Greenwich Village

POETRY, POLITICS, LITERATURE AND ART BY THE WOMEN OF NEW YORK

— TAKING CONSTRUCTIVE POLITICAL ACTION
— SPRING FASHIONS FOR NEW YORK'S NEW WOMEN!
— BRAINS OR BOMBS? THE NEW WEAPONS OF WAR
— "THE METAMORPHOSIS OF DORA"

POETRY BY

**DJUNA BARNES –
GEORGIA DOUGLAS JOHNSON
– ALICE DUNBAR NELSON –
MAY SINCLAIR**

Illustrations by
- Ethel Myers -- Florence Howell Barkley

towards land. He saw the tall figure of Charlton in the front, and then the slighter figure of the co-pilot behind, waving a hand to the crowd and tossing another handful of leaflets high into the air.

'If that's not Forsyth, then who is it?' he murmured.

He began pushing his way through the crowds, the two bowler hats following close at his heels, looking more than ever like a pair of flapping black crows.

CHAPTER TWENTY-NINE

The Orient Hotel
Manhattan Beach
Brooklyn, New York City

Not much more than a mile away from Dreamland, the Orient Hotel stood tranquil and serene among prize-winning rose gardens and sweeping green lawns. Luncheon was being served on the verandah, with a view over the sparkling ocean, where seagulls soared, and little boats danced on the white-tipped waves.

It was a world away from the busy avenues and stately buildings of the city, Anna thought, as she sipped her iced tea. Yet there was no doubt that the Orient Hotel was still very grand indeed – four storeys tall, with hundreds of rooms, and every modern convenience. Eva would have a shock if she ever came to visit Elffburg, Anna thought, recalling the old-fashioned crooked buildings, the narrow streets, the steep-sided mountains. Arnovia had never seemed further away.

'A decent sort of place, isn't it?' said Teddy Van Bergen, gazing around at the Orient appreciatively. 'Comfortable, I think – and a pleasant change.'

'A *change* is certainly the case,' said Mrs Alma Van Bergen, examining her crystal glass sceptically as if not entirely convinced it was the real thing.

'Oh, come, come, Mother. It's one of the finest hotels on the East Coast. Three different presidents have stayed here – not to mention the cream of the British aristocracy,' said Mr Van Bergen. Mrs Van Bergen looked a little mollified by this, as he went on: 'Besides, there's only a week left before the young ladies go back to Europe. We hadn't time to travel out to Long Island, but we couldn't possibly let Princess Anna leave without enjoying a little of the ocean breeze.'

'I imagine she'll get plenty of *that* on the voyage home,' said Mrs Van Bergen drily. 'Which reminds me – I must make sure the arrangements are in place for the young ladies' new chaperone. Where did I put my portmanteau?'

But Anna did not want to think of their return journey yet. She was staring out at the view of endless sky and sea, at the swooping seagulls, and at the distant shapes of buildings on the horizon. A group of young guests on their way to play croquet paused to look too.

'Look – you can see Dreamland. It's the grand opening today, isn't it?' said one.

'Say, why don't we walk down there and take a look?'

said another.

'*Dreamland* – no! We couldn't possibly!' exclaimed a third, with a delighted shriek, as they went on their way.

'What's Dreamland?' Anna asked, the name catching her imagination at once.

'Isn't it one of those amusement places at Coney Island?' said Evangeline.

At the mention of *Coney Island*, Mrs Van Bergen shuddered. 'A very vulgar place. All those ghastly thrill rides – and the most dreadful food!'

'Oh come, Mother,' said Van Bergen again. 'I've always thought it sounded rather fun. All those architectural marvels and lights. Quite a spectacle! Dreamland is the biggest of the amusement parks, I believe, and it's reopening today for the summer season. There's a big celebration – aerial displays, fireworks, all that sort of thing.'

'Could we go and see it?' Anna suggested.

'Heavens, no, my dear! It wouldn't be at all suitable. It's for *working people* – *not* young ladies, and certainly not a princess!' exclaimed Mrs Van Bergen.

'I don't see that it would do any harm to run them down in the motor, just to have a look,' said Van Bergen. 'If I were with them, I'm sure it would be quite safe.'

'Good gracious, Theodore!' exclaimed Mrs Van Bergen. 'Sometimes I doubt your common sense. You can't possibly take Princess Anna to *Coney Island*. After all the trouble we've taken to keep her safe and out of the way of the press, you can't plunge her amongst that rabble. The King would never forgive us. Besides, aren't you taking them to tour the shipyard?'

Mrs Van Bergen always had the last word. Even Evangeline never dared to argue with her, and now, the two girls were sent up to their rooms to change. Anna had already discovered that Mrs Van Bergen had very specific ideas about wearing the right clothes for the right occasion.

'Ugh! I can't believe we have to spend the afternoon at a *shipyard*,' sighed Evangeline. 'How dull!'

'I think it might be rather interesting,' said Anna.

Evangeline laughed. 'You're such a goody-two-shoes, Anna! You always like *everything* they take us to – even that awful boring opera.'

Anna just shrugged and smiled. It was hard to explain to Evangeline that the easy freedom they had here in New York was special to her. In Arnovia, if she visited a shipyard or went to an opera, it would be for an official royal visit. She'd have to wear a white frock and white gloves, and people would hand her bouquets. Here it was different: she could be lost in the crowd, watch the people, see what the world was really like. She wanted to make the most of every moment. Everything was interesting, and besides, you never knew when something unexpected might happen. If she hadn't known that already, she'd certainly learned it on the *Thalassa*.

Together, she and Evangeline went up the wide stairs

and crossed the landing. Anna registered that a door marked 'Ocean View' stood open. Inside, in a large and elegant parlour, one maid was arranging a vase of flowers, while another set plates and silverware on a table. It looked as if it was being prepared for a grand afternoon tea. Two boys in overalls and caps were struggling up the stairs behind them, carrying a large and obviously heavy wooden box.

'We're to set this up for Mrs Davenport's party,' mumbled one of them to the maids, who beckoned them inside at once.

Mrs Davenport. Anna was certain she'd heard that name somewhere before.

'Come on, Anna!' called Evangeline from above her.

Anna turned, almost colliding with a young man in spectacles, who was on his way down the stairs with a book under his arm.

'Oh – I beg your pardon,' she said.

He smiled at her pleasantly. 'My fault entirely, miss,' he said, before continuing down to the foyer below.

Anna ran on upstairs. If she'd looked back, she might have noticed that one of the boys in overalls was staring after the young man in spectacles. There was a puzzled expression on his face.

'Surely it couldn't be . . .' he murmured.

'What?' his companion demanded. Dressed in an overall, her thick curly hair tucked under a cap, even Anna's sharp eyes had not recognised the smart lady's maid from aboard the *Thalassa*.

'Nothing,' said Billy, though he was still frowning. 'For a minute, I thought I recognised one of the fellows from my cabin on the *Thalassa*, but it can't have been.'

Tilly glanced at the clock. 'Well, hurry up then. We've lost too much time already – we'll have to work fast.'

Ten minutes later, when Anna came back down the stairs with Evangeline, the boys in the overalls were gone. But down below, the quiet hotel foyer had become suddenly busy. Two or three black motor cars had drawn up, and several gentlemen were climbing out. At his desk, the concierge was talking to a lady in a large hat, while a party of young people went by with tennis racquets under their arms. Two waiters in white gloves were hurrying upstairs with trays of champagne glasses, while at the door, a young woman came haring in, followed closely by a young man in a boater carrying what Anna idly thought might be a big camera. She was just wondering where she had seen them before, when her attention was caught by a girl wearing a frilly white frock, white gloves and a hat wreathed in flowers and ribbons, sitting in a corner of the lobby.

As soon as she saw Anna coming down the stairs, the girl jumped to her feet. 'Oh my goodness! *Princess Anna!*'

Her voice was loud and carrying. Evangeline stopped short. '*Miss Zhang?*' she said in astonishment.

But no one heard her. Several heads had already turned to stare at Anna. 'That's her! Princess Anna of Arnovia!' exclaimed the young woman. 'I recognise her from Paris!'

'I say, it *is* her!' gasped a fellow with a tennis racket. 'I've seen her picture in the papers.'

'Isn't she the one who was kidnapped? Who's that with her? Surely it's young Miss Van Bergen?'

'Lucy, run and fetch Mother and Father. They won't want to miss this!'

'Fancy us staying in the same hotel as a real-life *princess!*'

Anna froze. The young woman was already at the foot of the stairs, making an awkward sort of curtsey. 'Your Royal Highness, may I introduce myself? I am Roberta Russell, of *The Daily Picture*, London,' she said, in a crisp English accent. 'I wonder if you could take the time to answer a few questions for our readers?'

All at once, the foyer seemed busier than ever. People were hurrying in, while at the same time Anna noticed several smart gentleman making a dash for the entrance, as if they wanted to get away. A camera bulb flashed before her eyes, making her blink.

'Do you suppose she'd give me her autograph?'

'Don't be an idiot, Dora. You can't ask a *princess* for her autograph. She's not like a Broadway star!'

Another camera bulb flashed and Anna blinked again. She'd had her photo taken many times in Elffburg, but those had been formal state occasions. She'd been carefully dressed in her white frock and green sash, her hair arranged by a hairdresser. Grandfather and Alex had been at her side, all of them waving courteously to the crowds. Now she was here, standing on the stairs of a hotel, in a perfectly ordinary afternoon dress, her hair fastened back with a simple bow. She could see the concierge trying to push his way towards them, but more people had appeared out of nowhere and he was struggling to keep order.

'Anna . . . what's happening?' hissed Evangeline in alarm. 'What are we supposed to do?'

Anna drew herself upwards, surprised to find that she knew exactly what to do. For a moment, she imagined Grandfather at her side, Arnovian flags waving above her head and then, with calm dignity, she began to speak.

Across the foyer, Mei knew she could not linger. They were already running behind; now she would have to race back to Dreamland as fast as she could. Just the same, she paused for a moment, wishing she could tell Anna she was sorry for what she'd had to do. But as she watched, she saw that Anna did not seem in the least bit disconcerted. Instead, she was talking to the reporters as graciously as if she were receiving visitors at a state reception.

Mei took off Miss Zhang's flowered hat and slipped away into the crowd – vanishing as if she'd never been there at all.

Charlton's plane made one final swoop over Coney

Island before it came gliding down, landing with the softest of bumps upon the grass. Sophie was breathless, her eyes shining. She'd forgotten how marvellous it was to be so high up. It had been splendid to see New York from the air: the glittering spires of Dreamland; the brown rooftops of Brooklyn; the great stretch of glittering silver-blue water and the jagged shapes of the Manhattan skyline beyond. It had reminded her of the night she'd arrived, driving through the city, that brief fizz of excitement about being in this new place. Now, the great metropolis seemed spread out before her, waiting to be explored. Almost, she'd forgotten what she was here to do.

'Jolly good, eh, Miss Grayson?' said Charlton. He was beaming too as he clambered neatly down, offering his hand to help her. 'She's a fine little plane, isn't she?'

'You fly her terribly well,' said Sophie approvingly as she took his hand and jumped down. But as she landed on the grass, her smile faded.

Standing in a row, waiting for them were three men. Two were tall and wore black bowler hats. One, smoking a cigarette was a little shorter, and his hard eyes were fixed on her face.

'Good afternoon,' he said in a hoarse voice. 'I think you know who I am.'

'Mr Molloy, I suppose,' said Sophie, keeping her head held high and her voice steady, though her heart was pounding. They'd always known this plan had consequences. Now, she was about to find out what they were.

At her side, Charlton looked baffled. It was clear he hadn't the least idea of what was happening.

'I say, Miss Grayson –' he began awkwardly.

But Molloy cut him off. 'We warned you,' he said to Sophie, tossing his cigarette end to the ground. 'We made things perfectly clear. But you chose to ignore us. Well – that was your mistake.'

The bowler hats stepped forward, and Sophie felt her panic rising. If she only had her pistol! But it was long gone and she had nothing to defend herself with. She looked around for a way out, but there was nowhere for her to go. The men were blocking her path.

'Now, look here –' began Charlton again, but no one paid him any attention.

Molloy took a step towards Sophie, and his hard face broke into a cold smile, driving an icicle of fear into her heart.

'No second chances,' he said, his smile growing wider. 'You're coming with us.'

CHAPTER THIRTY

Coney Island and Manhattan Beach New York City

At the Orient Hotel's Ocean View Suite, the Black Dragon waited alone, amongst the abandoned preparations for an elegant afternoon tea.

She sat very upright in a throne-like velvet armchair. Behind her was a heavy brocade curtain; on the small mahogany table at her side was a vase of deep crimson roses. She looked like a person in a painting, Sophie thought. The richness of her surroundings made the perfect setting for her diamond earrings, her velvet gown, and her hat adorned with ostrich feathers. Yet Sophie also saw a glittering fury in Mrs Davenport's eyes that made her feel clammy all over with fear.

'Sit down, Miss Taylor,' was all she said. She gestured with a hand to the armchair opposite her. A table stood between the two chairs, set with tall glasses and a plate of dainty cakes. It looked like somewhere two society ladies would have a companionable *tête-a-tête*, and yet seeing it, Sophie felt more frightened than ever. She faltered and took half a step backwards. But Molloy gave her a rough shove, making her stumble to the floor.

'That's enough,' said Mrs Davenport, waving her hand at Molloy in lordly dismissal. 'You can leave us. Go and take care of that other business, if you please.'

Molloy nodded and left the room, the bowler hats following. Sophie was glad to see them go, for the short time she'd spent in their company had not been pleasant. After being dragged off the field, she'd been bundled into a motor car, and strong-armed through a side door and up the back staircase of the hotel. She'd struggled of course, and tried to get away, but she hadn't stood a chance against the bowler hats, each of whom was at least twice her size. In response they'd tied her hands behind her back, painfully tight, grinning as if they were enjoying every second.

But any fleeting feeling of relief vanished when she saw the Black Dragon rise and cross the room towards her, her narrow eyes fixed on Sophie. To her horror, she saw something small and wickedly sharp shining in the Black Dragon's hand – a little jewelled knife. Instinctively she scrabbled backwards, but the Black Dragon was already leaning over her, and Sophie realised she was merely reaching around her back, to cut through the bowler-hats' restraints.

'That's better,' she said coolly, moving back towards her

chair. 'Sit down.'

Sophie scrambled to her feet. She swallowed hard, and forced herself to step forward. Don't let your enemy see that they intimidate you. That had been one of Papa's maxims – and it was a good one.

'It's been a long time since we last met,' Mrs Davenport said, sounding for all the world like a titled lady at a garden party, exchanging polite remarks with someone she considered her social inferior. 'Come – sit down,' she said again.

Sophie took the seat opposite Mrs Davenport, steeling herself for what was to come. But the Black Dragon merely pushed one of the glasses in Sophie's direction, ice cubes clinking. 'Would you care for a cool drink? Strawberry lemonade. A speciality of the hotel, I understand.'

Sophie took the glass warily. Mrs Davenport sat back in her chair, folding her hands. 'I was planning a little party this afternoon,' she said, watching Sophie through narrowed eyes. 'A number of important gentlemen were to join me. Some of them had travelled quite a considerable distance. Now, thanks to a spectacle down in the foyer, they are unable to attend. For many reasons, they did not wish to be spotted by members of the press.'

Mrs Davenport took a tiny sip of her lemonade, before she went on. 'I had intended for my guests to see a special presentation. But that too has been spoiled. The man who ought to have carried it out is missing. The firebombs that

298

he was to scatter on the Atlantic Line shipyard are gone. Theodore Van Bergen, who ought to have been *at* his shipyard, has been delayed and is still here at the hotel. And instead, copies of a *literary magazine* have been scattered all over Brooklyn.' She sighed, and picked up a copy of *LUNA* which was lying on the table at her side, beside the roses, a blue porcelain bowl and a small gilded statuette of a lion. 'I commend you on your taste, Miss Taylor. I'm interested in experimental poetry myself. But *this* is not what I intended.'

Her voice was cold and indifferent, but once again, Sophie saw a glitter of fury in her enemy's eyes. She felt a surge of triumph. They'd done what they intended. Whatever happened now, they'd succeeded in stopping the Black Dragon's plan.

But the Black Dragon was still talking. 'Of course, all you have really done is delay matters. There will be plenty more opportunities, and more firebombs. In fact, I believe Dr Snow is perfecting a more powerful formula as we speak. Do try your lemonade, Miss Taylor. It's *so* refreshing.' She gave Sophie a cold smile, and took another very small sip from her own glass, before she went on.

'My brother now – you know who my brother was, don't you?'

'Of course,' said Sophie, trying to sound calm. 'The Baron. John Hardcastle.' She thought of the photograph she'd seen: *John and Viola*. Sitting here, she could see the likeness between brother and sister for the first time.

'Indeed. My brother underestimated you, I think. Of course, he underestimated me too. He always thought he knew best, even when he was at his most reckless and foolhardy. My husband was just the same. He was a member of the society too, you know. How I used to cringe, watching them make their plans, knowing that I could have done so much better! But women had never been allowed to join.'

'But you're a member now,' said Sophie. 'Head of the New York branch.'

Mrs Davenport inclined her head graciously, as if receiving a compliment. 'Things have changed a great deal since my husband's day. The new master is different. Under Gold's leadership, the society has at last begun to enter the new century. The old guard – the likes of John and my husband – were rather crude in their thinking. But Gold is progressive. His approach is more subtle and sophisticated. He sees new possibilities for influencing world events in less obvious ways.'

'Such as putting pressure on the right people in places like Russia, or Arnovia, where there are already tensions?' suggested Sophie sharply. 'Or stirring up fears about foreign spies?'

Mrs Davenport nodded. 'Very good,' she said, like a schoolmistress praising her pupil's work. 'Of course, the society's real aim is to create division. By giving everyone else someone to hate, we create an atmosphere of chaos, in which we can thrive. Gold knows I understand that. He saw that I was quite able to fill John's shoes. He understands that women are capable of more.'

He understands that women are capable of more. All at once, Sophie was sitting in the dining room of the *Thalassa*, while Miss Russell talked and talked. *He knows that I'm capable of more.*

She'd got it all wrong – she saw it in a flash. Albert Moorhouse wasn't the Gold Dragon. Roberta had said he was old-fashioned and set in his ways, believing lady reporters capable of writing only about fashions. But the Gold Dragon was progressive. He saw new ways of doing things, and offered opportunities to women. He was a man who had connections all over Europe, and could spread chaos wherever he pleased.

He'd been there all along. She'd seen him with her own eyes, sitting at the luncheon table with Mrs Davenport and Florence Andrews. He fitted Leo's description perfectly. How could she have been so easily misled by the sight of the Black Dragon, whispering in Moorhouse's ear? It was so obvious now that *Moorhouse* could never have been the head of the *Fraternitas*. He might be a member, perhaps, but he was no leader. All his stories about spies were printed on the orders of someone else.

The Gold Dragon was someone far more powerful than Moorhouse. He operated his business across half a dozen European cities – and now in New York too. He was capable of organising something as grand and complex as an international air-race, and could influence everyone from an Arnovian Duchess to a radical young Russian. It was so clear to her now that she couldn't believe she hadn't seen it before.

Sir Chester Norton was the Gold Dragon.

The sun was sinking as Molloy stalked through the early evening crowds, his bowler hats close at his heels. He ought to have felt like a king surveying his empire as he strode through Dreamland; but the truth was, *she* was the boss. He'd never thought he'd answer to a woman, especially not a woman like her. Yet as the thought crossed his mind, he instinctively began to move a little faster. Even thinking about her made him nervous. He'd seen what she did to the people who crossed her. Not herself – for she wasn't the kind who got her hands dirty. But with that kind of money, that kind of power, she could have anyone do whatever she wished.

He hadn't enjoyed telling her that the presentation had gone wrong. Now he had to make it up to her, and fast. He quickened his pace, shooting sharp glances across the crowds. He'd never thought that kid Joey would show his face round here again. They'd made the consequences of returning to Coney Island quite clear. But some people were like that: always running headlong into trouble. Besides, *she* didn't even seem to care about Joey. It was the girl she wanted, the girl she said would be with him. 'Find one and you'll find the other,' she'd said. So where would Joey go?

Molloy left Dreamland, moving against the tide of people still surging through the gates, and crossed the street, making for Ruby's. The bar was busier than he'd seen it since last summer, packed with regulars and visitors. Leon was at the piano and a little crowd had gathered round to sing along.

Ruby nodded to him from behind the bar as he stepped through the door.

'Where's Joey?' said Molloy. 'You seen him?'

Ruby shrugged. 'How should I know? You were the one who took him away. Lost me my best bartender. Charley can barely pour a lemonade without spilling it.'

Molloy gave her a hard look. 'Don't mess with me, Ruby. Where is he?'

'I don't know, all right?'

'Where's Eddie then? In the office?'

He moved towards the back stairs, but Ruby shook her head. 'He's not there. He went over to the park.'

Molloy gave an annoyed grunt. Then he looked at Ruby again. 'What are you smiling about?'

'Why shouldn't I smile?' Ruby rolled her eyes. 'It's been a good day for business. You ought to be smiling too. Look at Dreamland! Even now, folk are still turning up.'

But Molloy didn't even give a flicker of a smile. 'You're

up to something, Ruby. I can tell. Joey *has* been here, hasn't he?'

Ruby folded her arms. 'All right. Fine. You win. He's been here. But he's gone now. He was with some girl, said he was taking her over to the dance hall.'

'Go – quickly,' Molloy instructed his bowler hats. Then he turned back to Ruby. 'I told you not to mess with me,' he growled.

But Ruby snorted. 'Oh please. You know, sometimes Molloy I think you forget that *I* knew you when you were just a kid. Bawling because you'd skinned your knee, or lost your baseball in someone's yard. Yeah, I remember. I know you're in charge now. Money in your pockets, those two thugs to keep everyone in line. But even so, *you don't scare me.*'

She folded her arms. Leon was still playing the piano, but the singing had stopped. Molloy had the distinct and unpleasant feeling that everyone in the place was listening. He scowled at Ruby. Who the devil did she think she was, talking to him like that? He'd make her sorry.

'I don't have time for this now,' he said, jabbing an angry finger at her. 'But I'll be back, Ruby. You can count on that.'

He caught up with his men by the dance hall. There was no sign of Joey, but as they scanned the crowds, they caught sight of Eddie with one of the girls from Miss Patty's.

'You seen that kid, Joey, around here? Or this girl?' He'd

been given a picture of the girl, torn from a newspaper. Now he showed it to Eddie, who squinted at it for a long moment.

'You know, I reckon I *did* see him around with that girl, a little while ago,' said Eddie at last – not sounding very certain. 'But I didn't think it could be him. I didn't think we'd be seeing him round here again.'

'So where'd he go?' demanded Molloy at once.

Eddie said he thought they'd been headed in the direction of the *Gondolas of Venice*. But when Molloy made it to the ride, there was no sign of Joey waiting in line, and the fellow on duty shook his head at the photograph. Dreamland was growing busier than ever, and Molloy found himself buffeted by pushing people as he scanned the crowds. A couple of girls actually bumped right into him, almost knocking him off his feet and smearing a half-melted ice-cream on to his shirt front, as they rushed towards the *Alps of Switzerland*. 'Oh, my! I'm sorry, sir,' the one in the frilly dress gasped, while her friend, who carried a large carpet bag, pulled her onwards. 'Come on!' They ran off together, giggling, while Molloy brushed himself down angrily.

He'd been left in such a mess that he had to stop to get some paper napkins to wipe off the worst of the ice-cream at a hot-dog stand. He showed the fellow serving up sizzling-hot sausages the picture of Lil.

'Yeah, I've seen her – maybe ten minutes ago?'

But before the fellow could say any more, there was the sudden sound of barking and shouting, and a little black dog came zipping out of the crowd, making a beeline for the hot-dog stand. Its lead was trailing behind it, and it bounded joyfully straight for the sausages, diving through Molloy's legs and almost tripping him over in the process.

'Hey!' Molloy yelled, grabbing at the nearest bowler hat to save himself. But the dog had already upset the sausages and bread, scattering bottles of mustard everywhere, and was racing off with a half-eaten hot dog in its mouth.

A young fellow came chasing after it, breathless and pink-faced. 'Sorry!' he called out as he passed the hot-dog stand, then disappeared into the crowd after the dog, crying: 'Lucky! Come back!'

It took several minutes before order was restored, and the flustered hot-dog seller could finish telling Molloy that he'd seen the girl heading to the Animal Arena. It was perhaps not surprising that Molloy was quite out of temper by the time he arrived there to find that Joey was nowhere to be seen.

Old Grandpops was leaning on the fence, watching the lion-tamer at work. 'Wouldn't want to be getting up close to a beast like that myself,' he remarked, as Molloy stalked up to him. 'Remember what happened to poor Jack Bonavita? Lost his hand to a lion. You see, these creatures, they don't want to be ordered about. Likely as not they'll turn on their captors one day. If *I* was that fellow,

I'd be watching my back.'

Molloy was not in the mood to listen to Grandpops babbling nonsense. 'You seen Joey? The bartender from Ruby's?'

Grandpops nodded very slowly. 'Nice kid. And a good bartender. Got manners, you see. Listens to us old-timers, which is more than I can say for some.'

'Has he been here? Have you seen him?' Molloy barked.

'Now let me see . . .' said Grandpops, seeming to become slower the more annoyed Molloy became. 'Has he been here? Yeah, he's been here. Mmm-hmm. Saw him just a minute ago, with a pretty girl in a white dress. Stopped to pass the time of day too – I told you the kid has manners. Now, where did they say they were going?'

'Come on, old man. Spit it out!'

'Easy there. Don't rush me. Memory's not what it was. Now let me think. Yeah, I got it. He said they were headed to *Hell-Gate*.'

Molloy did not wait to hear any more. *Hell-Gate* was on the other side of the park, back in the direction he'd come. But he was gaining on them. Joey'd been here just a few minutes ago, and Molloy knew all the fastest ways to cut through the park. He turned on his heel and stalked off, the bowler hats hurrying to keep up.

Hell-Gate had been one of the most popular attractions of opening day. Dozens of people were queuing outside, nudging each other in anticipation and excitement. A huge figure of a demon, eyes blazing, leered ominously down at them, while ahead yawned a dark cave. Several little boats bobbed about on murky water, waiting for the brave to step inside, before they were conveyed by a hidden mechanism into the darkness below. At the rear, people were emerging laughing and gasping and clutching one another's hands, shrieking over the horrifying groans, the ghoulish figures and ghastly red lights they'd experienced within.

Molloy went up to the fellow on duty, glad to see that it was Jake, one of the most reliable of the workers. He was an older fellow with a mechanical bent, who understood how all the rides worked and was always called on to fix any problems. Molloy knew he could count on him. 'Did you see a couple youngsters go in here just now?' he demanded. 'English accents. A tall fellow with curly hair, and a girl in white?'

Jake nodded. 'Sure. They're in there now,' he said, jerking his thumb at the ride.

Molloy nodded, his frustration beginning to fade. All at once, things were working out nicely. He glanced up at the demon, and gave a grim smile.

'Close up the ride. Shut it down. No one else is to go in tonight,' he ordered Jake. Turning to the bowler hats, he gestured towards the boats. 'You two - with me.'

He leaped into a little boat, the bowler hats following. He gave Jake a quick nod, and then they were off - swept by the whirring mechanism down into the darkness beyond.

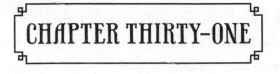

CHAPTER THIRTY-ONE

Coney Island and Manhattan Beach
New York City

S ir Chester Norton was the Gold Dragon.

Norton, who'd been there all along. Norton, whom she'd actually met in Paris, when she'd been investigating Professor Blaxland's death.

It changed everything. But Sophie knew she couldn't think about that now. Mrs Davenport was still talking, and she knew she must listen to every word.

'John had always been obsessed with the story of the dragon paintings, and the secret they concealed. The location of the Draco Almanac, the society's ancient book of knowledge, and the instructions to make a deadly weapon. In the end of course, he got carried away. It was all most *unfortunate*.' She pursed her lips disapprovingly and took a sip of lemonade. 'After all that, I decided to leave England.'

'You *had* to leave,' Sophie corrected her. 'The authorities were looking for you. So you fled London for New York. You stopped being Lady Tremayne and became Mrs Davenport.'

'Gold wished to set up a base for the society here. He saw the important role America would play in world events,' said Mrs Davenport airily. 'New York is full of possibilities.'

'But it's not London,' said Sophie suddenly. 'Or Paris, or Vienna, or Rome.'

Mrs Davenport shrugged. 'I can visit Europe if necessary. I was in Italy only a few weeks ago.'

'But you were recognised in Venice, and you had to leave in a hurry. Somehow, I don't think you'll be returning to Europe for a while, not even for your new season Paris gowns.'

'New York has perfectly good dressmakers.'

'But not like Maison Chevalier,' said Sophie, watching her carefully. 'That *is* a Chevalier hat you're wearing, isn't it? One of last autumn's styles, of course. It must be difficult to get the new ones here. As for your gown, it's easy to see that it's a copy of one of the new House of Worth models. Not a patch on the real thing, of course, but you won't have access to that kind of *haute couture* any longer. I suppose you saw a photograph and had your dressmaker copy it?'

Mrs Davenport gave her a thin, icy smile, but Sophie hadn't finished. 'The Cartier earrings you're wearing are copies too – of a pair made by Rivière for the Tsarina, if I'm not mistaken? And I notice your supply of French perfume is running rather low.'

Mrs Davenport's lip twitched with annoyance, and Sophie saw her point had struck home. Her time in the wardrobe had given her the opportunity to contemplate Mrs Davenport's clothes, but it wasn't only that. Everything Sophie had seen in Mrs Davenport's suite had been proof of her attachment to Europe – French operas, European paintings, novels set in Italy. Yet Europe was closed to Mrs Davenport now.

'Of course, I'd expect someone who worked as a *shop girl* selling hats and jewellery to notice such things,' the Black Dragon said, as if the very word *shop girl* was faintly ridiculous. 'You see, I know your history. But such details are scarcely of importance.'

'Still, it must be frustrating. And perhaps even more frustrating to know you'll never move in the same kind of circles here as you did in London?' Sophie suggested. 'New York high society hasn't welcomed you with open arms, has it?'

'New York is different,' Mrs Davenport interrupted. 'But there are many valuable opportunities for me here.'

For the first time, her voice sounded hollow, and Sophie pressed her advantage. 'Opportunities like owning an *amusement* park? *Quite* different to what you're used to. And it's such a long way from home. Isn't it strange to think you can never go back there – not to London, nor to your family's estate? You're no longer Lady Viola Tremayne, daughter of the Duke of Cleveland. And most likely you'll never see any of your friends or family in England again. Like your goddaughter Leo, for example?'

Sophie saw a shadow fall over Mrs Davenport's face. She got up from her chair abruptly and walked to the window, turning away as if looking at the ocean.

'There are valuable opportunities for me here,' she asserted again, as if Sophie hadn't spoken. 'John had visited before. He had connections that were useful to me.'

'Do you mean Molloy?'

Mrs Davenport turned back from the window. 'Oh no, I tracked *him* down myself. He was running a rather shoddy little operation in Coney Island, but I could see he had potential. And through him I got to know some other businessmen.'

'Such as Sai Wing Mock?' Mrs Davenport did not answer, so Sophie went on. 'Then you brought Henry Snow over, and set him up in the old Brooklyn Pickle Works, which you'd bought and turned into a laboratory.'

'I needed somewhere discreet for him to continue his work. Dr Snow is a brilliant young man, though his time in gaol disturbed him somewhat. He has become erratic, although his research remains exceptional.'

'Did he design the submarine?'

Mrs Davenport smiled. 'So you saw it? An impressive machine, isn't it? So *stealthy* – just perfect for carrying out sabotage. Think how they could be used in wartime! I shall soon be setting up one of my new factories to manufacture more. There's already been a lot of interest – from the British Navy, for one.' Seeing Sophie frown, she added: 'Oh didn't you know? One of the gentlemen I expected here today was a representative of the British government. Sent by Prime Minister Lockwood himself.'

Sophie stopped in her tracks. She must be bluffing. The British government wouldn't have anything to do with the *Fraternitas*. How could they?

Seeing her confusion, Mrs Davenport laughed. 'The *Fraternitas* works with many of the world's most powerful governments. Of course, Britain is one of them. Whatever little investigations your Secret Service Bureau may be involved in are no concern to us. We go straight to the top. The Gold Dragon and Prime Minister Lockwood know each other rather well. The Prime Minister has no problem accepting the services we offer – and he pays us handsomely in return.'

'*Services* like plotting disasters, or supplying dangerous weapons, you mean?' Sophie's voice was sharp. She'd long suspected that they couldn't trust the British government with a deadly weapon, but this was beyond anything that she had dreamed of. Could the *British Prime Minister* really be in league with the Gold Dragon? It seemed impossible, and yet it made a horrible kind of sense. Was that why, no matter how hard they worked, none of the Bureau's investigations had ever led them to Gold? Then a new thought struck her, even more disturbing than before. What if Lockwood knew that Norton was deliberately stirring up fears of German spies in his newspapers? What if it was all part of a deliberate plan?

'You aren't drinking your lemonade, Miss Taylor,' Mrs Davenport said as she returned to her chair, a cat-like smile on her face.

Her voice was oddly hypnotic, and Sophie found herself taking a sip from the glass. The lemonade was sweet and sticky, almost syrupy, but at least it was cold.

'I know who the Gold Dragon is,' she said. 'It's Sir Chester Norton, isn't it?'

But Mrs Davenport did not blink. She only carried on talking, as if Sophie hadn't spoken. 'I'd planned to show my guests our new firebombs. There are several varieties, ideally suited to being dropped from aeroplanes, whether on battlefields, military targets or on civilians. The devastation they cause is considerable. Now, of course, Dr Snow has the information in the Draco Almanac to help him strengthen his formula. With the instructions for making the *feu du ciel*, they will be more powerful than ever.' As she spoke, she took out a small, familiar book and laid it on the table, out of Sophie's reach. 'Thank you for bringing me this, Miss Taylor. Especially after all the trouble you went to in order to get it.'

She rested her hand on the Almanac. 'You see, *I* do not

underestimate you. On the contrary, I know what you're capable of. That's why I let you find this for me. I'd planned to take it from you in Venice but Forsyth bungled that. So, I arranged to have you bring it to me here in New York.'

'You used Joe to blackmail us,' said Sophie shortly.

'Forsyth wanted to kill him. He's rather simplistic in that way. But I saw at once that he might be useful. I felt sure you'd give up even the Almanac to save one of your own. I understand you, Miss Taylor – as my brother never did.'

'But if that's what you had planned, then why send Forsyth to steal the Almanac from me on the *Thalassa*?'

'That was a last-minute change of plan,' said Mrs Davenport. 'We didn't expect you to travel on the *Thalassa*. When we learned you'd be there, it seemed a fortunate coincidence. Forsyth was sent to take the Almanac before sinking the ship, since you would most probably go down with it.'

'But I didn't,' said Sophie. 'And the plan to sink the *Thalassa* failed.'

Mrs Davenport shrugged. 'No matter. It still offered us an excellent chance to test the new submarine. Thanks to the near miss with the iceberg, people are already beginning to feel uncertain about the Atlantic Line. Once we've destroyed its most important shipyard, and wiped out hundreds of workers, it won't last long. We simply cannot allow that sort of international collaboration to go on, you see. And the evidence we leave will make the Americans believe it's all the work of German agents. That is a strategy that has already worked extremely well in Britain.' She smiled, and gave the book a little pat. 'And, of course, I have the Almanac in any case.'

She looked so complacent that Sophie felt her temper flare. 'Why do you even *want* the Almanac?' she demanded. 'You keep talking about the society becoming more progressive, and *entering the twentieth century*. So why would you want a book of obscure old rituals and alchemy? It can't be just for the *feu du ciel*, no matter how powerful it might be. After all, Snow's already managed to create dangerous firebombs by himself. What possible use can the Draco Almanac have here – now?'

'You're right, of course. Most of it is gibberish,' Mrs Davenport acknowledged. 'John might have thought it was full of powerful ancient knowledge but I am not deceived. But that doesn't matter. Regardless of what's in it, the Draco Almanac has immense power. Can you imagine how impressed Gold and the rest of the International Council will be, when I present them with their long-lost treasure?' She smiled at Sophie. 'Its power comes from what it *symbolises*. A time when the *dragons will reign supreme . . .*' Her eyes darkened strangely, and Sophie felt a shiver run over her skin. Then Mrs Davenport's expression was cool and unemotional once more. She gestured to the plate of cakes. 'Would you care for something to eat?'

Sophie shook her head. She had never felt less like eating cake, but her throat was dry and she swallowed some more lemonade. Mrs Davenport drank some too, wincing slightly, as if its cloying sweetness was too much for her.

'But why do you want to impress them? Why be part of the *Fraternitas* anyway?' Sophie asked. 'It's not for the money, is it?'

Mrs Davenport shook her head. 'I do enjoy beautiful things, and it is pleasant to surround myself with them.' She touched the petals of the crimson roses at her side as she spoke. 'But no, not money. For John, it was a way to strike back against polite society. He had always been a rebel. But for me, it is really a kind of a game – or a puzzle. I believe you'll understand me when I say that I enjoy pitting my wits against those who oppose me. It makes one feel *powerful*, and goodness knows, I haven't always had the opportunity to feel that.'

'And Gold?' asked Sophie. 'What about him?'

'Oh, he's different. I really think he believes what he's doing is right.'

Sophie stared. How could attempting to sink an ocean liner full of innocent people, or dropping bombs in the middle of New York possibly be *right*?

'War is inevitable. Gold is simply helping things move along. Putting the society in the best position to profit. That's what we've always done, since our earliest days in Venice,' said Mrs Davenport. She touched the cover of the

Almanac again, lightly tracing the shape of the golden eye.

'But what about the lions?' said Sophie.

Mrs Davenport laughed. 'Lions? Oh, dear me! The Loyal Order of Lions was a credible threat once, perhaps, but no longer. You and Miss Rose may be quite capable, but even with the help of your little gang you can hardly expect to stop us. Remember, you're alone and friendless here. New York is *my* city. As we speak, Miss Rose and your friends are being dealt with by Molloy. I know very well she's here – where one of you goes, the other surely follows. So I'm afraid this is the end for the Loyal Order of Lions.'

'No – I don't believe so,' said Sophie steadily.

'There's nothing else you can do. Even if your friends escape, what then? *You're* still here. And you know there's no proof of anything I've told you.'

'Actually there is,' said Sophie. 'As a matter of fact, you've just given it to us.'

Mrs Davenport only smirked, but Sophie leaned forward, pushing back the heavy brocade curtain. It revealed an extraordinary machine rather like a gramophone. But rather than the usual gramophone horn, extending from behind the curtain was a long, narrow tube, which had been concealed from sight by the vase of roses at Mrs Davenport's side.

'The Edison Business Phonograph, Model D. Sometimes called the Stenographer's Friend,' Sophie announced.

Mrs Davenport stared at her, uncomprehending.

'It's a *dictation machine*. It's been recording your voice – every word you've said. It's captured our entire conversation on a wax cylinder that can be played back quite easily. It's been adapted to suit our particular purposes, of course. You're not the only one who works with a clever scientist.'

Mrs Davenport looked from the machine to Sophie, and then laughed. 'Very impressive, Miss Taylor. I suppose you found out about my gathering here. But this "recording" will hardly help you now. I can simply throw it into the fire, or toss it into the ocean.'

She finished the last of her lemonade. 'We've talked enough. Now, we come to the point. I dislike violence – it is vulgar and unnecessary. Instead, the drink you have just finished contains a powerful sleeping draught which will take effect at any moment. After that an accident will be arranged for you. Sea-bathing, I think. The ocean can be very dangerous.'

She looked at Sophie with satisfaction, as if expecting a reaction. But Sophie remained where she was. 'You're wrong,' she observed, her eyes fixed on Mrs Davenport.

'Really? Please, do enlighten me.' The Black Dragon smiled her cat-like smile.

'You said we were *all alone here*. But that isn't actually true,' said Sophie. 'If you know my history, you'll know I have some American connections. I was trained by Ada Pickering, of Pickering's Detective Agency. And then there's Mr Sinclair. I suppose you're aware that he is also an agent of the American Secret Intelligence Service?'

Mrs Davenport wafted a hand. 'Ada Pickering is retired. She's been in Colorado since last winter, for her health. As for Sinclair, he's in California, nearly three thousand miles away. He can hardly help you now.'

'Perhaps not,' said Sophie. 'But there's something else.'

Mrs Davenport did not ask what it was. A certain heaviness had overtaken her. Her smile was slipping away.

'You don't understand me as well as you think,' Sophie went on. 'If you did, you'd know I wasn't going to be fooled by a *glass of strawberry lemonade.*'

Mrs Davenport only blinked at her, as Sophie stood up. 'Why would someone who drinks dry martini cocktails, and likes her coffee bitter and black, choose something as sweet and sickly as this? To *disguise the taste of something* – like a sleeping draught, perhaps.' Her voice grew stronger as she added, 'It's a trick you've used before. In Venice, when you poisoned those chocolates for Mrs Knight?'

Mrs Davenport's face had turned pale, her eyes glassy. She grew paler still as Sophie added: 'That's why I switched our glasses.'

'You . . .' It came out sounding like a groan. Mrs Davenport slumped back in her chair, as if she could no longer hold herself upright.

'I did it while you were over at the window. I've been drinking your glass, and you've been drinking mine.'

The glass slipped from Mrs Davenport's hand, but Sophie reached out and caught it neatly before it fell to the floor and shattered. She placed it on the table, then reached for the Almanac.

'There is one thing you got right, though,' she said softly, as Mrs Davenport's eyes closed. 'How people tend to underestimate me – and my friends.'

She went over to the machine behind the curtain, switched it off, and removed the cylinders as Tilly had shown her. Then, glancing around the room, she spotted a familiar, battered old case in the corner, and smiled. A moment later, the cylinders and the Almanac were safely inside her attaché case, and Sophie was headed to the door.

On the threshold, she glanced back at Mrs Davenport, slumped in her chair, her silk dress rumpled, her hat crooked. Then she closed the door, turning the key and slipping it into her pocket. When it came to someone like the Black Dragon, you simply couldn't be too careful.

Outside the Ocean View Suite, a young lady in a white frock was sitting, flicking through a copy of *LUNA* magazine and humming to herself. When she saw Sophie, she grinned. 'She *did* go on a long time! Jawing on and on. I thought you were going to be there all night!' She gave Sophie a fond look. 'I *was* a bit worried when I heard her talking about *sleeping draughts*. I thought of rushing in to save you, but I ought to have known you had it all in hand. Really, it's worked out very nicely, because now we can leave her there until the authorities come to collect her.'

Sophie smiled back. 'What about Forsyth?'

'Safe and sound – and cross as two sticks about being locked up,' said Lil. She got to her feet, looping an arm round Sophie's shoulders as they walked off together. 'Really, it's awfully satisfying. I only wish Carruthers was here to enjoy it, too.'

Molloy winced as their boat dashed down a steep incline, spiralling downwards amongst a fountain of spray. He'd never actually ridden through *Hell-Gate* before – he had better things to do with his time – but he knew what lay ahead. The dark caverns might be made of plaster, but they were convincing. Unearthly sounds screamed and howled in their ears, and steam rose all around them. Red lights cast weird shadows and behind him, one of the bowler hats jumped as the shape of a ghastly figure loomed suddenly out of the dark.

Molloy ignored it all. He was squinting ahead, into the blackness, his expression grim. 'Let's find 'em,' he said, clambering out of the boat.

Outside, there were groans from the queue of waiting people as Jake shut the gate and hung up the sign saying: *Ride Closed – Come Back Tomorrow!* He whistled to himself as he began tidying things up, but then, a lad in overalls came racing over.

'You're Jake, aren't you? Can you come to the *Alps of Switzerland*? Somethings gone wrong with the mechanism! The ride's broken down – and they sent me to fetch you.'

Jake frowned. 'I'll come over in a few minutes,' he said. 'I've got to see the last few people out and close up the ride.'

'You better go *now*,' said the lad anxiously. 'There must be thirty people stuck on there – they can't get off and they're getting mad. Molloy isn't going to like it one bit. I can close up here for you.'

'All right,' said Jake. He tossed the lad the keys. 'Bring 'em back to me when you're done,' he said, and hurried away without a backward glance.

Billy smiled and watched him go. As he stood, jingling the keys in his hand, Joe came out from where he'd been hiding behind a large boulder made of painted papier-mâché. Still in her frilly white frock, Mei emerged too.

'Everyone else out?' Billy asked.

'Only Molloy and his men left in there,' said Joe, with a slow grin.

Billy grinned back. Together the two of them pulled the big metal gates across the exit, and then padlocked them shut. At the control box which operated the ride, Mei clicked off the mechanism that controlled the boats and then the lights too.

Just then, Tilly came wandering over from the direction of the *Alps of Switzerland*. She was carrying her carpet bag in one hand and casually twirling a small spanner in the other. She joined them as they looked up at the gruesome sign reading *Hell-Gate*.

'Best place for 'em, if you ask me,' said Joe.

Turning away, they wandered slowly towards the entrance of Dreamland. Tilly and Mei fell behind, linking arms, while Billy and Joe walked together, Lucky trotting at their heels.

Billy looked up at Joe. 'It's awfully good to have you back,' he said shyly. Then he glanced longingly at the *Shoot-the-Chute*. 'Do you suppose we've got time for a quick ride? I've always fancied a go on one of those.'

'Not by the looks of that queue,' said Joe. 'But I reckon we might have time for a hot dog.'

'Good idea!' said Billy immediately. Then frowning a bit, he added. 'But Joe . . . what exactly *is* a hot dog?'

Joe gave a little hoot of laughter. 'Come along and see.'

CHAPTER THIRTY-TWO

The Orient Hotel
Manhattan Beach, New York City

Under normal circumstances, the staff of the Orient Hotel might have been doubtful about the large party who gathered to dine that evening on the verandah.

For one thing, most of them were not wearing proper evening dress. The young ladies were in ordinary, if pretty, afternoon dresses. The two young men present were even more casually attired. It was not the *done thing* at the Orient, but after all the extraordinary happenings at the hotel that day, the staff merely shrugged their shoulders.

Besides, the old traditions were changing. *New York* was changing. The days of the Astors and Vanderbilts, of the city's 'Four Hundred' with their rigid social conventions, had passed by, heralding something new.

The elegant gentleman seated at the head of the table was part of that. He was so well-known, and frankly so rich, that really, as one waitress whispered to another, his guests could come to dine in their bathing-suits if they liked. Exquisite in his evening attire, an orchid in his button-hole and a small black dog squirming delightedly in his lap, Mr Edward Sinclair looked exactly as he did in the newspaper photographs.

Far less recognisable was the small, bright-eyed elderly lady at the end of the table, though had the staff but known it, she too was a person of some importance. She looked rather like someone's kindly grandmother, but her gentle demeanour was deceptive. In fact, Miss Ada Pickering, of Pickering's Detective Agency, was one of the sharpest people Sophie knew.

'*Retired*, indeed!' she said to Sophie, with a shake of her head. 'You know me well enough, my dear, to know that *retirement* is the last thing that interests me. But going to Colorado for my health was certainly an effective cover story when I needed to investigate that spate of gold-mine murders. Of course, no one suspected that's what I was there to do, so I was able to get on with it nicely. I'd just about wrapped things up when I got your message.'

It was wonderful to see her again, but Sophie was even happier to see the lean, sharp-eyed man at her side. Mr McDermott had been the first to see that she and Lil had the potential to become detectives, and it was he who had introduced them to the Chief and the Secret Service Bureau. Now, Sophie felt that they had truly been able to live up to the promise he'd seen in them, back when the idea of becoming young lady detectives had still seemed nothing but a wild and impossible dream.

Billy looked excitedly at her across the table. She knew he was eager for what was always his favourite part of any adventure – unravelling it all and piecing together the story. She knew he was longing to know exactly what had happened once the American Intelligence Services, summoned by Miss Pickering and Mr Sinclair, had swept in. But before they could begin, a cheerful-looking gentleman came bounding over to their table.

'Why, Sinclair – by all that's remarkable! What a pleasure to see you here! I thought you were out in California?'

'Evening, Van Bergen,' said Sinclair, shaking his hand. 'Yes – I only came back to New York this morning, and I've found myself in the thick of things already.'

'Ah – you mean the excitement here?' Van Bergen chuckled. 'Mother is quite put out about it. She's furious with me for bringing her to a hotel where a common criminal was arrested.'

'Nothing very common about *her*,' said Sinclair. 'You tell Alma that the woman arrested here this afternoon was a genuine English aristocrat: Lady Viola Tremayne, daughter of the Duke of Cleveland. The British authorities have been looking for her for a while. You don't get more of a top-drawer criminal than that.'

Van Bergen laughed. 'You know, that might just cheer

her up. But what brings you here, Sinclair? It's not one of your usual haunts.'

Mr Sinclair leaned back in his chair and sipped his champagne. 'As a matter of fact, I'm catching up with a few old friends.'

A little way down the table, Sophie was having a conversation with another old friend who had just appeared – Roberta Russell. For one way or another, Miss Russell *had* become a friend, of sorts.

'Thanks for the tip-off. We got the story about the princess, which Moorhouse adored. Then Charlie got a whole set of pictures of the Van Bergen family, who agreed to pose for us here at the hotel. But best of all, we were right here when those Intelligence Service fellows turned up.'

'Something about a Coney Island crime ring, wasn't it?' said Sophie innocently.

Miss Russell gave her a shrewd look. 'It's no good pretending this is all news to you. I simply don't believe that it could be a coincidence that you and the rest of your team are here on the spot.'

'I can't imagine *what* you're talking about,' said Sophie. 'But I'm sure it will make a splendid story for the newspapers.'

Miss Russell nodded, and lowered her voice. 'Of course, the *really* extraordinary thing is that we actually *met* the woman who was arrested. Believe it or not, she was supposed to be an investor in the *New York Evening Telegram*. Now it turns out that it was all a sham – she was here in New York under a false name, and was wanted by Scotland Yard all the time!' Miss Russell paused for breath. 'What can a woman like that have wanted with a *newspaper*, do you suppose? Either way, it was a narrow escape for Sir Chester. It's not at all like him to be taken in!'

'Will he allow the story to be published?' Sophie asked. 'I don't suppose he'll want to be associated with a criminal.'

Miss Russell shook her head. 'Oh no, he's perfectly happy for the story to run. After all, he barely knew the woman. He only met her a few weeks ago, when she approached him about investing. He had no *idea* she was using a false name.' Then, suddenly distracted: 'Oh, I say – is that Edward Sinclair talking with Van Bergen? Do you suppose we could get a photograph, for *The Daily Picture*?'

Charlie Walters was already setting up his camera.

By the time Miss Russell and Walters and Van Bergen had left, they had been served their first course. Mr Sinclair looked down the table at them all and smiled.

'A busy day even by Taylor & Rose standards. But thanks to your hard work, the Intelligence Services have been able to round up a number of criminals. First, Lady Viola Tremayne, a.k.a. Mrs Davenport – one of Scotland Yard's most wanted, and a person of interest to the authorities in New York. Second, Mr Molloy, a Coney Island gangster that the Intelligence Services have been interested in for some time. And third, Harry Forsyth – a former British Army officer, wanted for crimes of espionage. You may be assured we'll be sending *him* back to London for the British authorities to deal with.'

'But what is truly remarkable is that you've also provided enough evidence to convict them,' said McDermott. 'Not to mention pointing the authorities to a secret lab full of prototype weapons and dangerous chemicals. On the evidence they found there, the Intelligence Services arrested the head scientist, whom I recognised as an old friend of ours. Henry Snow, if memory serves.'

'Apparently he was poring over his notes, mumbling about *the age of the dragons*,' added Sinclair. 'They had to pry the papers from his hands to put the handcuffs on.'

'Altogether, a very impressive achievement,' said Miss Pickering, her eyes twinkling. 'But no more than I have come to expect. When Miss Taylor and Miss Rose set about a task, you can count on them to do it *thoroughly*.'

'Well, we have had some jolly good teachers,' said Lil, with a smile.

But Miss Pickering would not accept that. 'Your instincts are all your own, my dears. That kind of thing simply *cannot* be taught.'

'I'd very much like to hear how you worked it all out,' said McDermott.

'Oh, it was Sophie's idea really,' said Lil.

But Sophie shook her head at once. 'I might have been

the first to guess what they were doing, but the plan was a joint effort. It needed all of us working together to map it out. And of course Tilly was the one who came up with the really important part – the phonograph.'

'A very smart idea,' said Miss Pickering to Tilly. 'I'd like to speak to you about how it worked, my dear. My detectives would find a device like that most useful.'

'Well, I wasn't sure it would work at all,' Tilly admitted. 'But when Sophie was talking about how much we needed evidence, she said something about *capturing a conversation* – and it gave me the idea. I thought it might be worth a try.'

'We knew that we had a good chance of stopping Forsyth,' added Lil. 'We'd outwitted *him* before. But what would be really difficult would be proving that the plan had been masterminded by the Black Dragon, and tracing it back to the *Fraternitas*.'

'When Tilly suggested using the phonograph, we came up with the idea that I might deliberately allow myself to be captured, and then get Mrs Davenport to talk,' said Sophie. 'We planned it so that the recording equipment would already be set up and ready in the room here at the hotel.'

'How could you be sure she'd take you there?' asked McDermott.

'It was a gamble,' admitted Sophie. 'But we knew she'd want to be here, on the spot, and I couldn't see her hanging around an amusement park, or a factory. She'd much prefer a place like this,' she said, gesturing around her to the elegant surroundings of the Orient.

'That was smart,' said Sinclair, with an appreciative nod. 'You understood her. And you knew how to get her to talk.'

Sophie nodded. Now, she reflected that it had been the photograph tucked away like a treasure that had pointed the way. *John and Viola.* Families mattered, and whatever Mrs Davenport might think, she and her brother had not been so different in the end. Just like the Baron, she'd wanted to explain everything she'd done. To tell the story, as if she needed someone to listen.

'But weren't you afraid?' Sinclair asked.

'Yes, I was,' Sophie admitted. 'But I knew Lil was outside the door most of the time.'

'*Rather!*' said Lil. 'I was listening for all I was worth! I'd have been in there like a shot to back Sophie up if she'd needed me.'

'And in the meantime, you rounded up Forsyth – not to mention Molloy and his men?' said McDermott, looking around at the others.

'We had a bit of help from the folk out at Coney Island,' Joe pointed out. 'I hope none of *them* will get into trouble with the authorities,' he added a little anxiously. 'I know they're not always exactly on the straight and narrow. But they're good people. They were kind to me – and they helped when we needed it.'

'You don't need to worry about them,' said McDermott.

'The US Intelligence Services have got far bigger fish to fry.'

'You mean . . . the Gold Dragon?' said Billy in an awed whisper. 'Sir Chester Norton?'

But Sinclair shook his head. 'Unfortunately, in spite of your efforts, there's no evidence to suggest Norton was anything but an innocent bystander,' he explained. 'When the Intelligence Services spoke to him at his hotel this afternoon, he had a very convincing story. He said he barely knew Mrs Davenport, but she'd seemed charming and knowledgeable, and he liked the idea of taking on a female investor based in New York. He vaguely remembered the name Lady Viola Tremayne, but he'd never made any connection between her and Mrs Davenport. And he'd been nowhere near the Orient Hotel at any time today. His secretary vouched for him – a Miss Andrews?'

'So she's *Norton's* secretary, not Moorhouse's!' exclaimed Lil. 'Well it's no surprise *she* vouched for him.'

'But surely they won't just leave it at that? They can talk to the British government, and start a proper investigation of Norton together,' said Billy.

But Sinclair, McDermott and Miss Pickering were exchanging awkward glances. 'Let's just say that neither the Americans nor the British are keen to follow that line of investigation at this time,' said Mr Sinclair after a moment's pause.

'So what does that mean?' asked Mei, incredulously.

'He's just going to get away with it? Carry on at the head of the *Fraternitas* – and keep plotting against the Germans?'

'Unless Mrs Davenport decides to point the finger at Norton herself, but I should say that's most unlikely,' added Miss Pickering.

'She didn't even say his name to me in the hotel,' Sophie reminded them. Even when she'd been revealing all her secrets, Gold's identity was one thing the Black Dragon had kept to herself.

'But why? Surely they'll try to do something!' protested Tilly, in disbelief.

But Sophie thought she understood. Mrs Davenport's remarks about Prime Minister Lockwood had been lost from the recording. When she'd got up and gone to the window, it had given Sophie the opportunity to switch the glasses of lemonade, but it also meant she'd been too far away for the phonograph to pick up what she said. Would anyone, even the Chief believe what she'd heard? And what if he did? He reported directly to Prime Minister Lockwood – who 'knew the Gold Dragon rather well'. No wonder the British government was not keen to *follow that line of investigation*, Sophie thought.

Just then, a young man in spectacles came into the restaurant, and made his way directly to their table. 'Ah, hello Danny,' said Miss Pickering at once.

Sophie stared. The young man pulling up a chair at Miss Pickering's side was *Daniel Quinn*.

Across the table, Billy looked as stunned as she felt. 'It's you!' he exclaimed. 'So I *did* see you here earlier! I wondered if you might be working for the dragons.'

Danny chuckled. 'Not me. Well, she can *sometimes* be a bit of a dragon, I suppose, but not in the way you mean,' he added with a grin to Miss Pickering.

Miss Pickering raised her eyebrows. 'Mr Quinn is one of my detectives,' she explained. 'He's been in Europe for a time, carrying out various assignments for Pickering's, before he returned to New York on the *Thalassa*. Since he's been back, he's been keeping an eye on Mr Van Bergen. The US government was concerned that he might become a target, so they asked us to carry out a little surveillance to ensure he stayed safe.'

Danny grinned at Billy. 'You know, I had a few suspicions about you too, *Bill Smuggs*. Especially when you kept wandering off in the middle of the night, when you were supposed to be laid low by seasickness. Now of course I find out it was all a sham and that you were really thwarting a secret plot to sink the ship! I wish you'd let me in on a bit of the action.'

'I wasn't shamming! Even *Lil* couldn't act as well as that!' Billy protested, shuddering at the memory.

'Did you know who I was, when we met on the docks?' said Sophie in astonishment.

'No, I didn't, and that's the honest truth,' said Danny, looking at her earnestly. 'But I did think there was something different about you. Something kind of – *special*.'

Sophie was aware that Lil was grinning at her from across the table. To her enormous annoyance, she found she was blushing.

'Of course, Van Bergen has no idea,' Sinclair was saying from the head of the table. 'A fine fellow, but naïve. I don't think he has the least idea how close he's come to being drowned, or blown up. Probably ought to have a quiet word, to put him in the picture.'

'Or perhaps the Intelligence Services will put him wise,' said Danny. 'I've been with them until now. Mrs Davenport hasn't said a word, but the other fellow – what's his name, Forsyth? – is letting all kinds of secrets slip.'

'Not the identity of the Gold Dragon?' said Billy hopefully.

Danny shook his head. 'Oh no. He'll be too frightened to give *that* away. The *Fraternitas* have ways of handing out punishment, even to fellows in gaol. Still, I don't think the Gold Dragon ought to be too comfortable. I've heard word that Ziegler's sent one of his best fellows to New York on the trail of the *Fraternitas*. Apparently the Germans aren't too happy about the way they've been trying to set them up. If I was him, I'd be watching my back.'

But Sophie knew how clever and careful the Gold Dragon was. He was still out there, no doubt even now spinning a new scheme. After everything they'd done, they had not been able to stop him, or put an end to the *Fraternitas*. Perhaps they never would.

But they'd done what they could, and that was something. Perhaps it was enough, Sophie thought. Besides, what Danny had said had given her a sort of idea.

'The fireworks are about to start!' exclaimed Lil.

While the others turned to look, Sophie stayed where she was, watching her friends. Unexpectedly, she found herself thinking of the Black Dragon, who would be spending tonight in a gaol cell instead of her luxurious suite at the Waldorf-Astoria. Most particularly, she thought again of the photographs she'd seen in Mrs Davenport's bedroom – which, of all the clues they'd gathered, had been perhaps the most important. *John and Viola*.

Family mattered. Sophie had no family of her own any longer. But as she reached up to touch her mother's green beads, she reflected that the people around her now were really very like a family.

In the distance, fireworks began to burst over Dreamland, filling the night sky with glittering colours, like a million stars.

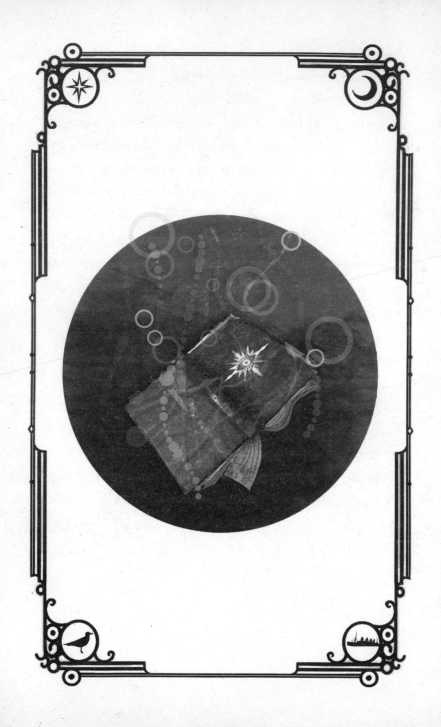

PART V

CHAPTER THIRTY-THREE

New York City

That night, after they'd said goodbye to Sinclair and the rest, the six friends walked together along the beachfront to Ruby's, where they found quite a party underway.

Leon was at the piano, Miss Patty at his side, belting out a tune. Eddie was helping Ruby behind the bar, and all the regulars were there, buzzing about how the cops had turned up to take away a fellow who'd been locked in the basement. There were all kinds of wild rumours about who he was. Some said he worked for Molloy; others that he was some sort of foreign spy up to no good. 'One of those anarchist fellows, I shouldn't doubt,' said Miss Patty. His arrest was already becoming part of the legend of Ruby's. Soon, rumours would spread that Ruby herself had been the one to catch this dangerous criminal and trap him in the basement. When questioned about it, she'd simply shrug and grin, as if she could tell quite a tale, if she chose.

But even more than the arrest of the man in the

basement, everyone was talking about what had happened to Molloy and his thugs. One or two of the regulars had been nearby when they'd finally staggered out of *Hell-Gate*, after almost two hours trapped in the pitch dark, with ghoulish wails and screams ringing in their ears. 'You ought to have seen him!' said Eddie, shaking his head in disbelief. Of course, the moment they'd emerged they'd been strong-armed into a waiting car by the Intelligence Services, who it seemed had been watching him for some time.

Grandpops was looking tremendously pleased with himself. 'I warned him!' he informed a dashing young gentleman seated beside him at the bar. 'I told him about the lions. He ought to have listened to me, that's for sure!'

Sophie realised that the young man at Grandpops' side was none other than Mr Charlton. 'Miss Grayson!' he exclaimed. 'Thank goodness! I must say I was rather concerned about what had become of you when you went off with those odd fellows.'

'You didn't have to worry about me, Mr Charlton,' said Sophie. 'I'm perfectly all right.'

'I'm very glad to hear it. May I get you some refreshments?' he added, shouting to be heard over the din of music and voices. 'You know, I rather like this place. Not much like the Grand Café Odeon in Vienna – but just as good a party, what?'

Joe was leaning on the bar, talking to Ruby. 'What'll happen to Dreamland, with Molloy in gaol?'

'Search me. I suppose someone else will buy it. What I do know is that Coney Island will be a better place without Molloy. Most of these folks'll be able to make a decent living again. Eddie's even giving up the numbers game.'

'I'm going to help Ruby run this place instead,' said Eddie, grinning. 'I heard she had a vacancy for a bartender. The numbers game is a racket anyway.'

'I *told* you,' said Joe to Leon, who had wandered over the bar to join them. '*And* dream books are a lot of nonsense.'

Leon shook his head. 'I don't think so, my friend.' He tapped the *Hand of Fate* dream book in his pocket. 'It told me I'd have *success in business*, remember? Well, that's just what I've got. A new piano – and what's more Miss Patty heard me play a few of my own songs this afternoon, and now she wants me to write some tunes for her new vaudeville show! And I reckon she wants your young lady to be the star,' he added, glancing back over to the piano, where Miss Patty was now sitting at the keys, while Lil led a rousing chorus of 'The Fairest of them All'. 'Perhaps the two of you will decide to stick around here for a while?'

Joe shrugged and grinned at him. 'Maybe we will,' he said.

As a matter of fact, Lil had already said she wanted to stay a little longer. The Circus of Marvels would soon be arriving in Coney Island, and she was keen to introduce Joe to her friends. Then there was the rather interesting invitation from Mr Sinclair to go out to California, where he was busy with a new business venture – a movie studio he was financing. 'The movies are the future,' he'd said, as he was smoking his after-dinner cigar. 'And we could use an actress of your calibre, Miss Rose. You'd be just right for the silver screen.' Joe had been captivated by his description of California's wild country – its oceans and deserts, horse ranches and farms. 'It sounds like quite a place,' he'd said.

It had been then that Sophie had known for sure that neither Joe nor Lil would be returning to London immediately. What was more, whatever they did next, they'd be doing it together.

They weren't the only ones who planned to stick around. As they'd walked through Greenwich Village together the next day, Roberta Russell had confided to Sophie that she too was planning to stay in the city for a time.

'Moorhouse says I could be *The Daily Picture's* New York correspondent, and I think that would be rather fun. It seems to me that there are a lot of stories to be written about this city,' she said, surveying the streets around them with interest.

They were walking towards the Moonrise Bookstore. After Miss Russell had shown an interest in the copy of *LUNA* she'd picked up in Coney Island, Sophie had offered to take her to meet Flora. As she'd expected, the two young women had hit it off straight away. Miss Russell had some good ideas about the next issue of *LUNA*, which was beginning to attract some interest since it had been scattered among the crowds at Dreamland. They had even begun talking about whether they might edit future issues together.

As for Charlie Walters, he would be heading back to London on the *Thalassa*'s return journey. He was looking forward to taking his portfolio of new photographs back to *The Daily Picture*. From the shots of the *Thalassa*'s arrival in New York, to his pictures of the Coney Island Crime Ring being arrested, not to mention his informal portraits of a young princess on holiday, he felt it had been a most successful trip.

Tilly and Mei would return home on the *Thalassa* too. Mei was eager to see her family, and Tilly to get started on some new projects in the workshop at Taylor & Rose. She was already talking of how she might refine the phonograph for use in future cases.

Billy was going with them – his suitcase stuffed with all the seasickness remedies he could find in New York's drugstores. He planned to spend the voyage working on a story – a mystery set aboard a grand ocean liner. 'If it turns out to be any good, I might have another stab at getting published,' he told Sophie, as the two of them took Lucky for a farewell walk in Central Park. Now she was reunited with Mr Sinclair, the little dog would be returning with him to California, where Sophie had every expectation she'd soon be popping up in a moving picture show herself.

'Perhaps you could try *Boys of England* this time?' suggested Sophie. 'Imagine seeing your story published alongside a Montgomery Baxter adventure!'

Billy grinned, liking that idea. He'd told her a little more about his story, as they'd walked together in the spring sunshine, with Lucky trotting at their feet. 'It's going to be about a group of friends who work together to solve mysteries. And a dog, of course,' he added, with a quick glance at Lucky.

Sophie said she thought it sounded splendid.

At first, she'd planned to join the others on the *Thalassa*. Carruthers had certainly made it plain she was expected back in London when they'd managed to put through a transatlantic telephone call to the Bureau. The line had been so bad she could hardly make out what he was saying, but his tone had been quite clear. 'What on earth have you been doing?' his unmistakable voice had demanded, sounding crackly as it came down the telephone receiver. '. . . the most extraordinary reports . . . the American Intelligence Services . . . giving away the Draco Almanac! The Chief . . . come back to report to the Bureau at once and explain yourselves!'

'I don't know what he's got to be so cross about,' Lil had said, as Sophie held the telephone receiver at a little distance from her ear, and more loud crackles and exclamations burst forth. 'We've got both Forsyth *and* the Black Dragon locked up, and all the evidence the Chief wanted. You'd think he'd be delighted!'

Sophie smiled. They'd already had a telegram from the Chief, congratulating them on their success, so she knew that he was pleased with them. Although he'd never have admitted it, she suspected the real reason Carruthers was so keen for them to come back to the Bureau was because secretly he rather missed them.

Yet after a little more thought, Sophie had decided that she too would stay in New York for a while. She felt no special hurry to return to London. That powerful longing to be back at Taylor & Rose investigating an ordinary case seemed to have left her – perhaps while she'd been swooping in the skies above Coney Island, or with Mrs Davenport at the Orient Hotel. Besides, it was not long until her eighteenth birthday, and New York seemed like a rather exciting place to spend it. She wanted to explore – see a Broadway show, go to the Metropolitan opera, visit the art museums and the New York City Public Library. She wanted to walk across Central Park, and wander the streets of Chinatown and Greenwich Village, and take a train out of Grand Central Station and see where she ended up.

Mrs Davenport had said New York was full of *opportunities* and Sophie saw now that it was true. There were doors opening for her here, if she wanted. Miss Pickering had made it clear there would be a job for Sophie, for however long she decided to stay. The idea of working with Miss

Pickering was appealing – and there was Danny Quinn, too. What would it be like to work alongside him?

Then there was Flora, who needed help at the Moonrise Bookstore. Miss Russell was working on *LUNA*, but Flora wanted to expand her business, and she was in need of advice. Sophie knew something about running a successful business, and she thought she might be able to help.

There was something else as well – something the friendly girl staying at the Maple Hotel had told her about, as they'd chatted over breakfast one morning: 'I'm meeting my cousin for lunch today. She's a student at Wellesley College – I'm going there myself in the fall, and I can't wait to hear *all* about it.'

She'd been amazed that Sophie had never heard of Wellesley. 'Don't you have women's colleges in England? It's a perfectly splendid place.' Sophie had listened to her explanations, fascinated by her tales of a lively community of young women, studying subjects like economics or political science. What would it be like to do something like that? She wanted to find out more, while she was here in the city. But before she thought about anything else, there were some important things she needed to do.

The first was a visit to the offices of the *New York Evening Telegram*. She'd dressed in her least noticeable clothes for the occasion – a plain dark skirt, a blouse with a little lace collar, and a straw hat with a ribbon bow. Alone, she made her way to Park Row, where Miss Russell had said she'd find the newspaper's headquarters. Near the entrance, she found a bench, and sat down with a copy of the paper to watch and wait – as Joe had once done outside the offices of Norton Newspapers on Fleet Street. As it happened, she didn't have to wait very long.

After only a short time had passed, Sir Chester Norton emerged from the entrance. He looked just as he had the first time she'd seen him, at a grand dinner in Paris – the same grey hair, smart clothes, and brisk, practical manner. He looked so very unaffected by anything that had happened that for a moment Sophie's convictions wavered. Could this really be the Gold Dragon?

Beside him walked Florence Andrews, still carrying her neat little briefcase. 'Don't forget, Sir Chester, you have the meeting with Mr Murphy at three o'clock,' she was saying, crisp and efficient.

Neither she nor Sir Chester noticed Sophie watching them as they made their way towards the waiting motor car. But the third person in the party – a tall, thin man in a grey suit – most certainly did. His eyes flicked over her with a look of quick, unspoken recognition.

'Now, Mr Lowe – as you're going to be my assistant here in New York, we must make sure you're up to date with all the activity of Norton Newspapers,' she heard Sir Chester say. 'Miss Andrews will bring you up to speed on some of the most important points . . .'

Behind the newspaper, Sophie smiled. The idea she'd come up with on the verandah of the Orient Hotel had delivered exactly the result she'd hoped.

She'd realised that the British government would block any further investigation of Norton. He was an ally of Prime Minister Lockwood, and it was in their interests to look the other way – especially if the *Fraternitas* were supplying them with weapons of war. It seemed that the Americans would not be investigating him either. But there was someone else who might. It had been Danny's words that had given her the idea. *Ziegler's sent some of his best fellows to New York on the trail of the* Fraternitas. *Apparently the Germans aren't too happy . . .*

Getting the message to the right place had been a challenge, but as she sat on the bench watching, she was satisfied her tip-off had worked. He might have looked different to when she'd last seen him on the Paris airfield, but the man at Sir Chester Norton's side was without any doubt the German secret agent she knew as 'the grey man'.

As she watched, he looked over at the bench where Sophie was sitting and gave her a quick, almost invisible smile.

Later the same day, she embarked on her second task, taking a pleasure boat out to Coney Island. While the other passengers admired the view and talked of the attractions they planned to see, she found a quiet corner of the deck. From her handbag, she removed a small, leather-bound book.

She hadn't told anyone that she'd taken it from the suite at the Orient Hotel. In the recording, Mrs Davenport had spoken of the Almanac, but she'd never said it was there in the room. No one had asked Sophie if she'd seen it. Now, only she knew the truth.

Standing on the deck, she weighed it in her hand for a long moment, looking at the gold eye glinting in the sunlight. She remembered what Mrs Davenport had said about its power, and what it represented. Then, she opened her hand, and let it fall into the churning grey-blue waters of the Hudson Bay.

A few hours later, she was sitting with the others in a café, where Danny had promised to introduce them to the best pastrami sandwiches in New York.

Sophie knew it might be the last time they were together for a while – certainly weeks, perhaps months, maybe even more. Billy, Mei and Tilly were sailing back to London tomorrow, carrying the case report that Sophie had prepared, which they'd deliver to the Chief. Once they'd reported to the Bureau, Sophie knew that Mei and Tilly would soon get things at Taylor & Rose back on track, with Billy's help. The agency couldn't be in better hands until she and Lil returned to London, and things were back to business as usual.

If they ever *were* back to business as usual. Sophie had a peculiar presentiment that nothing at Taylor & Rose would ever be quite the same. In fact, she'd begun to wonder if the gold letters on the glass door would one day read not TAYLOR & ROSE but instead LIM & BLACK.

Now, as she sat beside Lil in the café, Sophie felt it again – the sudden sense that everything was changing. But of course it was. They were all growing up. There were new adventures beginning that might take them anywhere. What she did know was that whether they were together or apart, in New York or London or California or anywhere else in the world, Lil would always be her dearest friend. They didn't need their names written on a door for *that*.

It was a jolly evening. They sat there for a very long time, making jokes and teasing each other, and munching sandwiches, and telling Danny stories about their adventures together. They were there so long that the café staff began to clear up around them, putting chairs on tables, and looking meaningfully at the clock. No one really wanted the evening to come to an end, but at last, Sophie rose to her feet.

Danny offered to see her safely back to the Maple Hotel, but she only smiled her thanks and said she didn't really need an escort.

He laughed. 'No, I guess you don't, huh?'

She did not make a fuss over her farewells, hugging Billy, Mei and Tilly goodbye and telling Lil and Joe she'd see them tomorrow, or perhaps the next day. On the threshold, she paused to open her umbrella. It had begun to rain again, and now the bright lights of the city were shimmering out of the dark.

For one last moment she glanced back at her friends, still sitting cosily together in the warm glow of light, behind the café's steamy window. Then she straightened her hat, grasped her umbrella in a neatly gloved hand and set out alone along the New York street – ready for whatever adventures this city might have in store.

A MONTH IN

Our correspondent Miss Roberta Russell explores the bright lights of New York City, from the elegance of Fifth Avenue to bohemian Greenwich Village - with photographs by Mr C. Walters.

In today's edition, Miss Russell (pictured top left with friend Miss Sophie Taylor) explores Coney Island. Discover 'America's Playground' including the new Dreamland amusement park and the exclusive Manhattan Beach resort, where Princess Anna of Arnovia is amongst the guests at the luxurious Orient Hotel. Plus the dramatic capture of the 'Coney Island Crime Ring' who were arrested by the American authorities with the assistance of London's Taylor & Rose Detectives. Read more on p5.

MANHATTAN

lso in today's edition:

ommander Charles Samson
ecomes first pilot to take to the
ir from a ship in motion - p9

Sports News: Tennis star Miss
dith Hannam wins Gold for
ritain at Stockholm Summer
lympics - p13

International News:
lysterious robbery and murder
New York City - police have
o leads - p25

AUTHOR'S NOTE

This story is fictional but like all the books in the *Taylor & Rose Secret Agents* and Sinclair's Mysteries series, it takes some inspiration from real history.

In particular, the RMS *Thalassa* is inspired by the real-life RMS *Titanic*, the grand ocean liner that sank on 15th April 1912 on her maiden voyage from Southampton to New York City. More than 1,500 passengers and crew died in the disaster, which occurred when the ship struck an iceberg in the North Atlantic Ocean.

The Waldorf-Astoria was a real hotel on Fifth Avenue in New York City from 1893 to 1929, when it was razed to make way for the construction of the Empire State Building. A new Waldorf Astoria was built on Park Avenue in 1931 and remains one of New York's most famous hotels to this day.

The Moonrise Bookstore is inspired by The Sunwise Turn, a bookshop in Greenwich Village which existed between 1916 and 1927. Founded by Madge Jenison and Mary Horgan Mowbray-Clarke, it was one of the first bookshops in America to be owned and operated by women.

Dreamland was also a real amusement park at Coney Island, Brooklyn from 1904 to 1911, when it burned down in a fire that originated in the *Hell-Gate* ride. In this story Dreamland is refurbished and reopened the following summer, but the real-life park was destroyed and never rebuilt.

Readers of the previous *Taylor & Rose* books will already know that the Secret Service Bureau is partly inspired by the real-life Secret Service Bureau, which was set up by the British government in 1909. Although initially small it soon grew, and was later divided into two divisions, one dealing with counter-espionage at home, another gathering intelligence abroad. Today we know these as 'MI5' and 'MI6'.

Some of the technology that appears in this story, including 'Marconi' wireless telegraphy and the Edison Business Phonograph are real innovations of the early 20th century. Similarly, the powerful firebombs used by the *Fraternitas Draconum* are based on the new firebombs that were dropped from aeroplanes for the first time during World War I. During the war, Germany developed a 'Fireplan' in which German bombers were to strike London and Paris, engulfing each city in a blaze so big it could not be put out. A plan to firebomb New York City was also discussed. Thousands of bombs were stockpiled in preparation, but in the end the 'Fireplan' never took place. However, firebombs would later be used to devastating effect by both sides in World War II, including in the bombing of Dresden, Germany and Tokyo, Japan.

For more information as to the historical background in *Nightfall in New York*, visit www.katherinewoodfine.co.uk.

ACKNOWLEDGEMENTS

A heartfelt thank you to the fantastic team at Farshore, especially Sarah Levison. As always, enormous thanks to Karl James Mountford, whose glorious illustrations have brought so much to this series, and to designer Laura Bird for creating such beautiful books. Thank you to all those in the team, both past and present, who have been part of the *Sinclair's Mysteries* and *Taylor & Rose Secret Agents* – including Lindsey Heaven, Sarah Bates, Lucy Courtenay, Bhavini Jolapara, Ellie Bavester, Pippa Poole, Ingrid Gilmore, Cally Poplak, Lydia Silver, Amy St Johnston, Rebecca Lewis-Oakes, Siobhan McDermott, Dannie Price, Alice Hill, Maggie Eckel, Benjamin Hughes, Júlia Sardà (who beautifully illustrated *The Clockwork Sparrow* and *The Jewelled Moth*), Hannah Sandford and of course, Ali Dougal. It's been a joy working with you all on these books.

Special thanks to my most excellent agent Louise Lamont, for being the very best companion through eight adventures with Sophie and Lil. We may not have made it to New York for this one, but thank you for the *sachertorte*, *Babylon Berlin* discussions, reassuring and motivational lockdown phonecalls, and appreciating every single *Titanic* reference in this book – as well as for all of your wisdom. Huge thanks also to the brilliant team at ILA especially Clementine Gaisman and Alice Natali.

Writing this book in a pandemic without access to the British Library was quite a challenge. Thank goodness for bookshops – in particular my local Lancashire indies Storytellers Inc and Ebb & Flo, and of course, Waterstones – which were my go-to for the all-important research books.

Particular thanks to my family and friends – especially my Mum and Dad who are my biggest champions, my husband Duncan and my daughter Rose, who brought some extra exuberance to the writing of this book! Thanks also to all my wonderful author friends and publishing pals for all your enthusiasm and cheerleading, which is always so very much appreciated. Particular thanks to Nina Douglas for lockdown chat and encouragement when it was needed most.

In this story, Greenwich Village bookshop owner Flora is named for Flora Cardell-Ree, who was a winner in the Books to Nourish auction, raising money for the food redistribution charity FareShare. Huge thanks to Flora and Tori Cardell-Ree for supporting the auction and making the winning bid – and to Sarah Shaffi and Chloe Mavrommatis for organising Books to Nourish.

Finally, thank you to everyone who has been part of Sophie and Lil's journey. I'm enormously grateful to all the booksellers, librarians, teachers and bloggers for their wonderful support for the books – and especially to the readers of all ages, who have joined me on this thoroughly delightful adventure.